Also by Nina George
Available from Random House Large Print

The Little French Bistro

The Book of Dreams

The Book of Dreams

a novel

—//—

Nina George

Translated by Simon Pare

RANDOM HOUSE
LARGE PRINT

Translation copyright © 2019 by Simon Pare

All rights reserved.
Published in the United States of America by
Random House Large Print in association with Crown,
an imprint of Crown Publishing Group, a division of
Penguin Random House LLC, New York.

Originally published in Germany as **Das Traumbuch**
by Knaur Verlag, an imprint of Verlagsgruppe
Droemer Knaur, Munich, Germany.
Copyright © 2016 by Nina George. This translation
simultaneously published in Great Britain by Simon and Schuster,
UK Ltd., London.

**Interior art by istock.com/andipantz
Cover design by Michael Morris;
hand lettering by Alane Gianetti
Cover photographs: (paper) Katerina Sisperova/iStock/
Getty Images; (cityscape) Scott E. Barbour/
Digital Vision/Getty Images**

The Library of Congress has established a
Cataloging-in-Publication record for this title.

ISBN: 978-1-9848-4676-1

www.penguinrandomhouse.com/large-print-format-books

FIRST LARGE PRINT EDITION

Printed in the United States of America

10 9 8 7 6 5 4 3 2 1

This Large Print edition published in accord
with the standards of the N.A.V.H.

I dedicate this novel to my mother, Jutta Marianne George (May 18, 1939–September 27, 2017), and beloved wife of Broad Jo.

She always delighted in traveling to all kinds of imaginary worlds with me.

———⫻———

Maybe our lives are nothing but stories that are being read by other people.

The Book of Dreams

DAY ONE

Henri

//

jump.

The fall only lasts a few seconds. I can hear the engines of the cars above me on Hammersmith Bridge. Rush hour. I smell the city, the fading fragrance of spring, of dew on the leaves. Then I plunge into the cold water and it closes over my head. I strike out with my arms, gathering speed as the receding tide carries me with it. Despite being more than thirty miles away, the sea sucks the river toward it. My body has not forgotten the tug of the tide; it's as if I never left the sea, although it's over twenty-five years since I last bathed in the Atlantic.

Finally I reach the girl.

The river is dragging her along. It wants to own her. It's intent on breaking down her body into its constituent parts, severing her hopes from her

3

fears, ripping the smile from her lips, and cutting off her future.

She's sinking into the muddy waters. I dive and pull her closer by her hair. I manage to catch hold of a slender, slippery upper arm. I tighten my grip and gather my breath for the coming struggle. Salty, ice-cold water floods into my mouth. The Thames wraps me in its embrace.

Her face, with eyes the color of the wintry sea, floats toward me. She's pinching her nose shut with the fingers of one hand, as if she had merely jumped into the lukewarm, chlorine-tinged water of a swimming pool. In fact, she has fallen overboard, one of the many pleasure craft carrying tourists along the Thames. After climbing onto the second-highest bar of the boat's railings, the girl had tilted her face to catch the May sunshine when a chance wave slapped against the hull, raising the stern and tipping the whole boat forward. The girl didn't make a sound, but her eyes were brimming with boundless curiosity.

From Hammersmith Bridge we watched her fall—the kissing couple, the beggar in the threadbare tuxedo, and me.

The beggar jumped up from his "turf," a piece of cardboard in a sunny spot against the suspension bridge's green rail. "Oh my God!" he whispered. The couple turned to me. Neither they nor the beggar moved a muscle—they simply stared at me. So I clambered over the green cast-iron railing, waited until the small figure surfaced below me, and jumped.

The girl is gazing at me with more trust and hope than a man like me deserves. Of all the people in this city who might have been in a position to rescue her, it had to be me.

I lace my arms around her frail, wet body. The girl kicks out, and her feet catch me in the head and mouth. I swallow water, I breathe in water, but I still manage to make myself buoyant and push for the surface. The world grows louder again. The May wind feels mild on my wet face; the waves send spray into my eyes. I turn onto my back to form a bobbing, watery cot and haul the girl onto my chest so she can breathe and look up at the blue sky. In this position, we float down the Thames past brick facades and wooden boats moored to the muddy banks.

The kid splutters and gasps for air. She seems to be about four or five. I don't have a clue about children, not even my own.

Samuel. Sam. He's thirteen and he's waiting for me. He's always been waiting for me. Forever. I was never there.

I start humming Charles Trenet's **La Mer,** that majestic hymn to the beauty of the sea. Scraps of the French lyrics bubble up into my mind. I haven't spoken my native tongue since I was eighteen, but now it comes flooding back.

As I sing, I gradually sense that the girl's heart is

settling into a calmer rhythm. I feel her little lungs pumping and her trust piercing the film of water and fear between us. I hold her tightly and use one arm to propel myself on my back toward the bank, where there is a small jetty. My clothes are soaked. I kick my legs like a frog and my ungainly one-sided crawl makes me look like a one-armed bandit.

"It's going to be okay," I whisper. I can hear Eddie's voice clearly inside my head, as if she were there, whispering in my ear: "You're not a good liar, Henri. It's one of your greatest qualities."

Eddie is the best thing that never happened to me.

My shoulder bumps into one of the floating barrels supporting the jetty. There's a ladder within reach. I grab the girl by the waist and lift her up, pushing her tiny feet higher and higher until she finds a handhold and wriggles out of my grasp.

I follow her. I climb out of the river; pick up the exhausted child, who is desperately trying not to weep; and carry her past yellow, red, and gray houses back to Hammersmith Bridge. The girl entwines her arms around my neck and buries her face in my shoulder. She's as light as a feather, but she gets heavier and heavier as I walk along, pursued by the nagging thought that I really need to hurry now to meet Sam. I must go to him. I must. My son's waiting for me at his school.

The same couple is still standing there on the bridge, holding each other close. The woman looks at me in a daze, her eyes wide and shiny. The kohl swooshes at their corners and her beehive hairstyle remind me of Amy Winehouse. Holding up his smartphone, the man keeps saying, "I don't believe it. I don't believe it, man. You actually got her. That was unbelievable."

"Were you only filming or did you think of calling for help?" I hiss at him.

I put the girl down. She doesn't want to let go, and her tiny hands cling to my neck before finally slipping through my wet hair.

All of a sudden I feel very weak and lose my balance. Incapable of standing upright, I stagger out into the road. The little girl screams.

Something big and hot sweeps into view over my shoulder. I see a twisted face through glass. I see a black bonnet, glinting in the sunlight, swipe my legs from under me. And then I see my own shadow rising at breakneck speed from the asphalt to meet me, and hear a noise like eggshells breaking on the rim of a china cup.

The pain in my head is a thousand times more intense than the agonizing twinge you feel when you bite into an ice cream. Everything around me goes quiet. Then I melt. I melt into the ground. I sink down, faster and faster, as if I were plummeting into a deep black lake beneath the asphalt.

Something is gazing up at me expectantly from the lake's murky depths. The sky is receding all the time, its arc farther and farther overhead. As I seep into the stone, I see the girl's face up above, staring sadly at me with her oddly familiar eyes, which are the color of the sea in winter. Her oceanic eyes are now indistinguishable from the lake above me. I merge into the lake and its waters claim my body. Women and men cluster around the shores, obscuring the last patch of blue sky. I hear their thoughts inside my head.

The woman in the Mini tried to swerve out of the way.

The light of the low sun. It must have been the blinding light. She didn't see him.

From the way he stumbled out into the road, I thought he must be drunk.

Is he alive?

I can make out the beggar in the threadbare tuxedo as he pushes the other people aside, offering me a fresh glimpse of the sky—the never-ending, beautiful sky.

I close my eyes. I'll rest for a while and then get up again and continue on my way. I can just about make it there on time. It'll take a while before the roll call for Fathers' and Sons' Day gets to Sam and me, to V for Valentiner, his mother's surname.

Dear Dad,

We don't know each other, and I think we should do something about that. If you agree, come to Fathers' and Sons' Day on 18 May at Colet Court. That's part of St.

Paul's School for boys in Barnes. It's on the banks of the Thames. I'll be waiting for you outside.

Samuel Noam Valentiner

I'LL BE RIGHT with you, Sam. I'm just having a little rest.

Someone pries open my eyelids. The lakeshore is far, far away, high above me, and a man is calling down from the rim of the hole. He's wearing a paramedic's uniform and gold-framed sunglasses. He smells of smoke. I can see my reflection in his shades. I see my eyes go dull and glaze over. I see the paramedic's thoughts.

Come on, his thoughts echo inside the hole I'm in. **Don't. Don't die. Please, don't die.**

A long shrill beep draws a straight line under my life.

Not now!

Not now! It's too soon!

It's . . .

It . . .

The long beep swells into a final drumroll.

I jump.

DAY FIFTEEN

Sam

2:35 p.m. Samuel Noam Valentiner. Patient visited: Henri M. Skinner.

Fourteen times I've written these same words, but every day I have to register again. Every day Mrs. Walker pushes the black clipboard toward me with a form on which I must enter, in capitals, the time, my name, and the name of the patient I'm visiting.

The name above mine is Ed Tomlin. Ed Tomlin also visits my father, always a few hours before me while I'm still at school. Who is he?

"I was here yesterday," I tell Mrs. Walker.

"Oh, I know that, darling."

The woman at the Wellington Hospital reception is lying. She doesn't recognize me at all. Lies have a particular sound: they're whiter than someone's normal voice. Her name is printed in capital letters

13

on the sign above her left breast: SHEILA WALKER. She calls me "darling" because she can't remember my name. English people are like that: they hate to tell the truth—it's rude.

Sheila Walker's body bears the shadows of many years. I can tell, just as I can tell with most people. Some have many shadows, others fewer, and children have hardly any. If they do have shadows, then it's because they come from countries like Syria and Afghanistan, and their shadows grow longer as they grow up.

Mrs. Walker has experienced a lot of sadness, and she's so preoccupied with the past that she neglects the present. That's why to her I'm merely a boy in a school uniform whose voice is breaking— with embarrassing effects. Maybe when she looks at me she sees a beach and her empty hand, which nobody has held for years.

I was here yesterday and the day before, though. And the one before, and the eleven days before that too. I cut one teacher's lesson one time and another's the next, sometimes in the mornings, sometimes in the afternoons. Today it's French with Madame Lupion. Scott said I should make sure that I spread the missed lessons across all subjects so the teachers don't catch on so quickly.

Scott McMillan is a specialist at cutting class, Googling, and doing things nobody else does. He also excels at chess, drawing, and getting bad marks at school. At everything, in fact. He's thirteen, has an IQ of 148, can fake anybody's handwriting, and has a rich father who hates him.

My IQ's a mere 144, which makes him "very gifted" and me "gifted," or as Scott would put it, **"Moi le Brainman,** you my smart-ass sidekick, **mon ami."** Le Brainman is currently going through a French phase after polishing up on his Mandarin and an African dialect that features lots of clicking sounds.

I'm thirteen too. I'm a synesthete—or, as some boys at my school call me, a synes-creep—and my father's in an induced coma. That's like a long-lasting anesthetic, except for the fact that he has small suckers in his brain that are supposed to relieve the pressure, a machine that takes care of his breathing, another one that keeps his blood cool, and yet another one that eats and pees for him. They intend to wake him up today.

Nobody at school, apart from Scott, knows that my father's in a coma. That's partly because nobody knows that Steve, my mother's husband, isn't my real father. Except for Scott, who once said to me, "Man, at one fell swoop you could be the most interesting boy at school—well, for one wonderful week at least. Give it some thought: you might not want to pass up this opportunity. Being the mystery kid could be one of the greatest things that ever happened to you. It'd work like magic on the girls too." There **are** no girls at our school.

Scott and I are the only thirteen-year-olds at

Colet Court to have been invited to join Mensa. Scott calls this high-IQ society the "wimps' club." My mum says I should be proud of myself, as one of only two Year Eight students among the nine hundred or so young Mensa members in England, but being ordered to be proud leaves a nasty taste in my mouth.

If she knew I was here, she might give me up for adoption. Never speak to me again. Send me to boarding school. I've no idea how she'd react.

"Thank you, darling." Sheila Walker's voice reverts to its normal color as she picks up the sign-in clipboard from the counter and types my name into the computer. Her long fingernails make a bright green clatter on the keyboard.

"You need to go up to the second floor, Samuel Noam Valentiner," she says emphatically, as if I didn't know.

The intensive care unit on the second floor is for patients wrapped in silence and loneliness. That's why they're sent here, to the Wellington Hospital's neurology department. The London Brain Centre— the NASA of brain departments.

Sheila Walker hands me an A4 map of the hospital, the same one I received yesterday and the day before. With energetic swishes of her red felt-tip she circles where we are now—"We're here"—and where I have to go—"You need to go there"—and marks the shortest route between the two points—"You'd be best taking that lift over there, Samuel."

Mrs. Walker would be well suited to working at an information desk in the tube. "Turn right for Kensington, straight ahead for hernias, and the morgue's on your left after the vending machine."

"Have a nice day, Mr. Valentiner," she says.

"You too, Mrs. Walker," I reply, but she's no longer paying attention.

MY MOTHER came with me to the hospital on the first day. As we waited for the lift, she said, "We don't owe your father a thing, you know. Nothing. The only reason we're here is because—"

"I get it," I interrupted her. "You don't want to see him. You promised yourself you wouldn't."

After a second she angrily retorted, "How come you always get **everything**, Sam? You're not old enough!" She gave me a map of the hospital. "I'm sorry. It's just that your father drives me up the wall. Oh, Sam."

She wasn't pleased that I had secretly asked my father to the Fathers' and Sons' Day at Colet Court. "He won't come anyway," she said at the time. Her voice suffused me like a fragrance, like the scent of rosemary in the rain, sad and muted. At that precise moment I could feel how much she loved me. All at once I could breathe properly, as if I were standing on the world's highest peak. The ball of phlegm that usually clogged my chest was gone.

Sometimes my love for my mum is so over-powering that I wish I could die so she'd finally be happy again. Then she'd be left with her husband, Steve, and my little brother, Malcolm. A normal family—just father, mother, and child, rather than father, mother, child, and me, the kid who never looks anyone in the eye, reads too much science fiction, and is a permanent reminder of a man she can't stand.

"Listen," I suggested. "I'll go in on my own, but only if I can stay for as long as I want and you wait for me in the cafeteria."

She gave me a hug. I could sense how much she wanted to say yes, and how ashamed this made her feel.

My mother hasn't always been like this. There was a time when she worked as a photographer and traveled to war zones. She was afraid of nothing—of nothing and nobody. But then something happened. That **thing** was me, an accident, and everything changed. Now she sneaks through her own life, as if she's constantly trying to duck out of harm's way.

"Please, Mum," I said, "I'm almost fourteen. I'm no longer a kid."

My mother ended up going to the cafeteria, and I went up alone to visit the second floor and the man who became my father because my mother slept with him once during what she refers to as an "embarrassing moment." She's never told me where and why it occurred.

Sheila Walker has already forgotten me as I make for the lift and take it to the second floor. The first thing I have to do there is put a smock over my school blazer, disinfect my hands and lower arms, and cover my mouth and nose with a white oval mask.

The brain center's intensive care unit is like a large, brightly lit warehouse. There are beds along three long walls—A, B, and C. Rails run just below the ceiling, allowing blue curtains to be pulled around each bed to form a separate cubicle. On a raised platform in the center of the hall are several counters equipped with computer monitors and controls. Doctors sit there watching screens or making phone calls. Every patient has been assigned his or her personal nurse.

It resembles a refugee camp, because the coma patients aren't called by their names, only by a combination of a letter and a number. "A3, glucose level falling." "B9, restless." None of them is real anymore. My father is C7. One of the "zombies."

On my first visit, the right side of his head had been shaved and then daubed with orange iodine tincture. Lengths of white adhesive tape had been stuck on his face to hold the breathing tube in place, and his skin was blue, green, and purple—the colors of night, strength, and dreams. When I entered the ward, I felt as if liquid concrete were oozing into my stomach and hardening with every breath. That lump of concrete has been inside me ever since.

I've already told you that I'm a synes-creep. I experience the world differently from other people. I see sounds, voices, and music as colors. The London Underground sounds steel gray, like a bagful of knives. My mother's voice is soft, like soft gauze on a frozen lake. And purple. My voice is currently colorless, but when I'm scared it turns bright yellow. When I speak it's light blue, like a baby's playsuit. It's breaking at the moment, and ideally I would say nothing further until that's over.

People who know who they are and what they're capable of have green voices. Dark-green voices, serene and majestic like a wise old forest.

For me, numbers also have colors. The figure eight is green, four is yellow, and five is blue. Letters have personalities: R is aggressive, S is sly, and K is a covert racist. Z is cooperative and F is a diva. G is upright and strong.

When I enter a room I can tell which emotions have been felt in it most frequently. With someone like Mrs. Walker, I can sense how heavyhearted she is by the density of the shadows surrounding her.

I can't look another person in the eye. There's too much there, and much of it I don't understand. Sometimes I'm afraid that their gaze will tell me they're about to die, which turned out to be the case with our housemaster at Colet Court and our neighbor Mrs. Logan.

People with synesthesia used to be regarded as pathological. Pathologically shy, pathologically over-sensitive, a real burden on their families. Children who have it are always screaming, quick to tears, and peculiar in other ways too. When they grow up they often turn out to be borderline, complete schizophrenics, or prone to depression. Many kill themselves because they can't cope with the world and the way they see it. Hypersensitive crybabies. If there were any pills to treat this condition, I'd be gobbling them like Smarties.

THE FIRST TIME I walked through the ward of the "zombies," it felt as if their souls were bleeding colors. I perceive that kind of thing, although I'd rather not. Then I caught sight of the man in C7. I felt nothing.

It was weird. I've never felt nothing. Only that once. The stranger was lying motionless on his back on an aluminum bed. The shadows around him were thick, the color of the moon. His eyes were closed, and he gave off nothing. That nothing worried me, but only in a strange, standoffish way.

I sat down carefully on the edge of his bed. Still nothing. I was relieved. If I didn't feel anything, then I wouldn't be obliged to miss my father all the time, keep thinking about him. I could stop searching everywhere for him. I didn't need to come here again. My mother could make peace with herself at last.

Then I saw the scoobie. That scoobie changed everything. My father was wearing a plastic bracelet on his otherwise bare right wrist. It was dark blue, light blue, and orange. I'd woven it two years earlier and sent it to him by post. My mother had claimed that he wouldn't wear it. He'd throw it in the bin.

I believed her, as always, even if I kept hoping that she was wrong. But she managed to convince me that my father was the man she had always described him to be: hard-hearted, self-centered, inconsiderate.

But he was wearing it. He was wearing my stupid, childish plastic bracelet in my three favorite colors—midnight blue, sea blue, and the orange of a summer sunrise.

I've no idea how long I sat there, staring at the plaited plastic—a cheap charm that changed everything. All I know is that after a while the head of intensive care, Dr. Foss—"Call me Fozzie, lad!"—came over to me, laid his hand gently on my shoulder, and told me in a nasal voice that my father had been very lucky. His skull was fractured, but the swelling was no longer putting pressure on his brain and the cerebral cortex had barely been affected.

Luckily, God walked past and barked, "Samuel, don't believe a word Fozzie says. We'll have to operate on your father a few more times and only then will we be able to see where we went wrong."

God's real name is Dr. John Saul. With his blond hair, his broad shoulders like a rower's, and his big sideburns, the director of the London Brain Centre resembles a Viking. Whenever he enters the intensive care ward where the "zombies" live, wearing that aura of silvery coolness about him like an invisible cloak, the nurses and doctors catch their breath. They all pray that he'll be able to perform a miracle. Behind his back they call him God, because he knows everything—including the fact that they call him God. And Dr. Foss, in his green cord trousers, his curry-colored socks, his finely checked purple shirts, and his suspenders, is his Holy Ghost. He models his hairstyle on John Cleese and takes tea for half an hour every afternoon while playing Quiz Battle on his smartphone in its tartan case.

The night after that first hospital visit I talked to Scott via Skype while my mother had quiet sex with her husband, Steve. Scared of having another nightmare, my brother, Malcolm, was desperate to sleep in my room. As he fell asleep it was as if his spirit were walking down a long flight of stone steps into the dark. I could hear his footsteps, but unlike my father he was close, very close to the surface, and I could still sense his presence.

I told Scott that my father was "away." Scott was sitting on the toilet. The McMillans have more toilets in their mansion than my mother Marie-France's terraced house has rooms. We live in Putney, Scott in Westminster. If Putney's Swatch, Westminster's Rolex.

We searched for "traumatic brain injury," "artificial coma," and "cerebral cortex" on Google, or rather Scott did while I stared into the darkness, listening to the tapping of his fingers and to Malcolm's deep breathing. I thought about the scoobie and how I couldn't get through to my father under his thick fluffy duvet of anesthetics.

"Wow, Michael Schumacher was put into an artificial coma after a traumatic brain injury," Scott lectured. "If the person doesn't die straightaway, then—"

"Shut up." If he didn't say it aloud, then it couldn't happen. It simply **mustn't** happen. Not now. Not like this.

"Of course you don't want to hear it, but you have to. Or do you want to let them lie to you? They always lie to us—at first **because** we're children, then later because we're **no longer** children." Scott took a deep breath. "Now, listen to Brainman here. The cerebral cortex is the site of our personality. If it tears, you become either a vegetable or wildly aggressive. One day your dad might wake up and be so aggressive that he runs amok. Or kills himself.

Or you. Or thinks he's someone else. Some people come back and can do inexplicable things."

"What kind of things?"

"You know, see auras, speak Tibetan, or hear thoughts."

I didn't tell him that I'm sometimes capable of two of those three things.

He resumed his typing and mumbled, "Aha, you have to hold his hand. If he squeezes your hand, he's still there."

Malcolm turned over in my bed with a sigh. I could feel his presence very clearly, even though he was sleeping and dreaming. My father, on the other hand . . . My father was somewhere beyond dreams.

"Where else might he be?" I asked Scott.

"This is crazy," he whispers instead of answering me. "I've stumbled across a self-help forum for people who've met God or someone while they were in a coma."

"What do you mean, 'or someone'? Who? Elvis?"

We laughed and then the light came on in Scott's toilet. He cried, "Oh shit, my dad!" and hung up. I was left sitting there in the dark at my desk.

If he squeezes your hand, he's still there. I had to find out if my father was still there.

When my mother had finished making love with her husband, she went into Malcolm's room, as always, to say good night. When she didn't find him there, she knocked on my door, carried my sleepy brother to his own bed, and then came back to see me.

"I'm not going to sign that indefinite visitor's permit for you, Sam. I don't want you going to the hospital all the time. You need to focus on your exams, you know? That's the most important thing right now. If you want to go and see him again in a few weeks' time, fine—we can talk about it."

My mother pays almost nineteen thousand pounds per year for me to attend Colet Court School, so it's my fault that she doesn't have enough money and is unhappy. But my mind was entirely on the scoobie, so I just said, "Okay."

"Your father never took care of you, so there's no reason you should look after him now. That may sound harsh, Sam, but it's for your own good, do you hear? Otherwise, you'll just end up being even more disappointed."

Again I said, "Okay." What else could I say? At last I knew where my father was. In C7. And I knew he was wearing my scoobie. She was wrong about him. Or was I? In any case I knew I would go back there to squeeze his hand. For as long as it took until, one day, he returned that squeeze.

But I kept those thoughts to myself—the first time I'd ever hidden something really important from my mother. By no means the last, though.

———— // ————

ON THE SECOND day Scott brought a great stack of printouts about brain injuries to school for me.

"Virtually everyone shows signs of delirium when they wake up from an induced coma," he told me during the lunch break, which we spent on St. Paul's School's carefully tended hockey pitches behind the assembly hall instead of at the dining hall. Once we'd passed our exam with top grades, we too would become so-called Paulines. Everyone at St. Paul's went on to have a brilliant career—at least that's what the mothers of Paulines said—and they all knew by the age of sixteen what they were going to study and do with the rest of their lives.

Nothing could interest me less at the moment.

"Delirium—what a scary thought! Hallucinations and nightmares. You no longer know who you are or who anybody else is. Your dad might think you're an orc or a synes-creep."

"Oh, kiss my ass."

"Here? Word would get around, **mon ami**."

I didn't react to this. For the very first time I couldn't bring myself to laugh at one of Scott's jokes. He watched me closely through the square inch-thick glasses he'd recently started to wear, of his own free will, in order to look like a geek. "Know why? Because of the girls." There are no girls at Colet Court.

"When are you going to go and see him again, Valentiner?"

I shrugged. "My mum won't let me."

Scott tugged at the three hairs on his chin that he's been trying, unsuccessfully, to sculpt into a beard. "She can't stand the fact that you like him, **mon copain**. Jealousy. Like my dad. It rankles him that my mother loves me. The same problem all fathers have at the birth of their first son," he stated pompously. He's known that he wants to study psychology since he started seeing a psychotherapist at the age of nine near St. John's, the church with the unicorn on its coat of arms. He intends to specialize in psychosis and somatic delusions.

Now, however, he was observing a group of older St. Paul's pupils, who no longer had to wear a school uniform but were allowed to wear whatever they liked—as long as it included a jacket, an ironed shirt, and a tie, as well as full-length trousers. They were holding the doors open for one another.

"Where exactly did the accident happen, Valentiner?"

"On Hammersmith Bridge," I replied. "Yesterday morning." As we stared into each other's eyes, the penny finally dropped in our highly gifted but idiotic brains. It always takes geniuses longer to understand the easiest thing. We're totally and embarrassingly unequipped for everyday life.

"**Merde,** Valentiner! That's just around the bloody corner from here! Your dad was hit as he—" Scott stops abruptly.

Yes, it would seem that my father . . . was on his

way to see me. He was going to come! My sense of joy blazed for one bright second, but then the full force of my guilt came crashing down on me. If only I hadn't sent him the email, he'd never have been on that bridge. If I hadn't invited him to come, he wouldn't be lying in a hospital bed now, half-dead. If I hadn't . . .

"Valentiner?" Scott asked.

I couldn't answer.

"Valentiner! Whatever you may be thinking right now, check this out and then think again!"

He was holding up his smartphone. It's approximately fifty-three times more expensive than my own, and on it I could see a shaky video Scott had found on YouTube. He wasn't the only one—it had 2.5 million hits. The film's title was "A Real Hero" and it showed a man swimming in the Thames. The camera zoomed in, and the blurred footage showed the man diving into the water and resurfacing a few seconds later with a wet bundle. It was only when he had made it to the bank that it became clear that the bundle was a girl. The man carried the child to Hammersmith Bridge. The picture shook as he strode toward the camera and said, "Were you only filming, or did you think of calling for help?" Four seconds later the car smashed into him. The film broke off. The man was my father.

"Your dad's a cool dude," Scott said dryly. "You should tell him that one day."

The bright burst of joy and energy that had

swept through my heart when I caught sight of my father in the film gave way to a dark shadow at Scott's words. My yearning to tell that living father everything—everything I thought, everything about who I am—turned to despair as I was reminded of his now motionless figure. Motionless and cut off from the world.

Slowly I pulled out the permit that my mother had refused to sign and showed Scott a picture of the back of her Visa card, which I had secretly photographed with my smartphone that morning, just to be on the safe side. I hadn't actually meant to use it. Until now. Until the film.

"Can you do this one?"

"Easy-peasy," said Scott, taking my mobile and the piece of paper, and spiriting his fountain pen from its case.

SO AT MIDDAY today I rubbed sand in my eyes and pretended to my French teacher, Madame Lupion, that I'd suffered an allergic reaction. Then I set off for the Wellington with bright red eyes that were still itching and weeping.

No one paid any attention to me in the Underground. No one ever says anything on the tube, and no one looks at anyone either. People act as if they're alone in the world, even when your face is being pressed into your neighbor's armpit. The air is seventy-three times more polluted down there than it is aboveground.

Sheila Walker didn't comment on my eyes either. They really do sting.

Dr. Saul is sticking a sheet of paper to the wall of the waiting room as I enter. It reads: "This is a specialist neurological clinic, not a clubroom, so no slurping your tea and no chatting." I try to sneak past God without being seen.

"Hold it there, Samuel! What's the matter with your eyes?" he snaps without turning around. He carefully sticks down the last corner of the poster. His lower arms are powerful, and his fingers never shake.

"I . . . I have an allergy, sir."

"Oh yeah? Well, so do I, Samuel: I'm allergic to liars."

"I might have gotten some sand in them," I answer tentatively, adding a reverent "sir," just in case.

God turns to face me. He has one blue eye and one green. His right eye, the blue one, is cold, whereas the green one is warm—two different men staring out at me from the Viking face framed by strawberry-blond sideburns.

"Some sand, eh? You look as if you slept face-down on the beach. Trying to blind yourself? No? Ever heard of neuronavigation?"

"N-no, sir," I stammer.

"Then come with me," he purrs, and leads me up to the next floor and into the magnetic resonance imaging demonstration room.

"Allow me to present . . . the monster," Dr. Saul says. "This is a functional MRI scanner. It measures brain activity. Bloody thing cost two million pounds and is regarded as England's first mind reader. It's so smart that we hardly understand how it works." He points to a chair and says, "Sit down, tilt your head back, and open your eyes wide!" He trickles a few drops onto my eyeballs. This immediately relieves the stinging.

All at once it strikes me that God is very often very alone. Dr. Saul switches off the lights and turns on the projectors. The whole wall is suddenly plastered with images of slices of brain. My eyes feel better in the dark.

He runs his fingers slowly, almost lovingly, over the projections on the wall. "Here's a splendid aneurysm. We plug it by entering through the upper thigh and working our way along the veins. Ooh, how about this one! A wonderful example of a hemangioblastoma, as snug as a pea in a pod." His voice changes from black to light green to pink as he traces the outlines of different brains. God loves brains.

"Have you ever peered into someone's soul, Samuel?" he says, beaming a microscopic view of the brain onto the wall. "These are the two halves of the brain, as seen from the spinal cord at the bottom of the neck. It's as if you were climbing up a tunnel from the neck, striding down a long corridor to the end of the brain stem, and then stepping from the cerebellum into the center of the brain. The secret chamber, the seat of our humanity."

He enlarges the picture until it takes up the entire wall. It looks like a cathedral, with veins for buttresses and cells like high vaulted ceilings. It's magnificent—magnificent and very weird.

"A church built of thoughts," I whisper.

God pins me with his two-colored gaze, as if until this point I had been unreal to him, a simple offshoot of C7, and am now becoming real. His cool eye becomes warmer, then he gives a slow nod. "Exactly, Samuel," he says softly. "The brain is a church built of thoughts."

He abruptly flicks the lights back on and is once again a blond Viking with the forehead and shoulders of a bull. "Okay, you're wondering if your father's going to die, right?" Nothing holds any fear for God, not even the toughest questions.

He picks up a marker and draws a big black dot on a whiteboard. "This is 'waking,' okay?" He writes **Awake** next to the black dot and draws five concentric circles radiating out from it. At the edges, above, below, and on both sides of the largest circle, he writes the word **Death**. Inside the circles, from central to outermost, from the black dot, he writes **Numb, Asleep/Dreaming, Unconscious, Coma,** and **Brain-Dead.** The marker squeaks on the board.

"There are a variety of forms of life on the margins of death," God explains. Tapping the area marked "Coma," he takes a different pen, a red one this time, and draws three lines. "Deep, medium, and light coma. But it is in these areas, Sam, closer to the core," says Saul, shading in the rings marked "Asleep/Dreaming" and "Unconscious," "much closer to being awake, that your father is presently living. Do you see? Closer to life than to death. Do you understand?"

I nod. Has God noticed that he describes unconscious and coma as places rather than states?

Dr. Saul tosses the markers casually onto the table.

"A word of advice," he barks as he leaves the room. "Use toothpaste instead of sand next time."

ON MY WAY to take the lift back down to the second floor, I run through all the things I want to tell my father today. Maybe I'll mention Saul's model. The disc world.

I wonder if you dream beyond the sleep zone, and if a medically induced coma is similar to a true coma or not. And if you know that you're in a coma. I don't know I'm dreaming when I dream.

Is being in a coma like being alive, except that you don't know you're alive? Like in **The Matrix**?

In recent days I've had an occasional impression that I can feel my father. There was something restless about him, as if—and these are thoughts I will never reveal to Scott—he was searching for the path leading back to reality through a maze of darkness and fear. I now know that might be the case. If waking and sleeping and coma aren't states but places, then my father is currently on a journey between those places. Or worlds. Or zones that get darker and darker, the closer they are to death.

Waiting for the lift, I imagine these worlds as one gigantic subterranean space. They rest on top of one another like discs and become more unfathomable the further you advance from the waking point. Nobody knows what it's like at its outermost edge. Maybe a lot different. Maybe coma isn't a dark zone. Maybe it's identical to life in the waking zone, where I'm now sitting and hoping that my father will respond to my pressure and squeeze my hand. Hoping that just once he will approach the waking zone, through all the different levels and zones and degrees of darkness, via the staircases and corridors that appear abruptly through the fog of medication and dreams, allowing him for a few short moments to navigate a path through all the intermediate zones between waking and death, and surface.

If he squeezes my hand, he's still here. "I'm here, Sam, I'm here. Even if I'm elsewhere. I'm coming back."

But so far he hasn't squeezed back. Not after the first operation, nor after the second, when they mended his ruptured spleen and pinned his broken arm, nor after a further ten days.

Maybe today?

Eddie

―――//――――

"You look a bit cross today, Mrs. Tomlin."

"I'm not cross, Dr. Foss."

"Of course not. My apologies."

"I'm **furious**. There's a difference, wouldn't you say?"

"Certainly, Mrs. Tomlin." Dr. Foss remains as friendly as a butler pouring tea, but I can hear my voice getting louder. My fear is howling inside me like a wounded animal.

"Are you actually doing anything, or are you simply allowing him to wither away in order to save money?" I snarl.

Dr. Foss is standing behind me, but I can see his face in the mirror in the brightly lit, tiled room in which, every day for the last fourteen days, I've put on a smock and taken it off again, disinfected my hands and lower arms, and pulled a white oval mask over my mouth and nose. Dr. Foss purses his lips almost imperceptibly and stares at the floor. I've hurt his feelings. Hallelujah. In a sense, I am grateful that there are still people with feelings to hurt in English hospitals. You need to have some feelings in the first place for them to be hurt, and if you have feelings, you can empathize.

"I'm sorry, I'm not usually like this. Or I hope not, anyway."

Dr. Foss flashes his engaging smile and says, "Of course not," and ties the turquoise smock behind my back. The way he stands and walks and goes about his work brings to mind either an expensively trained royal valet or a well-educated aristocratic spy. He's one of those very rare gentlemen who would remain on the deck of a sinking ship until every woman and child had been winched to safety. He's even kind enough to push the elastic band of my face mask a little higher on the back of my head. Gingerly, as if I might explode.

I use my elbow to pump some disinfectant gel from the dispenser mounted on the tiled wall and rub it into my hands, which are shaking. Suntanned hands with ink stains on them, quivering like little wings.

"Be patient with yourself," he says gently.

Ha, me of all people! I'm never patient with myself. Most of the time I don't even like myself. I push the button again so I don't have to meet Foss's gaze.

"Every patient needs someone to believe in them. Believe in Mr. Skinner, Mrs. Tomlin. If he has a good reason to wake up, then . . ."

I feel like asking Dr. Foss which book of motivational axioms he's quoting. I want to yell at him that I'm not a good reason for Henri Skinner—not good enough, in any case. After a totally weird three-year, on-off relationship during which I sometimes didn't see Henri for months on end, he made it abundantly clear to me two years ago that I wasn't the woman with whom he wanted to spend the rest of his life.

It was the first time I had said to Henri, "I love you. I want you, forever and beyond, in this life and every other."

He replied, "I don't want you." And the world went dark.

I've only just stopped feeling ashamed. I've only just stopped missing him. I've only just controlled the yearning for which there are no words and no logic. I've only just begun to contemplate the possibility of starting a new life, with another man. And now Henri has erupted into my days, my nights, and my desires again.

When I heard the police officer say his name—"Do you know Henri Malo Skinner?"—three memories came flooding back: the heavy, fluid heat of his body on mine; that night on the beach beneath the green shooting stars when we told each other about what we'd been like as children; and his expression as he walked out.

Henri had entered my name into his mobile and written, **In case of emergency,** on a slip of paper stuck into his passport, and had even put my name in his living will. Which all came as just as much of a shock to me as the phone call from the police fifteen days ago. The police officers—an awkward fat man and a fidgety red-haired woman—were quite annoyed when I told them that I wasn't Henri's partner or fiancée or cousin, and that I had last seen him about two years ago, at about quarter to nine on the morning of October 2, 2014.

I love you. I want you, forever and beyond, in this life and every other.

I don't want you.

And then I slapped his face and threw him out.

"Get lost!" I shouted, while what I really wanted to say was, "Stay!"

"Get out!" I roared, while inwardly begging, "Love me!"

"Get lost, for hell's sake!" really meant, "Go before I humiliate myself any further!"

He left.

I'll never forget his face when he turned around one last time by the door. It was as if he couldn't fathom this departure and was looking back at the flip side of our love and wondering how he'd happened to cross the boundary between the two. Such desperation in his eyes.

I almost cried, "Stay!" and "It doesn't matter, you don't have to love me." I'd have meant it. My love was greater than my desire to be loved, and it was worse that he didn't want my love than not being loved in return. I don't have a clue if that's normal.

For two years I missed Henri every day, then I met Wilder Glass, who desires me, who does want me. I'm no longer the same woman who loved Henri Skinner so much that she was ready to spend this life and every other with him. No, that old me is an empty shell, and the thought of it sends ripples of shame over my skin.

Yet here I am. The woman he didn't want but whose name he nevertheless put in his living will. I'm the person for emergencies, for dying but not for life. **What the fuck?**

Wilder doesn't know I've been coming to the Wellington every day for the past two weeks. Some of the time he thinks I'm at readings or with agents, at others I'm meeting promising authors, genre writers and utopians. I've a lot on my plate as a publisher, and so Wilder doesn't inquire and he's never jealous. Wilder David Stephen Ptolemy Glass has too much class, too expensive an education, too much sense, and far too enviable a reputation in literary circles ever to be jealous of anyone.

I hate lying, and yet I do it as naturally as if the truth weren't even an option. What is truth, anyway? A question of sufficient imagination. And how are you supposed to tell your partner why all of a sudden you've started to take care of an ex-boyfriend you've never mentioned? The mere fact of not having mentioned him would arouse any other man's suspicions, but maybe not Wilder Glass's.

I don't know why I'm here, but I can't help myself. It would cost me too much energy to deny myself, so I subject myself to this torture and get on with it.

There are signs and posters all over the place here. There are some bloody rules in the changing room, because presumably, without them, most visitors would beat and shout at their relatives to get some kind of reaction out of them.

1. Behave calmly, kindly, and respectfully in the patients' presence.
2. Avoid hurried movements and walk quietly.
3. We do not talk about patients; we talk to them.
4. Approach patients slowly and always so that they can see you and will not be startled when you touch or speak to them.

EVEN MARRIED COUPLES don't treat each other like this. Henri hasn't moved a muscle in these two weeks. He hasn't blinked or moaned. Nothing. Frozen in an invisible block of anesthetics and pain-killers, cooled by the machines that have adjusted his body temperature downward. The depth of his sedation is measured every eight hours. Minus five on the Richmond scale means unreachable; minus three and he'd have dragged himself back into the world; minus one and he'd be awake. I imagine him valiantly trudging toward minus one through a black void.

"Ready, Mrs. Tomlin?" Dr. Foss's voice is quiet and respectful too. To him everybody is presumably a patient, suffering from some illness or other.

"Yes," I answer, but I'm not. I'm afraid. Fear is a rampant creeper tightening its tendrils around my heart, my stomach, and my head, trying to force me to run to the end of the earth and hide there in the darkness.

Dr. Foss looks at me with soulful eyes. He's a huge bear like Baloo. His boss, Dr. Saul, is a huge asshole. He isn't thrilled that I want to be there during the attempt to wake Henri up.

"You're afraid, Tomlin"—Dr. Saul calls me Tomlin, as if he were a drill instructor and I a soldier—"and your fear disturbs me during my work and infects Mr. Skinner."

Dr. Foss interjects, "Dr. Saul doesn't mean it like that, Mrs. Tomlin."

Dr. Saul whirls around. "Don't you ever again dare to suggest that I don't mean what I say! Never again. It's an insult to my intelligence, which, unlike you, I do not spoil with flattery. Their relatives' worry is toxic to these patients."

Whether it's as a soldier or a trembling impediment to Henri's recovery, I am here. I breathe, and with each exhalation, I seek to blow my anxiety somewhere far over the horizon. An author I publish taught me that trick. It had something to do with martial arts, a way of suppressing memory.

Blow it away. Maybe Dr. Saul is correct and my panic is poisonous. Then again, maybe not. I don't want to run the risk, so I decide not to be scared and I blow my fear a long, long way away.

"Are you sure you're ready, Mrs. Tomlin?" Dr. Foss asks.

I nod. Another lie. **Breathe out, Eddie.** I've had no idea what I've been doing here for the past fifteen days—I just do it.

We walk past A and B, past the cubicles, each with a bed in it, and in each bed an individual fate. Fingers quiver, eyelids twitch; the battle for life goes on in silence, far below the surface. I read somewhere that an induced coma is exactly halfway between life and death.

Is Henri already thinking in the language of the dead? He's lying in cubicle C7. I go over to the bed and reach for his hand. Dr. Foss adjusts his tie and carefully loosens Henri's cooling sleeves. "The brain doesn't like being inactive for a long period of time. It's like a car: if it simply stands around, its condition deteriorates. Machines like to be used, then they run smoothly."

Dr. Saul stands there like a stocky blond tree at the head of Henri's bed, a brain scan in his left hand. He rolls his eyes in irritation at the head of the intensive care unit. "Oh for God's sake, Fozzie. Do stop butchering metaphors in my presence. The brain is not a machine, or else we'd have some idea of how it works. It's like leavened dough: we knead it this way and that until we run out of ideas. In this particular case, we don't have the foggiest idea what's going to happen. Got that?"

I know Dr. Saul's right, but I dearly wish he weren't.

Dr. Foss smiles at me, and his smile says, **Yeah, well, that's what he thinks, but after all, he is the best.**

The fearful creeper shoots out its tendrils into all my muscles at once. Into my tummy, shoulders, and neck. Every strand of my being is as taut as a drum, and I hold my breath, as if I want to bring time to a standstill so the worst cannot happen. Time pays no attention to me and catapults me back ten years into the past.

"DON'T LET ME die in the hospital," my father whispered as the paramedics carried him past me on a stretcher following the heart attack that had struck him down as he dined alone at the kitchen table. A steak, rare, with mustard and a salad containing fresh watercress. The piece of gorgonzola he'd planned to have for dessert with cherry jam was standing on the sideboard.

More and more often my father would eat alone in the kitchen. My mother had long since given up even liking him, but at seventy she was too tired to leave. My father still loved her, after all this time, throughout their fifty years together. He loved the doors and walls that separated them from each other in their home because he knew that she was in the next room, on the other side of the wallpaper and the thick, muggy silence. That was enough for him, and the affection with which he gazed at the walls behind which she sat, somewhere, never failed to break my heart.

Following his panicked call—"Eddie, my girl, I think something bad is happening to me"—I made it back from my publishing house almost at the same time as the paramedics arrived, and as I held his strong, rough, increasingly dry hand all the way from the kitchen table to the ambulance's wide-open doors, he begged me not to let him die in the hospital. I promised him that I wouldn't.

I followed the ambulance to the hospital on my motorbike and then tailed the ambulance men all the way into the green-tiled casualty department with its aluminum doors. I ignored the doctor, whose job was to pummel hearts back to life with his electric-shock machine and his pride, as he tried to prevent me from entering this cramped corridor of misery, fatigue, and human suffering. I ignored him as he tried to explain to me that other rules applied at the end of a person's life than during it, that love no longer had anything to do with it, only adrenaline and oxygen, and that I'd get in the doctors' way.

I stayed, even though I'd have much preferred to run away, screaming. I stayed with my father as they cut open his trousers and shirt, as they fixed needles and catheters to him, as they talked to him but actually looked at him less and less. The classic, robotic triage you'd find in any casualty department on a Friday night: drunks with injuries from broken glass; battered women; lonely little grandmothers; ironic, cynical police officers; the odd distraught relative, propelled this way and that like a lost pinball, surrounded by cynicism and frenzied activity. In the midst of it all lay my father on a thin turquoise sheet and a hard stretcher, apologizing to every doctor or nurse who examined him: "Sorry for the inconvenience. You must have more important things to do." As if a heart attack were just an embarrassing mishap.

Once they left us alone in the green-tiled room for a while. What if he died now? How was I supposed to stop him?

He gave me a labored smile. His face seemed so foreign. His features had aged on the way from home to the hospital. He took my hand. I placed my other hand on top of his and he put his other one on mine—a stack of four hands—while his pulse lurched up and down, and his heartbeat scratched a jagged electric landscape on the monitor. I didn't know at the time that we were already saying our last goodbyes.

NOW THE SAME beeping, red LED mountains decorate Henri's screen as they did my father's. Signs that he is alive. Signals from his desperately battling heart. A heart monitor, a breathing monitor, a blood pressure gauge, a pulse gauge, an oxygen density sensor, a lung machine, a pulmonary bypass that makes a soggy, chugging sound like a ship's engine, an electroencephalogram. The CT scans of his fractured skull are projected onto the wall.

"Should he stop breathing spontaneously before we remove the tracheal cannula from his throat, you can go and get yourself a coffee, Tomlin."

"And you can behave yourself."

Dr. Saul raises his eyebrows. "Let's get started," he says.

Sam

I join two doctors in the lift. One of them presses three, the other five. I'm not brave enough to push past them and press two. It's embarrassing, but I really can't do it. Scott would say that I'm one of those people who deliberately walk the wrong way to avoid hurting the feelings of the person I asked for directions. He's right.

"Going to the veg compartment?" Floor Three asks Floor Five cheerfully.

"Yeah. I've got one with about as much brain activity as a can of beans."

"Are we still playing squash this evening?"

"Sure. Eight o'clock."

Floor Three gets out, but Veg Floor stays and starts whistling through his teeth. "After you," the doctor says when the lift reaches the fifth floor— the veg compartment.

"Thank you, sir," I mumble. **Fantastic, Valentiner. Damn.**

A set of double doors swings open in front of us with a gentle thud. I'm just planning to get back into the lift as soon as the doctor is out of sight and go back down to the second floor when a nurse comes through the doors.

"You can go straight in, love."

"Thank you." **Damn, damn, DAMN!**

I've now gone too far to admit that I'm in completely the wrong place, so I walk decisively along the wide corridor—and she follows me! This unit is completely unlike the warehouse downstairs. The corridor is carpeted. The air is pleasantly cool and it's very, very quiet. There's none of the tension you feel in the intensive care unit with all the bright lights and alarms and the constant vigilance and injections and incisions to ward off approaching death. This floor is like the forgotten attic of an old house.

What do I do if the nurse follows me to the very end of the corridor? What do I say? "Oops, wrong building. I meant to go to the intestine department, actually."

There are photos on the doors here. Laughing, friendly faces, and under each one, a name.

On the first door: "Leonard." The photo shows a man wearing blue overalls and a Manchester United scarf and sitting on an excavator. I can hear someone sobbing quietly on the other side of the door.

The second door: "Elisabeth." The photos show her holding up a tart. Behind the door I hear a man's voice saying, "Now breathe out. I'm turning your wrist to the left . . . Yes, nice and relaxed, as if you were whipping cream . . . good . . . to go with scones."

After two or three more doors—"Amanda" and "William" and "Yamashiro"—I've understood the principle: the pictures are of the people who live on the other side of those doors. In the veg compartment. I'm willing to bet they no longer look like they do in the photos.

"Then again, frozen vegetables don't resemble the pictures on the packaging either, **mon ami**." I hear Scott inside my head making comments that I would never allow to cross my mind.

The nurse is still tailing me. I continue along the corridor, calculating that I'll probably have to walk straight into the end wall because I can't think of anything else to do. I'm coming to the last door, which is ajar. The sign on it reads "Madelyn."

Soft piano music flows from the room. The gentle sounds are so at odds with the surroundings that I wonder if this isn't a dream—a long, bad dream in which I'm waiting for my father outside school and he never turns up because he's dead. I stop and close my eyes. That's how you wake up: by screwing up your eyes in your dream. When this has no effect, I raise my hands. Stare at your hands while dreaming and you'll wake up. Still nothing changes. This must be reality. When I lower my hands again, the corridor is empty. There's only me, the music, and the half-open door.

Then three things happen all at once. I notice that although I've felt cold for the past two weeks, suddenly I don't—the music is like a mild breeze, thawing my bones. Also, the lights flicker. And time starts to thin. I get the feeling that a single tiny movement would be enough to change my life forever. I reach the end of the corridor and, with it, the end of my old life.

I'm going to walk back, get into the lift, and take it down to the second floor. Exactly. That's exactly what I'm going to do. But no, I don't do any of those things. I stay where I am and a feeling takes shape inside me that I'm about to find something I didn't expect to find.

Instead of going back to the lift, I watch my hand, as if of its own volition, take hold of the door handle and push the last door in the corridor a little farther open.

A low white bookshelf with a blue teapot full of red tulips on top of it. Curtains by the window. Paintings and photos on the walls—landscapes, faces, mountains from above, and underwater scenes. And on the very edge of the bed, her legs covered by an ankle-length nightie, sits a blond girl surrounded by music. The girl looks straight at me. She doesn't blink. She simply stares at me, and I completely forget not to meet her eye.

Standing in front of her, with her back to me, is a small woman with curly red hair in a nurse's uniform. She's combing the girl's hair. ". . . and in the evening, when drops of dew cling to the tips of the blades of grass, my two little tubby tots emerge from their sofa cave and lick the grass, and their catlike eyes watch the stars breathing."

I think the nightie has unicorns on it, but they may be ducks. I'm not sure. The girl stares at me, and something in her blue gaze pierces my skin, perhaps reaching places you see only if you can look through people. The music washes up the walls, converges in the middle of the ceiling, and sprinkles down onto my head.

"Did you know that stars could breathe, Maddie?"

For a split second I can sense some movement in Madelyn's glassy gaze, like a fish swimming from one hiding place to another at the bottom of a deep lake. No, it isn't a lake—it's the wind in her eyes, a gust of music, and the movement was a raven taking off and spreading its wings. Madelyn has ravens in her eyes, and I tumble into this sky full of ravens.

"The world is so beautiful when you're a star looking down on us all," the nurse continues. "On the cats in the grass, on girls sleeping with open eyes, and on boys standing in the doorway with their jaws on the floor." With these last words, the nurse turns to face me. She has a face like a leprechaun's, with laughter lines arcing from the corners of her eyes to the corners of her mouth. The name on the badge pinned to her dark-purple blouse is Marion.

Nurse Marion says, "Hello. Have you come to visit Maddie?"

So what does this smart-ass sidekick do next? I slam the door and run away, even though part of me is left standing there by the door, because at the end of the corridor is a girl who can see through me into other worlds, as if I were made of crystal and all of reality is no more than a glass bubble with her floating inside.

My feet pound the carpet. Her name is Madelyn. Ma-de-lyn. I'm simultaneously happier and sadder than I've ever been in my entire life.

Eddie

They work like a team of Formula 1 mechanics. Dr. Foss raises the head of the bed and dabs Henri's eyelids with a cotton swab, while Dr. Saul taps his patient's knee, a nurse draws the blue curtains around the bed, and an anesthetist removes the sedative drip from the catheter in the side of Henri's neck.

I know there's going to be no "awakening" like in the movies. He's not going to open his eyes and say, "Hey, Ed, got any decent whiskey in this joint?"

First, his reflexes will return. Spontaneous breathing. Blinking. Swallowing. Then there'll be pain. Pain will permeate every corner of his being before swelling into a torrent of dread.

For days he will be enveloped in hallucinations like thick smoke, although Dr. Foss claims that they use a mild sedative and tranquilizer at the Wellington, leading to fewer delirious visions. As if that were reassuring: two nightmares instead of three.

I believed Dr. Saul when he said, "We know more about the surface of the moon than we do about the inside of our own heads. That's a fact. We have no idea what goes on in the brain when it releases a rush of interleukin-2 in the event of serious inflammation. Nor do we know which harmless sensory perceptions manifest themselves as panic and nightmares for Mr. Skinner, or turn Dr. Foss here into a singing pumpkin."

Dr. Foss added indignantly, "We do, however, presume that Mr. Skinner doesn't dream. Narcosis completely stifles a person's ability to dream."

"We? I don't. Is that invisible friend still with you, Fozzie?" asked Dr. Saul.

My creeping fear grows and grows. Each of us is like an archive of themselves. Demons start to crawl from the drawers, compartments, and safes of my memory.

TEN YEARS AGO in that casualty department, I felt anxiety on a scale I'd never previously known. That's when it was born. It grew inside me like an invasive plant, quickly and greedily, wrapping itself around my organs and gradually crushing them. The thought that my father might die, just like that, in his prime, filled me with panic.

His eyes shone like fjords in the shortest midsummer night. I stayed by his side until they took him away to intensive care and put in the first of three stents. No doctor came to see me after the operation, as they do in those TV hospital series, to say, "Don't you worry, Mrs. Tomlin. We're treating your father and four weeks from now he'll be back outside, mowing the lawn." There was no one in charge—only stressed, impatient nurses. No doctor, no one to take responsibility.

I stayed with my father. Once he asked, "Is your mother coming?" and I lied, saying, "Yes, tomorrow." She didn't pay him a single visit in his last three days.

At the end of those three days my father died on the hospital floor on his way back from the toilet. According to the man in the next bed, his last words were, "At long last I enjoyed a really good night's sleep," before he collapsed in "convulsions," as my mother would later refer to them. "He was in convulsions, Edwina. There was no point in fetching him back a second time, you know. There was no more oxygen in his brain. He wouldn't have been the same. Like a child . . . or worse." I hated her for the relief in her voice—amazement too, but above all relief—and for her impatience, her acute impatience, when I burst into tears.

ON THE EVENING it happened, I was sitting in the office of my publishing house, Realitycrash, because I'd nipped in to pick up the manuscript I was editing, an incredible book that was to be my next lead title. I was longing to tell my dad about it.

I publish novels of magical realism. Not fantasy: there are no elves, no orcs, no vampires. Utopias and dystopias, stories about alternate realities, other planets, one world where there are no men and another devoid of adults—anything that's potentially only three steps from our own reality and represents a scientifically plausible form of the miraculous.

I'd only left my father alone for a couple of hours in that hospital, which smelled, like this one, of antiseptic and anxiety. His room had a view of a canal and the golden roofs of London, and we would watch people playing with their dogs on the towpath.

A nurse declared that my father's prognosis was positive; his collapse had been merely a shot across his bows. The doctors, who were incredibly young, would never look you in the eye or say a word as they hurried along the corridors, their white coats fluttering behind them as a symbol of their importance.

Dad's bows were obviously less sturdy than everyone had assumed, for two hours later he was gone. I stood in his room, the manuscript in one hand and my motorbike helmet in the other, and his bed was empty.

Suddenly there was a doctor in charge. He led me to my father, whose eyes no longer shone like fjords but were now empty blue discs. His body was still warm, or at least slightly warm, and I sat down beside him in the empty farewell room, took his rapidly cooling hand in mine, and read the book to him. I didn't know what else to do.

A nurse came to tell me that she was going home. I continued to read to him. Another nurse came to tell me that she was starting her shift. She came back later and said that she was going home now too. For a night and a day I held a vigil for my departed father. I whispered, "Good night, moon. Good night, room. Good night, Dad," and in the early hours it felt as if he were standing behind me with his hands on my shoulders and telling me, "Now you'll always know where I am."

The worst thing imaginable had happened. My best friend was dead. My childhood was dead. There was no one left to love me.

"DON'T GET your hopes up even a jot," says Dr. Saul. "There's only a very slim chance that a person who wakes up after such a serious accident will be able to think in a logical fashion. We're talking less than a nine percent chance. Do you understand that, Mrs. Tomlin?"

"No, I'm just a poor, stupid woman, doctor."

Dr. Saul scrutinizes me. I stare back at him. I want Henri to come back as I know him. As the man who morning, night, or in the middle of the day would appear in my kitchen, upstairs from my publishing house, and softly say, "Hi, Eddie. I'm tired. Do you mind if I lay down?" At my place he was able to sleep. Sometimes for three days in a row. Even asleep, he was the pivot and fulcrum around which my weeks and days and emotions revolved, powered by his presence alone.

I'm crazy to still love Henri, even if now the flame is low, as low as it goes, just big enough to hurt but not burn me.

The beeping of the heart-rate monitor accelerates.

"What's wrong?" I ask Dr. Foss, who frowns. "Is that normal?"

No answer.

His heart is racing, it's speeding . . . no, those aren't the tripping steps of Henri's treacherous heart, they're . . .

The blue curtain parts to reveal a boy's face with a sprinkling of freckles and wide-open eyes, followed by a lanky body in a navy-blue school blazer, matching trousers, and a light-blue polo shirt under a turquoise visitor's smock.

The boy rushes over to the bed. I feel my heart tighten at the sight of his eyes above the mask and the way his face ages from one heartbeat to the next. A despairing moan escapes his lips. "Dad?"

Wait a second. Dad? Henri Skinner has a son?

Sam

There are about a thousand people clustered around my father. He looks as if he's sleeping so deeply that his heart beats only once per hour. They've removed the thin blue sheet from his body. My father seems to be wearing a vest of skin the color of baking powder; only his arms are tanned. He has electrodes stuck to his chest—strange eyes with long blue lashes that connect him to machines.

I think of Scott and Michael Schumacher and the fact that someone can simply go missing in the middle of his life without dying.

"Dad?" My voice sounds like a yellow four, feeble and small, and I hate it.

"Sam. There you are. Your father'll be glad," says Dr. Foss.

I reach instinctively for my father's hand, as I've done every day for the past two weeks. But

61

his arm shoots up before I can touch him, and I shrink back, bumping into Fozzie Bear. My father groans and his arm thrashes the air, then drops to one side. His body twists and rears up. It reminds me of a garden hose.

Dr. Foss pushes me aside. Backs close ranks in front of me to form a wall. Beyond them I can sense my father, as if he were breaking through the zones, racing through the disc world and the rings of life—coma, unconsciousness, sleep/dreaming, numbness—and heading straight for the center—waking—and at the same time it's as if the darkness were pursuing him, so dense and close that it's already embracing him and pulling him back. I can feel my father's presence more distinctly than ever.

"Dad!"

"EEG. Ventricular tachycardia. No pulse," someone says.

Hands pass each other syringes, needles, probes, and tubes.

"Defib, three sixty."

A red eye joins the blue electrodes on my father's chest.

"Dr. Saul? Ventricular fibrillation?"

"Stay calm, kids. Keep calm. Glucose level?"

"Three, two, one." A buzz and then a bang like two car bumpers colliding. The darkness dissolves like black smoke. Now my father is with us. He's fully here!

Lighthouse, bombs, milk churn: those are the

images that race through my mind. I have no idea where they come from. No, that isn't true. I do know, but I don't understand. I see shadows on my father, and bravery and despair. And the images inside him.

"Cardiac massage thirty, two." Fist on fist, pressing down on my father's chest. A sound like spaghetti shattering.

"Cardiac arrest."

There, a gap between the smocks. My father's eyes are open. He can see me. He's looking at me!

"Dad!" I whisper.

It must cost him an immense effort. My father's gaze steadies. Yes, it seems as if he's waking up. He's coming back. He stares at me, his face a question mark.

"Keep calm. Gently does it. Mild hypothermia. Time, please."

"Five seconds, Dr. Saul."

An ear-splitting noise, high and shrill.

"Adrenaline."

"Seven."

"Get the boy out of here!"

"Eight, nine . . ."

It's quiet. So quiet, apart from the screaming. Dad gazes at me, but his presence is fading, dissolving, and he's so sad, so infinitely sad and . . .

"Prepare antiarrhythmic amiodarone, and be quick. We're at eleven. Critical now. I don't want him to die after bringing him back, you hear me?

And please get the boy out of here. He won't stop screaming!"

"Outcome!"

A hand reaching for mine and a voice that sounds calm, deep, and safe like a dark-green eight says, "He isn't dying, Sam. He can't. He forgot how to many years ago. Sam? Come on. Come with me!"

The shrill noise condenses into my own screaming and fragments into words. "No! No! No!" It turns into rage—rage at my father and hatred for all doctors because they do everything wrong. Then the sensation of falling and falling and falling.

And suddenly this stranger is there, this woman with incredible gray-green eyes like a wolf. She's there and she catches me before I come apart.

Henri

———— // ————

I'm falling. And then I see my own shadow rising at breakneck speed from the asphalt to meet me and hear a noise like eggshells breaking on the rim of a china cup.

I'm falling for the umpteenth time, and something is watching me fall. It seems to be watching me closely, opening for me. A mouth. A huge open mouth. Now the bottom of the lake opens up for me and sucks me toward it. But then I'm hurled upward again. I rush up through the black funnel, as if an angler has caught me on his line, his hook driving deep into my heart, and is now reeling me in. I rise up hard and high from the lake into dazzling light . . .

"Adrenaline."

"Seven."

"Get the boy out of here!"

I lose my balance. I throw up my arms, but it feels as if I don't have any. I want to break my fall and then I see the boy, looking at me, and he cradles me in his gaze.

"Eight, nine, ten," counts a voice, but then screaming drowns it out.

I see the neon tubes beyond the flashing lamps. I see the smocks and tubes, hear the machines, and I feel the hardness of the bed.

I'm here! Please, I want to say, **I'm here!** Nobody notices me. Apart from my son.

Somebody holds my hand, and I recognize the shape of the fingers, the texture of the skin, and the firmness of the muscles underneath. I know this hand. It belongs to . . . Eddie.

Hold me, Eddie . . . I don't want to die. Hold me, I beg you!

Then I see myself. I see myself reflected in a metal pole with two drips dangling from it. I see my face. It's lopsided, my head battered. I see my eyes glass over and turn smooth and hard, and beyond them I see myself disappearing into myself, into the depths.

Eddie! Hold me!

She holds me tight, and I try to drag myself back into the room by her hand, back to life, but I don't have the strength.

And then something inexplicable happens: her hand lets go of mine. I fall into a bottomless pit, and above me, far above me, something closes. A huge glass barrier, like a tinted shop window, closes, as I sink and vanish into myself. It shuts, and the lake freezes over. A hard, dark, impenetrable layer of ice or glass cuts me off from the world. The glass appears to be rising while I slide deeper and deeper, and the colors fade, as do all sounds and smells. There's a silent absence of life in this . . . nonworld.

Eddie no longer loves me, cries my heart, which has stopped beating.

Eddie

D r. Saul kicked us out.
"Take her to the chapel!" he said, and that's where we are sitting now, in the quietest room in the hospital. It's as quiet as on the bottom of the ocean.

The boy has curled up in my arms with his eyes closed and is scraping his thumbs against his index fingers. He rubs them incessantly, whispering the whole time. I hug him, and it's as if his head and the crook of my arm are made for each other. I'd like him to know that his father squeezed my hand before I had to let go to catch him. I'll tell him in a minute. In a minute.

His name's Sam. He's Henri's son.

Henri has a son.

I hold him tight—Henri's son from a life I know nothing about. In awe, the same way I've held every one of my friends' or employees' newborn babies. In awe that such small, energetic life exists. It always feels as if life, however tiny, comes into the world fully formed.

Sam whispers something over and over again, and eventually I manage to make out the words of his prayer. "Come back!"

I join in, silently at first before whispering those words too. "Come back!" we whisper until our words are in step, and together we pray to our fathers: "Come back! Come back!"

Eddie

I shut my eyes and draw the boy a little closer to me.

Dad, help me! I think. This time I don't shrug off the touch of his hands on my shoulders, the same touch he gave me on the night he passed over to the other side.

When he died . . . **Oh, tell it the way it is, Edwina. Dying is the proper word! It's got nothing to do with going away. Going away means the person is going to come back, and that's not going to happen. He's gone. For good. For the rest of your life. And whatever you might have felt, assume that it can't have been real! He's gone forever.**

In a flash I feel the anguish of knowing that I'll never again hear my father outside my body, only inside me. My memories of my father—his voice, his smell, and the rhythm of his footsteps on asphalt—are like gently fading stars.

Sobs shake Sam's body.

I feel Dad's hands on my shoulders and hear his voice in the darkness. "Shush, Eddie, shush, my little Winnie. Come here! Come here and listen to me. Are you listening?"

That's what he would always say to me when I woke up in the middle of the night, gasping in fear. My dad would sing to me. He sang whatever came to mind. Sometimes he put to music a poem he had recently read in one of the forgotten books in the lighthouses he oversaw. Or he would sing straight from the gut, composing one-off melodies without lyrics.

He would cradle me as softly as one would a petrified bird in a warm hand, while I, resting against his chest, listened to the sounds, which next to his beating heart were released into the world.

"You mustn't think," he told me once when I asked him how he managed to sing wordless lullabies that were never written down and never would be. "Don't think. Follow the image you see inside you and slowly re-create it with your voice. Don't search for words to capture your pain and your consolation. Seek out a place and sing it."

Henri

———//———

"We're nearly there," my father says reassuringly. He's sitting behind me, the way we always sit, and he's rowing. There are lobster pots between my feet.

The often raging Iroise Sea is smooth and has taken on the metallic-blue, almost translucent glitter that the Atlantic usually only gives off shortly before sundown. I feel the warm rays of the sun on my back. As warm and bright as just now in that room . . .

Just now? How come? What room?

A bridge. A whiff of tar. A falling sensation, down and down, and a glass lid closing over me. A hand letting go of me as I drown. These frightening memories dissipate and disperse like smoke. I must have dozed off and been dreaming. That sometimes happens when we go out in the small blue rowboat, which is usually propped on its side against the garden wall of Ty Kerk, Malo's house near Melon, and which Grandpa Malo and my father, Yvan, caulk on windless winter days. It spends the rest of the year in the water.

I can feel the warm light on my hands and legs, all over my skin, making me drowsy but also filling me with an enormous sense of well-being. It's as if a shadow slides off me into the water with a sigh and quietly floats away into the distance. The whole scene is relaxed and peaceful, like the first day of the holidays when two months without school lie before you, as infinite as the great blue sky.

I half turn. My father smiles at me. I look ahead again. It's so quiet. Where's the wind? Where's the grating of the waves on the sand and rocks? Why is the sky so still? Everything's wrong.

Then I notice what's missing: the familiar outline of the coast and islands. The lighthouses have also vanished. This isn't real. No sea in the world has as many lighthouses, surrounded by waves and islands and huge blocks of granite, as the raging Iroise Sea at the western tip of Brittany, where the waves of the English Channel and the swell of the Celtic Sea and the Atlantic meet with a crash.

But where are the lighthouses of La Jument, Pierres Noires, and Le Four? Where is the Molène archipelago and the island of Ouessant, beyond which, as ancient legend has it, infinity begins?

"We're nearly there," my father repeats.

I glance over my shoulder. He's smoking a filter-less cigarette, holding it between his thumb and forefinger as always, but the smoke smells strangely faint. He's wearing his sea face—extremely calm, his eyes accustomed to staring into the distance and coping with the vast expanse of water, which is unlit and immense at night and a huge, fierce, foaming creature by day.

My father, Yvan, is wearing a blue-and-white-striped fisherman's sweater with three buttons on the left shoulder, a pair of faded jeans, and no socks. Yvan Le Goff always goes without socks from April to October. He was wearing the same outfit on the day he died over thirty years ago.

I leap to my feet so quickly that the boat rocks. I jump away from my father to the other side of the bench.

My father died when I was thirteen, at the age of forty-two. He's dead.

"You died," I whisper. "I was there."

My father doesn't reply. He keeps on rowing. The blue boat glides silently over the unruffled surface.

I really was there.

WE WERE ROWING out to check the lobster pots by the buoys. It was in the middle of lobster season.

But then my father turned his back on the open sea, something he never normally did. It's the

Breton fisherman's number one rule: "Never turn your back on her!"—"her" being the sea, the most unpredictable woman on earth. My father, however, was gazing at the land. I was trying to keep the boat on an even keel and thinking of the fib I was hatching for him and my grandfather later. I'd tell it casually so they believed it. I'd never lied to either of them before.

"This is a good spot, Henri. Keep the boat still!" my father called, grabbing hold of the slippery rope hooked onto the floating buoy, whose other end was fastened to the trap dragging along the sea bottom.

I planned to tell them that I was going to cycle to the **fest-noz** in Porspoder, whereas I was actually meeting up with Sionie, who'd promised me a kiss.

"What's this?" my father asked, tugging on the rope. The boat rocked. He still had his back to the sea.

A gull cackled angrily as it flew overhead but then fell abruptly silent. It's never a good omen when seabirds fall silent. I glanced up at the gull and just then I spotted the wave. It was big. Far too big.

"Dad!" I cried, but it was already upon us, a gray, raging wall of water, out of whose center a patch of blackness was exploding. The wave came crashing down on the boat like a hammer blow and next thing . . .

———— // ————

75

FOR A SECOND my skull splits with the pain—stinging, white pain. I sink down onto the bench and clutch my head in my hands. I hear a high-pitched wail like a saw, then the pain vanishes. I immediately pull my fingers away. This can't be happening.

"Leave them!" my father says.

Them? Are they really here? Below the surface, silently floating, attached to invisible threads anchored to the sea bottom? Deeper than I know the Iroise to be? Of course, at some stage you'll always touch the bottom, but what I just saw was floating over endless, impenetrable depths, with clouds scudding over the bottom.

"We're here," my father announces.

The boat has gently run aground on an island. It's perhaps a hundred yards wide and two hundred yards long. It's covered with hummocks and granite that glows gold in the sun, with a fine sandy beach running down to the water's edge. On the shore stands a blue wooden door in a frame. The door is half-open. It's identical to Ty Kerk's front door.

Ty Kerk. Grandpa Malo's pancakes, cooked over the open fire, then, straight from the hot griddle, spread with Breton sea-salt butter and sprinkled with sugar. Feeling pleasantly sleepy by the fireside on an autumn evening. Treading on crunchy snow and frosted pastures. Stars in a mauve sky.

Ty Kerk. The only place where everything was always fine.

Father's death. My fault.

Eddie's laugh. Her hand in mine on the table while we read. And me shattering my Eddie, setting a torch to her loving heart.

Sam's thumb in his clenched hand. Seeing my child once and then never again.

My father jumps out of the boat and stows the oars in the bottom. "Come on!" he calls. "We've almost made it. You're almost home." He walks over to the door, then looks back and waits for me. Obediently I follow him. Is he going to give me a hug? Hug me again at long last?

I know there's a wonderful place beyond that door. There, nothing will ever end. We'll know all the joys of this world. I will now pass through that door, and it will close behind me. Finally, I will be with my father and my grandfather again. The two poles that hold my world together, my up and my down, my breath and my pulse, my moon and my sea. My day and my night.

Come back! two voices whisper inside my head. I ignore them.

I quicken my pace. Beyond that door lies Ty Kerk, Malo's house between the stars and the sea. On nights when the raging Iroise hurled its waters against the cliffs and the waves leaped higher and higher, the two-hundred-year-old granite house would wheeze and creak like a ship on heavy seas, but it always resisted.

My father smiles and walks through the door.

Grandpa Malo will be sitting at the small wooden table by the fireplace, reading, and intermittently quoting, poetry or Proust. My father, Yvan, is bound to be making something in the far corner of the room: driftwood picture frames or a lamp whose shade is made of Breton drinking bowls, with a gnarled walnut tree stump for the base. My father will be mocking Grandpa's quotations or saying nothing, absorbed in converting an object into something different. My father understands things but has never understood people.

The door opens, inviting me in. Everything will be consigned to the past—all hardship, all torment, fear, pain, sadness, longing, all humiliation and anxiety, all . . .

Eddie's smile. The way she observes me when she thinks I'm still asleep and I appear not to notice that she's looking at me. Eddie, love of my unlived life, mother of my unborn children.

"Henri?" my father asks kindly, poking out his head from behind the blue door. "Are you coming?"

Come back! whispers the mild breeze, whose caress I suddenly feel on my skin. It's coming from somewhere, from the landless sea, the same sea under whose gray-glass surface figures are floating upright with open eyes, as if they are asleep and dreaming and don't realize where they are.

Back—back to where?

I stop and listen out.

Sam. His little thumb tucked into his fist while he slept.

A gust of wind pushes the door farther open, just a touch. Isn't that the fireplace? Can't I hear Grandpa Malo too, reading under his breath a **marvailhoù,** one of the old, occult Breton stories about the in-between world? Maybe he's just reading my story. Maybe we're all stories that someone is reading, and maybe that will save us before we ultimately expire?

A momentary recollection of the Eternal Reader, a monk in the mountains on the border between Austria and Italy, who read all day every day, from dawn to dusk, because he wanted to keep the people in the stories alive.

My father casts me a worried glance. "Henri, please. It's not good to hesitate for too long. Doors never remain open forever."

What's holding me back?

"Henri, I beg you! It isn't good. You shouldn't linger in between for too long."

In between? What does that mean? In between what?

My father stares at me as he used to do, as if to say, "Didn't you ever listen? Didn't you listen to Malo when he explained the sea's character to you?"

The sea is a woman. She knows every shore and protects the dead who sail out in their barks past the Île de Sein until they come to islands that feature on none of this world's maps. The sea is time's lover. Together, the sea and time gave birth to death, dreams, and humans; they are their off-spring.

"It's easy to get lost at the crossing points. Come on, Henri! I beg you. I don't want to lose you again."

He doesn't want to lose me? What? I lost **him**.

Unexpectedly, the door slams, opens again gently and crashes shut again, opens and then closes. The blows ring out like thunder. They're threatening, a message that says, "You'd better hurry up!"

Each time the door opens it's a request, a lure, a sweet tug, an invitation to curl up in the coziest sun-warmed corner of Ty Kerk and enjoy the quiet shelter and safety, punctuated by my father's occasional humming, Malo's quiet laughter at what he's reading, the dog's wheezing, the cats' purring, and the crackling of the fire. Everything would be fine forever more.

And yet I don't move. I don't know where I find the strength to resist this temptation.

My father says, "Oh, Henri, it's all over. Look!" He gestures to me, and all at once I am hit by a wave of emotion so intense that it permeates every cell in my body. It's overwhelming; it invades me and I'm flooded with images and feelings and knowledge. And then I see it. I see everything.

I see the things we regret most when we die and the final seconds start to tick, during which there's no possibility of catching up, no more making good. I see that, and it strikes me as logical. How stupid we humans are to forget it, death after death after death, and life after life! I also forgot. Worse: every time I had a chance to advance into the center of my life, I took a step back.

"Time's up, Henri. Let go!"

Of course. That's what I deserve from my time on earth—to be let go and forgotten, for it wasn't a life. What wouldn't I give not to have hesitated when I ought to have jumped, not to have run away when I ought to have stayed, not to have remained silent when I ought to have spoken out! Part of me is aghast at myself.

I traipse slowly back to the small blue boat. My father stands motionless on the shore of the island, arms dangling by his sides, a boundless sadness in his wide, calm sea face. "Henri! It's not so easy to get back. You'll get lost in the middle. In the middle of everything, do you understand?"

I don't know what he means by "in the middle of everything." I can't feel the sand under my feet; I can no longer feel anything. Even as I'm pushing the boat out into the sea, it feels as if I'm not pushing it with the force of my muscles, but that it's being moved by my will alone.

My father slumps onto the sand, his eyes fixed on me. He wrings his hands.

I climb uncertainly into the boat and take up the oars. The sea tries to knock them from my hands, so I clutch them more tightly.

"Watch out! Don't leave the boat, and avoid the storms!" my father calls after me. "And if you fall into the water and night comes . . ."

I'm no longer listening to what he says because the sea of the dying has caught hold of the boat and is pushing it away from the shore fast. I lean on the oars. They tremble, they resist, but they obey my command as I pull them hard, again and again, through the frothing, rolling waves.

I don't know whom I should beseech to let me come back, even if it's only to open my eyes and look at Eddie, whose face is the last thing I want to gaze upon in life before I close my eyes forever. Sam too, to tell him that I was on my way; I was on my way.

The island with the open door is already slipping below the shimmering blue horizon. I scan the sea and glimpse a number of granite reefs jagging up out of the waves like dark claws. I think I can see a hunched figure on one of the many scattered rocks, a whale-shaped islet. It seems to be a girl with long blond hair, who's merely sitting there, gazing out to sea.

"Hello!" I cry.

The girl doesn't so much as glance around.

I can't see any coastline. In the direction from which I've come the sky is blue and benign, but behind me the darkness is gathering into towering mountains of cloud. There are claps of thunder and the longer I look, the more certain I become that something is splintering the water over there.

There! I shade my eyes. **Yes, over there!** Invisible cliffs, against which the waves pound and crash, falling back as milky froth, subsiding, and being thrust against the bottom and the rocks and an invisible barrier. The sea's roaring. A never-ending line of cliffs, a wall of glass, and inside it . . . Fog?

I sit down on the rowing bench. **I must rescue the girl,** I think, but when I peer at the whale rock where the child was sitting a second ago, the girl is gone.

I feel the current straining at the blue boat's bows. The tide is turning. It's going out. The roaring grows louder, as if the sea has been transformed into a gigantic waterfall, cascading thousands and thousands of feet into a thundering, black chasm.

I turn round in the blue boat. The waves loom like mountains, houses upon houses high, grinding, bursting, and shattering against the barrier. I can now see that it is a sort of pipe that is smashing the waves. Not a glass pipe, but one filled with fog and night. My fear tastes of blood.

In winter the coast of the Iroise Sea suggested that the heavy, gray-blue, rolling sea was bent on taking a running start, leaping onto the land, and advancing over the waves of grassy hummocks to drag people from their beds. The waves hurl themselves against this tube of darkness and scudding shreds of fog every bit as brutally. I almost believe that I can see stars being sucked through it, treetops and mountain peaks and the shadows of cities appearing from it now and then, but so briefly that I can't be sure if I'm seeing properly. The pipe stretches out left and right to the landless horizon. All along it, waves hurl themselves against this barrier and bounce back in a mass of seething foam. The sky has also peeled back, yellow as pus, gray as smoke, and toxic.

The boat rises and falls, listing dangerously low on both sides. Spray flies over the gunwales.

I lean forward to peer into the whirlpool forming directly in front of the barrier. What is behind this border at the edge of the sea of the dying? What is beyond the barrier . . . or inside it? The whirlpool gapes beneath me like a waterfall. It begins to tug my boat down into the deep and toward the pipe, and all I can think is, **Yes, I want to find out. I want to find out what's there!** For an instant the boat teeters on the watery brink before plummeting down, end over end. I feel like I'm being torn apart, head, arms, and spine.

Please. Please! PLEASE!

Suddenly a great, flat, chill surface looms over me, and then the shadow comes crashing down on me like a giant hand, swiping me into the sea and into the pipe. I'm falling, I'm being washed away, lights and colors and voices wrap themselves around me. I'm sinking, I'm dissolving, I'm falling ever faster. I'm falling and . . .

Sam

I hear her heart beating close to my ear. I can smell her perfume and feel her fingertips resting lightly on my hair, as if my skull were made of fine glass. I can hear the crackle of her panic and her surge of hope, but there's something else beneath those things. Something warm and good that enables me to breathe.

I can hear her breath and then, with my soul snuggling against her heart, I hear her breath become a note. The note becomes a tune, a breeze, but it's not like Madelyn's piano music. This wind has been scouring the earth for a long time and is now slowly rising, growing brighter, as it continues its quest over the cool, silvery, frost-rimmed, icy coating of a long, broad, frozen river. It is changing into a warming ray of sunlight, which captures the sparkling silence and then alights on a motionless ice sculpture, inside which a heart is beating. My heart.

Her singing warms the ice until the melody envelops my heart, and the mild breeze carries me away over thousands of mountains and dark woods, back to where all is bright and fine.

TWO HEARTBEATS LATER, the chapel door opens. Dr. Saul comes over to us, sits down on the floor, leans his head against the wall, and shuts his eyes. Eddie stops singing.

"Samuel," Dr. Saul says. I know it's not a good sign when God calls me by my first name.

DAY SEVENTEEN

Eddie

D r. Saul turns the brain scan, the EEG, and a very complicated-looking sheet of paper with lots of little boxes and entries around on the table so that Sam and I can see them. I read the words "Innsbruck Scale" and "Edinburgh-2 Scale." I read Henri's score of six on the Glasgow Coma Scale, written in marker pen. Alongside this it says, "Medium-deep to deep coma." If his score were three, he would be brain-dead. Fifteen, and he'd be the man I once knew.

I glance at Sam. His expression is hard and far too grown-up. He's fiddling with his thumbnail under the table, but otherwise he's utterly still.

"Following his eight-minute cardiac arrest, Mr. Skinner has slipped into a coma. A coma is not an illness—it's the brain's reaction when it needs to protect itself. The patient withdraws into himself, shutting himself off from the world that is causing him pain and anxiety."

In my mind's eye, I picture Henri retreating from his life, raising his hands like a shield. Basically, a coma is therefore the logical extension of his general response to life: **I'd better get out of here!**

I'd rather not entertain that thought, but I'm so angry with him. I'd love to smash something here and now. I don't know if I'm going to be able to cope with this on my own. I'd like to ring Wilder and beg him to come to the hospital, but Wilder doesn't even know I'm here. He doesn't even know that Henri was part of my life—and still is, in a very twisted, surreal way.

Always the same. Always the bloody same. Henri, the man who's never there and yet always there.

Dr. Saul takes out a piece of paper and starts to draw circles on it. "I've already explained this model to Samuel." He taps on the center point, which stands for **Awake**. A series of circles rippling outward from that point are marked **Numb, Asleep/ Dreaming, Unconscious, Coma**—and **Dead**. Dr. Saul makes a first cross in the unconscious zone— "He was here"—then a second cross in the dead zone—"and here"—and then marks a third one in **Coma**. It's too close to the edge, too close to **Dead**, for my liking. It's right on the border.

"They're places, not states," whispers Sam.

I say the first thing to detach itself from the swirling tangle of thoughts in my head. "Will he come back from that place?"

Dr. Saul takes only a second to answer this question. One second. The length of an adult's heartbeat when that person isn't scared; the time it takes for light to travel 186,282 miles; the time it takes for it to dawn on you that you don't want to live without someone. But how heavy a second of fear is!

Why wasn't Dr. Saul quicker? Was he weighing up whether to lie to us? No. I don't like him, but he isn't a liar.

Slowly and deliberately he says, "We don't know."

At least there's some hope. He doesn't say yes. But he doesn't say no either.

"But now he's almost dead?" Sam asks with the shrill voice of a teenage boy whose voice is breaking, pointing to the small, lonely cross on the outer edge of the concentric circles.

Dr. Saul nods. "Yes, Sam. But he **is** alive, only differently. Do you understand that? In a coma you're still alive. You're merely in a particular state. It's a borderline condition—a crisis, of course, but that doesn't make that life any less important than the one you or I or Mrs. Tomlin leads. That's why here we say that someone is **living** in a coma rather than **lying** in a coma."

"But two days. This isn't the beginning of forever, is it?"

Dr. Saul once again takes too long to answer my question. Far too long. **Please say that Henri could potentially wake up tonight or tomorrow or one day.** The pain has returned—the pain of never again hearing my father's voice outside my own body, but only inside me. Only in my memories. Memories like slowly dying stars.

Thinking of Sam tears my heart apart. Losing your father before you've even gotten to know him—it's too soon. Such loss never heals. I'd love to take the boy's hand, but it's as if he's clinging to himself. How like his father.

Once again, I've caught my breath, and Dr. Saul interprets my involuntary release of air as a sign of skepticism.

"Comas are a severely under-researched phenomenon, Mrs. Tomlin. We don't know enough about them and grope our way through the dark using statistics that tell us very little about why and how they occur. The figures suggest that two days is generally the beginning of forever, but not always."

"Is he scared?" Sam asks. His thumb is now bloody from scratching. He bites his lip.

"We don't know how a coma patient feels either, Sam. We can presume that he feels **something**, and that's what the scans show too." Dr. Saul points to the printouts. "Some of my colleagues believe that in a coma the brain is assailed by all the same words and images and emotions that flood it when the person is awake and completely relaxed. One group is convinced that the limbic system and the reptilian brain take over, safeguarding a minimal amount of stand-in brain function. Then there are the engineers. They regard everything we feel and think—love, hate, worry, songs by the Rolling Stones—as electronic chatter between our synapses and think that the soul is nothing but a fairy tale. For them, a coma is like a power cut to the system."

Sam taps his trembling forefinger on the cross again. "Can he see the dead from there?"

Dr. Saul doesn't hesitate for a second this time. "No," he replies. "Your father was clinically dead, Sam. Patients who have been reanimated often tell me that they've seen what awaits them on the other side, and their accounts are all pretty similar: tunnels of light, a floating sensation, voices, waiting relatives, relaxation . . . But . . ."—here Dr. Saul screws up his eyes—". . . we have explanations for the majority of those sensations and experiences. The lights at the end of the tunnel can be explained by loss of vision during a physical collapse. The feeling of flying or floating above one's own body is a typical symptom when the brain area responsible for equilibrium and balance fails. The dissolution of the boundary with one's own body is also due to the failure of—"

"I think we've got the message," I say, interrupting him. Sam dug his nails into his chair while Dr. Saul was overwhelming us with this torrent of specialist knowledge. The information is of no use to Samuel. He wants something else, hope maybe, and knowledge doesn't bring hope. "You believe in your statistics and you reject everything else."

"I don't believe in anything at all, Mrs. Tomlin. Not in statistics, not in experts, and incidentally, in case it reassures you, I don't believe for a second that I know all there is to know."

"That really is hugely reassuring."

He shrugs. "What do you want to hear? Near-death experiences? Angels, God, rebirth? Or whether people in a coma leave their bodies and travel through time and space? What can I tell you? I'm a neurosurgeon! We simply don't know if Henri Skinner can see anything or not, where he is at the moment, or what he feels. All we have is our scans, and they don't even show us if he can hear, see, feel, or smell."

Sam gulps audibly. Glancing at him, I see that his eyes are wet with tears, which he is straining to hold back. I lay my hand, palm up, on the armrest of his chair. I would love to hug him with all my strength.

"But I can feel him," he whispers hoarsely.

"You may wish you could, Sam, but that's impossible," says Dr. Saul, and his voice is full of sympathy.

Henri's son's tears are now running down his cheeks, and his voice breaks as he says more loudly, "I can!"

"Sam, kidding yourself won't help."

The boy claps his hands to his face, and now my blood is boiling at the fact that Dr. Saul isn't even tactful enough to spare the boy such torment.

"You're a horrible little bastard, Dr. Saul," I remark.

"That is possible, Mrs. Tomlin. My wife said the same, shortly before she asked me for a divorce. By email, so she wouldn't have to speak to me even one more time." He tidies the papers spread out on the beige table, but I can see he's affected by Sam's silent sobbing. The boy's shoulders are shaking. There isn't another sound or movement. It's a moment of shared solitude. Dr. Saul's only love is his work, Sam's missing his father, and as for me . . . I hadn't realized how hardened I'd become over these two and a half years without Henri.

I get to my feet, kneel down in front of Sam, and take this little bundle of misery in my arms. He weeps and clings to me, and at that moment I know that, whatever happens, I'm going to have to deal with it.

After a while Sam stops crying and whispers, "It's okay. I'm all right." I sit down again.

Dr. Saul pushes the living will Henri signed over two years ago across the table. I look at the date. Shortly after I declared my love for him and he turned it down. And he still put my name on his living will? What the hell did the imbecile think he was doing?

But there's another problem with the directive: my signature is missing.

"If Mr. Skinner continues to live in a coma, he will need rehabilitation but above all he will need emotional continuity. Not just for a few days, but for weeks, months, maybe for the rest of his life—however long or short that might be."

The doctor leans forward, and his different-colored eyes are piercing now. "Sam, you're thirteen years old. I like you and you're more intelligent than most people I know. That's why I shall always refuse to lie to you or to treat you like an idiot by telling you about angels or Jesus at the end of the tunnel." Now he turns to me. "But I'm not going to impose on Sam what I'm willing to impose on you, Mrs. Tomlin." He taps on the living will. "When someone's on the brink of death, it always unleashes an endless series of humiliating bureaucratic procedures. If you sign this, you'll be taking on responsibility for Sam's father. Can you do that, Mrs. Tomlin? Can you take responsibility for a life, or for a death?"

Dr. Saul leans back. His leather chair creaks.

For hell's sake! I feel like screaming at Henri. I'm sitting here and I have to answer an asshole's question about whether I'm willing to take responsibility for your life! Why did you do it, Henri?

"Consider very carefully whether you want to do this and whether you're capable of doing it. Think about whether you'll be there for Henri Skinner, to talk to him, move him, stand by him wherever he may be, live with him—if you wish to put it that way—more intensively than you've ever lived with anyone before. Every day for an absolutely indefinite length of time."

Forever, that means. Forever, in this and every other life.

I want to say something, but he won't let me speak. He lifts his hand—the calloused hand of a carpenter—and immediately continues, "No, please! You don't have to give me your answer now, Mrs. Tomlin. Not today. I wouldn't take it seriously if you did. You're in a minor state of shock, high on emotion and adrenaline. You really want to stick it to me and prove yourself. And you know what? That's good! It shows you're a real trouper, not easily shaken. Difficult and annoying maybe, but reliable."

He gives me a copy of the contract I, as Henri's representative, would sign with the hospital. My eyes devour the figures. A bed in the Wellington Hospital's rehabilitation department costs half a million pounds per year. Henri's health care, paid for by his press insurance plan, will cover two years of treatment. So two years is the average time the British state grants a person to recover from death. I feel like breaking something—for example, Dr. Saul's collection of delicate jade crabs, turtles, and seahorses, which he has lined up on his shelves in front of his hundreds and hundreds of books.

I read the passage that states, "The patient's legally appointed caregiver is entitled . . . ," and then read it again, more slowly this time. I'd have the power to decide all treatment and medication. I'd have the power to have the life-support machine turned off. I'd have the power to let Henri die.

"Give yourself twenty-four hours or, better, three days. Talk to someone who can tell you if you're biting off more than you can chew. Do you know anyone like that?"

"Yes, I do," I say. "Do you?"

He chuckles. "Not many. By the way, do you love him?"

"Sorry?"

"Do you love Henri Skinner?" Dr. Saul repeats.

"Is that a precondition?"

He slowly shakes his head. "No. It makes things harder actually."

I'd be crazy if I still loved him. Henri may not have wanted me in his life, but I'm fine for managing his death. Love him? No, I'm not that crazy. I could do with a whiskey.

"Taking care of a person in a coma is like marrying somebody who'll never say they love you," he says more calmly. "And yet you must give him all the affection and strength you have. All your love too, if you feel any for him, that is. With no prospect of a happy ending. You'd spend a large part of your life with someone who isn't there."

Really? That's nothing special. I'm used to that with Henri.

Dr. Saul leans back in his chair. I roll up the living will and the contract into a tight bundle.

So here I am, and all my plans from three weeks ago have turned to dust. Henri has come roaring back into my life like a comet. There's no way out. Sam looks at me, and his eyes are overflowing with hope, fear, trust, and deep determination. As if his gaze could force me to decide.

But I can't. I'm not going to get hooked on that drug again. I was addicted to Henri. A total junkie.

My feelings turn into a wild beast. I've starved myself to keep it under control, but now it's stirring again. **Come on,** it growls, **let's do it!**

All those hundreds of nights! All those hundreds of thousands of tears! All those times I avoided men with a physique or gait like Henri's, guys who used his cologne, bore his name, or loved Zaz, Amy Winehouse, and Bob Marley. All those times I thought of him in spite of myself. All the memories I shunned.

My love beast tells me those torments are irrelevant. **Come on,** it growls, **let's love.**

No. NO.

Sam

"I'm going to see your father. Want to come along?"
Eddie asks me. Her voice is oscillating between
red fury and greedy longing, as a bright silvery tear
trickles from her eye. She wipes it away impatiently
with the back of her hand, leaving a black smudge
on her fingers and cheek. A second tear trickles from
the other eye. Two twinkling eyes, from which the
wintry sea is now streaming. The sound of her singing lingers in my ears. I imagine her singing to my
father too. My father and her together.

It strikes me that she knows everything and I
know nothing. I want to ask her a thousand things,
but one question is at the forefront of my mind.
Did he ever mention me?

He looked at me as he died, and for one never-
ending instant I knew who he was. I could see the

shadow years, the warmth and benevolence drain-ing out of him, and I sensed that he knew me. It was a reunion.

Maybe I'm only imagining all of this, just as, long ago, I used to have imaginary friends. What do I mean, long ago? "Rational thought isn't one of your brain's strong suits, **mon ami**," Scott would say.

"No, I'm not coming because . . ." I search for an excuse. Everything's all muddled up. My entire being is sore and hot, but simultaneously numb and cool, as if it was snowing and scorching in Dr. Saul's office at the same time.

The idea of Eddie's leaving hurts. The idea that she perhaps loves my father also hurts. As does the idea that she might not love him, but that's a dif-ferent kind of hurt.

Her tears have cleansed her eyes. "Okay, never mind. They won't have any use for us in the in-tensive care unit anyway. Is your mother picking you up?"

"Of course," I lie.

"Good," Eddie says. "I wouldn't want to leave you alone right now. I really wouldn't, Samuel."

She looks at me, and it's hard to meet her eyes and deceive her.

"Otherwise, you could come to my publishing house and I'll drop you home later. Do you read fantastic novels?"

"Fantasy?" I shake my head.

"Not fantasy—fantastic. In the sense of augmented reality. Fantasy, on the other hand, involves stories about elves, vampires and orcs, Gandalf, gargoyles, and witches. Fantastic novels, or speculative fiction, are closer to reality." Her voice is greener now, less red than before. "Speculative fiction focuses on ideas that are theoretically possible: tears in the space-time continuum, time travel. Back to the future, sort of. Speculative fiction is a reality crash—and that's the name of my publishing house. So, do you read fantastic novels?"

I nod and let those words resonate in my mind. **Publishing house, home, fantastic, reality crash.** They describe a completely different world from mine, but they're close, as if we were two books that happen to be next to each other on a bookshelf when a fire breaks out, and the covers melt and our letters get mixed up. I've no idea what Scott would make of this. He'd probably make a comment like: "Marty McFly meets Elizabeth Bennet?"

The big hospital lift arrives, and the door slides open. Eddie blocks it with one foot and waits. If I go down with her, she'll insist on keeping me company until my mother arrives. But my mother isn't coming to pick me up because she doesn't know I'm here. She mustn't find out either. Not yet anyway.

The door begins to close, but Eddie forces it open again with her elbow.

"Why didn't your mother come with you today, Sam?"

"She had to take my brother, Malcolm, to the dentist." My voice is white, lit up by this barefaced lie. "He gets scared on his own, and I—"

"You don't."

I nod. How I wish the ground would open up and swallow me! "I need to go and wash my hands," I mumble.

Eddie shoots me a quizzical look, then steps into the lift at last. She raises her hand as the door slides shut and parts her fingers between the ring and middle fingers. Mr. Spock's Vulcan salute. I instinctively return the greeting. I stand there as the lift travels downward, still holding up my hand as if I'm the last Trekkie, forgotten in the galactic mists—and only after what feels like a thousand years do I press the button to call the other lift.

SHE'S SITTING DOWN, hunched over a book in which she's calmly making notes with a pen. She hasn't spotted me yet, and I could slip past her. That would probably be the best thing to do, but as Scott le Brainman would say, "You can't ignore the fact that there are many other lives you could be living. And they're only thirty seconds and one expulsion away."

She glances up as I knock gently on the window of the nurses' common room.

"Oh, hello there, young stranger!"

"Hello, Mrs. . . ." Quickly I read the name embroidered on the breast pocket of her nurse's uniform. "Hello, Nurse Marion."

She puts a bookmark in the book she's reading and shuts it. The words **Madelyn Zeidler** are written on the page marker. "And who might you be?"

"Samuel Valentiner, Nurse Marion."

"Valentiner, eh? I don't believe that we have a Valentiner up here for you to visit, do we?"

I shake my head.

"So what can I do for you, Samuel?"

"I wanted to ask how Maddie is." It happens just as I pronounce her name: a completely unfamiliar heat shoots into my cheeks. "And to apologize for eavesdropping recently. I'm sorry about that."

The heat is now spreading in all directions— into my cheeks, across my scalp, down my neck, and I think I can even feel it on the soles of my feet. What is it Scott calls puberty? "Probably the most embarrassing time of a man's life. And it lasts until you're about seventy."

Nurse Marion takes her time. She leans back in the blue office chair on wheels, crosses her arms, studies me, and at the end of this long lead-in, asks, "And why do you want to know how Maddie is?"

Why? Why have I thought for two days solid about my father and Madelyn, even dreaming about them, I'm sure? I have pictured her name in my mind and breathed it.

"Because I can't help it," I finally say.

Nurse Marion looks at me strangely again, and in her eyes I see two women—a young one and an aging version—and it almost sounds as if it's the elder questioning the younger when she says with a smile, "Life's an uphill struggle, eh?"

I don't really know so I keep quiet. Quite abruptly the nurse pushes herself out of her chair and says, "Come on, let's go and see if Maddie would like to tell us how she's feeling today."

The nurse is barely taller than I am, and her ginger locks bounce back and forth before me as she strides along the corridor toward the last room. "By the way, I'm the ward sister here. If I'm not here, I'm either on night duty or checking on patients down in the intensive care unit."

There's no time to get anxious: Nurse Marion is already knocking on the last door. She pushes it open and announces softly, "Hi, Maddie, we've got a visitor. The young man who dropped by two days ago is here again. His name's Samuel. May we come in?"

Maddie answers, "Of course, we're just warming up."

It isn't Maddie who says this, obviously, but a woman in a pair of white trousers and a blue blouse with her name embroidered on it—"Liz." She's in the process of doing something very strange with Madelyn, while the latter lies on her side on a quilted mat on the floor, gazing up at me. The woman has taken one of the girl's feet in her hands and is massaging it gently, twisting it this way and that. Classical music is playing in the background.

"More Tchaikovsky today, Maddie?" Nurse Marion asks.

"Hi, I'm Liz, Maddie's physiotherapist," says the woman, stretching out a little finger in greeting, as she turns the girl's foot in all directions and then begins to bend her knee.

I want to say, "Hello, Madelyn," but it suddenly feels as if I have a gigantic, invisible cookie caught in my throat, preventing me from speaking. My tongue, mouth, and voice all desert me as I run my eyes over her face, her cheeks, her wrists, all dainty and beautiful.

A catheter is hidden under Maddie's nightie and tracksuit bottoms, and two tubes are connected to her index finger. There is a vial of eye drops on the table next to her. Further dropper bottles on the table by the door contain other medicines. There are machines by her bed, monitoring the oxygen in her blood and her heartbeat on a constant basis. She is obviously fed through a tube that vanishes into the skin next to her collarbone. Another tube protrudes from her neck; it's hooked up to the ventilator.

All the same, I can sense as little of Maddie as any non-synes-creep would. I cannot see who she is. There's nothing but frozen ice on a silent river.

She is completely enveloped in something that feels like an electrically charged, icy air bubble. She's staring at me, but she cannot see me. We have that much in common, at least.

"Liz, this is Samuel. He'd like to ask Maddie how she's feeling today."

No, what I'd really like to do is crumple to the floor.

"We're dancing, but we're just coming to the end of the first act. After that, she has a speech lesson and ergotherapy. It's a pretty busy day."

Liz proceeds very carefully and cautiously, yet I'm concerned that Maddie is in pain. Her features are impassive, though, and her eyes stare off into the distance, far beyond the walls of this room. I try to concentrate even harder on her.

Nurse Marion picks up a clipboard from a small table over by the window. The tulips in the vase are orange today.

Maddie's face shows no emotion as Liz manipulates her feet and legs. The red-haired nurse kneels on the floor, gently touches the girl's fingers, puts a soft ball in one of her hands and then the other, and, after each test, makes some notes on her pad.

Not so fast, I think. **You'll scare her.** But now Nurse Marion runs a feather along Maddie's bare lower arms. I get the tickles just from watching.

Her hands, I think. **She needs to be taken by the hand.** And no sooner have I had this thought than something stirs inside her, deep below the surface.

"I'll come back later to do the tactile test. How's Maddie's dancing today?" Marion asks, as if this question includes some kind of code word.

The physiotherapist is kneeling behind the girl. Almost imperceptibly she shakes her head. Maddie can't see this, but I can. "No response," Liz mouths.

I watch Maddie, who's allowing her arms and legs to be yanked around like a puppet's, but this time I detect no movement beneath her impassive expression. Her coma seems very different from my father's, though. She keeps so still that it's as if she doesn't **want** to be found, but she's not as distant and immersed as he is. She's in there somewhere, hoping that nobody will come across her, like a little girl playing hide-and-seek.

I don't need to ask how she is. She's not well. Not well at all. Wherever she is, she's completely alone. I peer into her eyes and strain even harder to feel something more or communicate that I know how she's feeling. And yet I have my doubts. Maybe I'm just imagining all of this.

"May I come again tomorrow, Maddie?" I ask her after a while.

Since she doesn't immediately say no, I interpret her silence as an "Oh, all right then."

"I'm going to escort you back to the lift now, Sam," says Marion in a calm, friendly voice, but beneath the sweetness I pick up a hum of irritation.

What have I done wrong? Have I done something wrong?

———//———

WE'VE BARELY ENTERED the nurse's common room when Marion hisses, "If you think you're going to pay the occasional visit to a girl in a coma for some kind of thrill, Samuel Valentiner, perhaps even take the odd covert snap to boast to your school friends until it eventually gets tedious and you don't feel like coming, I'm warning you that we will never, I repeat, **never,** let you in here again. Do I make myself clear?"

Wordlessly I nod and feel my cheeks grow hot again.

"Good, I'm glad. It hasn't been clear to the sightseers who've come up here in the past to ogle some vegetables. If it's clear to you, then I won't need to have a word with your dad about his son poking fun at helpless children, and—"

"You wouldn't have far to go. My dad's on the second floor."

Marion exhales slowly and closes her eyes, as if she were pulling herself together. Her anger dissolves like a tablet in water. "I'm sorry, Samuel. I'm very sorry to hear that." Her blue eyes are gentle now, but they are brimming with questions.

"We don't give up easily here, Sam," she says gravely.

"May I come again?" I ask, to preempt any further questions about my father, for that'd be like walking across a bed of nails. "I don't mind asking Maddie's parents for their permission."

Marion rubs the root of her nose. "Oh, sweetie," she eventually says, her voice despondent. "If only it were so easy." She takes a deep breath. "Madelyn's special."

"I know," I say.

"No, you don't. You don't have a clue, Jon Snow." She smiles and flicks open the book she was writing in earlier. She hands me a newspaper cutting, then continues. "Madelyn Zeidler is eleven years old. For the past seven years she has been studying dance with the Elizabeth Parker Dance Company in Oxford. She's won sixteen prizes and a scholarship to the Royal Academy of Dance here in London. She's performed in two music videos by the French singer Zaz, each of which has had more than a million views on YouTube. She can do flips and twists and hold her breath for two minutes underwater. But unfortunately . . ."

It's this "unfortunately" that is described in the article. Seven months ago, the Zeidlers were traveling to Cornwall for a family holiday when one of their tires burst. Their motor home skidded onto the wrong side of the road, where it collided with a lorry transporting four show horses. Three horses, the driver, and almost everyone in the motor caravan died: Maddie's mother, Pam; her father, Nick; her brother, Sebastian; her grandmother Catherine; Maddie's aunt Sonia; and her uncle Nigel. Maddie and a mare called Dramatica were the only survivors.

MADDIE SOLE SURVIVOR AS FAMILY WIPED OUT, runs the headline.

"Madelyn is all alone in the world, Samuel. She has no close relatives, not even an uncle, a cousin, or some shrill spinster aunt who wears oversize earrings. She's a ward of the state."

So the Queen takes care of her, I think, because any other thought makes my head hurt.

"At first, Maddie's old dance teacher, Elizabeth Parker, came from Oxford a few times and showed Liz and the other physiotherapists here how to keep Maddie's body moving. She showed us and Maddie videos of Maddie dancing, and noted the things Maddie does and doesn't like." She holds up the book. "But then Mrs. Parker tripped over a loose paving slab and broke her hip, so nobody visits her any longer."

"Definitely not the Queen," I mumble.

Marion has a pained expression on her face. "It's Madelyn's birthday in twenty days' time. She'll be twelve. Her first birthday without a family, surrounded by strangers in a place that isn't her home." Her voice quavers with compassion, full of sunny gold—a rare color in today's world. "You see, Sam? She has nobody. And if you make friends with her—"

"Then I'm responsible for her."

Marion's blue eyes shine. "Yes. That's correct, Sam. Can you do it? Do you want to? Are you genuinely willing to be responsible for someone you don't know?"

The same question God put to Eddie earlier. Only now do I understand how she must be feeling. The air feels heavier, and many things that once seemed important no longer have any significance.

FIVE MINUTES LATER I'm standing beside C7. I have no idea how or why I came to be here or what I expect from my father. I want to tell him about Maddie, Eddie, and the rest. Tell him I'd no idea I was like Jon Snow.

I hear Scott say, "He's in a coma, Valentiner. Why can't you get that into your thick skull?" But who else am I supposed to talk to? I can't think of a single other person with whom I could discuss the fact that I don't want to leave a girl I don't know alone at the end of a corridor. Only him.

Or Eddie. She knows all about reality crashes. But if I told her about Maddie, then I'd have to tell her about my mother and everything else. So I'm here, having pulled on the rustling smock and put on the stupid mask through which I sound like Darth Vader with a bunged-up nose. I'm here because my father looked at me, and there was something in his eye that gripped me and wouldn't let go.

Now my father's face is a no-man's-land. His wrinkles are silent. They're no longer laughing, no longer suffering or thinking. His body too is more hunched than before, like an abandoned house.

I search for him. With Maddie just now, I detected a distant glimmer of loneliness and expectation. I think of God's circles. My father is on the outer edge of life. I try to find him. "Hi, Dad," I say quietly.

When someone's ill, seriously ill, you tend to forget all his or her other characteristics. Timothy, a boy in our class, contracted a rare form of cancer and died a year later. All anyone who remembered him ever said was how brave he was, as if fighting cancer had been his full-time job. Nobody mentioned that Timothy had also been the best at cannonball dives into the pool and had once rescued a kitten from a tree. So I try to view my father as not only sick, as more than almost dead. He would know what I should do.

God comes up to the bed, breaking my concentration. "Samuel."

The two of us gaze at my father, and I reach for my dad's hand and squeeze it. He doesn't squeeze back.

"He isn't there," I whisper.

"No. His soul's left its home." Dr. Saul's voice sounds different, as if he himself has just woken up from a long slumber.

"Will it ever find its way home?"

"If we take good care of it, yes."

I lean forward, gently kiss my father's inert cheek through my face mask, and whisper in his ear so quietly that God can't hear, "I'm going to take care

113

of Maddie's home and of yours too. And I'm going to find you."

AS I EMERGE from the Wellington into the outside world, which bears almost no relation to life inside the hospital, it takes me a few seconds to recognize the leather-clad figure leaning against a powerful motorbike and staring at me with some concern.

"Hi, Sam," Eddie says. "Your mother isn't really picking you up, is she? Because she didn't give you permission to come here in the first place, right?"

"Y-yes she did," I stammer.

She hands me a helmet that's a little too big for me. "You're as bad a liar as I am. Come on, let's go."

Eddie
//

The gray streets of London stream past like rivers of sun-baked asphalt beneath the wheels. I feel the thrum of the motorbike's accelerating engine between my legs and in my stomach and biceps. I catch whiffs of typical city aromas as they fly by. London always seems to smell of food wherever you go—doughnuts, chips and fried rice, hot soup and crispy waffles. There's no other city in the Western world where the fragrances of fresh cooking are so present.

I keep the 500cc BMW on a tighter rein than usual with the boy snuggling against my back. He's precious cargo, the son of the man who was my sun and my moon. Who was with me as I breathed and slept, a fount of desire and tenderness. My greatest failure. My greatest love.

Sam shows natural balance in the saddle and no

sign of fear. Making this boy's acquaintance has filled me with an absurd surge of joy, despite the terrible circumstances that brought us together.

Coincidences, my father used to say, are surprising events whose meaning only becomes apparent in retrospect. They're a chance to change your life, and you can either seize that opportunity or spurn it. My mother hated that attitude. Coincidences scared her, whereas for my father they were a source of happiness and curiosity.

WHILE SAM was upstairs, I dropped in to see Henri. Fozzie Bear was reluctant to let me in. "Okay then, but only for a minute."

How awfully quickly a minute passes! Henri seemed so drained. I told him what I'd wanted to tell him over two years ago but didn't. Now, though, I whispered that old prayer to his silent body.

"Don't go!"

We were always reaching for each other's hand when walking, talking, or eating. When we read, each of us would hold a book and yet at the same time we would maintain contact through our fingertips. I can still feel his forefinger circling my fingertip, faster when his book got tense, and more slowly when he relaxed.

His hand caressed me. His hand, his eyes, his laughter, and his body—they all caressed me. When he told me he didn't love me, it was as if he'd suddenly pulled out a gun as we held hands and shot me through the heart.

SAM AND I reach the East End and we soon turn off into Columbia Road. He gazes around wide-eyed as I let him dismount in front of Café Campania, which is next door to the old tulip warehouse where my publishing offices and flat occupy the two upper attic floors above an advertising agency and a tailor's shop.

His face is red and his eyes all shiny from the ride, and he seems younger than when we set out. When he stepped out of the Wellington in his blue suit, he resembled an earnest, pensive little old man who was nonetheless determined to endure the wicked tricks life plays and the even crueler wiles of death. Now, in his school uniform, with his rucksack on his back, he actually looks like a teenager again.

"Have you ever been to the East End before?"

He shakes his head and drinks in every detail of his new surroundings. On weekends Columbia Road metamorphoses into London's flower market. It's one of the few remaining roads in the city that hasn't yet degenerated into a typical pedestrian zone populated exclusively by Zara, Urban Outfitters, Primark, and their ilk. There are over eighty small proprietor-run shops here, each boasting a different-colored front or awning. It looks like the world's longest street café on a sunny day.

I sometimes forget that the experience is drabber and less kaleidoscopic in other London streets.

Sam, whose Colet Court uniform marks him out as a member of the status-driven middle class, takes his first tentative steps in this world, like a hypersensitive cat pricking up its ears and testing the air with its whiskers.

I tuck my helmet under my arm and go into Café Campania to order two cups of freshly brewed oolong tea and a plate of scones. My editorial team at Realitycrash Publishing comes here every day for coffee, as I've set up a beverages tab to compensate somewhat for their paltry salaries.

I've held dozens of meetings with authors around Campania's cast-off classroom and kitchen tables, which Benito and Emma have lovingly collected, refurbished, and decorated with pots of herbs. Those writers described their imaginary worlds to me, each hoping I would publish their manuscript and turn them into an author so that they might devote their lives to storytelling.

How I would have loved to sign them all, because every one of the writers I invited to a meeting after reading through their manuscript had a talent for conveying a message beyond words. That's the magic of literature. We read a story, and something happens. We don't know what or why, nor which sentence was responsible, but the world has changed and will never be the same again. Sometimes it takes us several years to realize that a book tore a hole in reality through which we could escape from the pettiness and despondency of our surroundings.

Emma prepares a small tray, and when Sam timidly approaches, his eyes glued as always to the floor, she shakes his hand and says, "Hi, I'm Emma. And who are you, handsome companion of my favorite publisher?"

He blushes and mumbles his name. He's standing a few feet from the table with an old globe on it where Henri and I would sit when he returned from his encounters with the world's most amazing people and I didn't have enough in my flat to make breakfast. His flights often landed very early in the morning, so he would slip the key from its hiding place in the courtyard wall and let himself into my loft while I was sleeping. When I opened my eyes, he'd be sitting on my bed with his back to the wall, watching me. How many lonely evenings did I spend hoping that he'd be there when I woke up the next morning?

"Sam?"

He turns to me, and for a split second I glimpse the young Henri in the schoolboy's features. My longing for Henri, his warm body, his skin, his scent, and his voice, is tearing my heart apart.

We sit down on opposite sides of the table. I spin the paper globe, whose continents have been re-created from old sepia maps. I stop it with my finger on South Sudan and tap a tiny blue ink mark.

"Your father was here," I say quietly. I spin the ball again. "And here," I say, pointing to the Canadian Rockies, and then repeat the process several times, pointing to Kabul, Colombia, Tierra del Fuego, Moscow, Damascus, Tibet, and Mongolia. Henri would draw dots on this globe with a pen to show me where he'd been.

Sam runs his finger over the surface. "I've got all his reports and portraits at home," he whispers. His eyes are very bright and piercing. "He learned to ride in Mongolia. In Canada he met the professor who walked out on his family one day and went to live in the wilderness. And in Damascus he tracked down a former tutor of Arab princes and princesses." He touches the various spots again before asking, "What is he like?"

He says "is," not "was."

I study the pen marks and recall every single time Henri made a new one. He never made a fuss, never made a show to emphasize "Look at all the places I've been." He did it seriously and meticulously, as if this small globe were the only record of his search. Only now does it strike me that that's what it was—a search. Henri was scouring the earth for himself.

"He was . . . ," I begin, then swallow to relax my constricted throat and correct myself. "He's the best listener I've ever met. When your father listens to someone, it feels as if the speaker is the most important person in the whole world. He can get anyone to talk. It's as if you perceive who you are better in his presence, and by simply being there he encourages you to express things of vital importance to you, which you've never voiced for fear of being laughed at. Or because you weren't aware of them. Henri inspires people to reveal their true selves."

Memories cascade over me, for instance the lilt in Henri's voice on the odd occasion he forgot to mask the fact that he's a Frenchman who changed his name from Le Goff to Skinner.

"Your father's from Brittany. Actually, he ran away from Brittany, leaving everything behind: his mother tongue, his dead father, his dead grandfather, and the graves of his mother and grandmother. I didn't realize how lonely a person can be until I met Henri. Having no one who knew you before you knew yourself, no one to love you just for being you. Having only yourself to fall back on cuts you off from the world."

Henri spoke perfect English, but he never talked about himself, let alone his emotions. Who knows, perhaps we are incapable of expressing who we really are in a foreign language.

I recall our last conversation. It was here, and Henri had followed a cup of tea with several shots of whiskey. There were dark circles around his eyes. He was a driven man who was both running away from himself **and** searching for his true identity. He'd never be fast enough to throw himself off his trail. I've noticed that genuinely special people never recognize that they're special.

"I'm writing about drug barons in Myanmar, who categorize the world into the poor, the rich, and addicts. I'm going to meet a woman who lends her uterus to other couples and divides the world into guilty and not guilty. The couple bear no guilt for their childlessness, but this allows her to make up for the guilt she believes she bears from a previous life. I've spoken to an eleven-year-old prodigy called Jack who's already a better musician than Coltrane or Cincotti. Jack says that when you love something you must practice, and when you're good at something you must practice even harder. What else are our long lives for? Those are the little fellow's precise words. Just goes to show that he's smarter than any of us."

That's what Henri told me the last time we talked. He'd arrived in London so stressed and so desperate that I felt like screaming, "What's the bloody use of all this? Let's be together. I love you so much. I love you, everything about you. Let's be together for this life and every other. I can never get enough of you."

He told me about dozens and dozens of people, and yet he never mentioned his son, Sam.

I spin the globe. It rotates only briefly, and yet those revolutions catapult me back two years into the past.

"I'm writing and traveling, drinking and trying

to keep the nights at bay. Dawn is my foe. In Iceland I meet Etienne, a Canadian ocean cartographer who's settled in Iceland and sees the world as most people will never see it—as the blue planet, whose principal feature is water, not land. Reality is flux," Henri says, running his finger along the coastlines on the magnificent globe. "The areas we've explored are far smaller than those we know nothing about. In other words, we can see the world, but we don't know it. We are dwarfed by reality."

I quote this last sentence to Sam. He nods, and I see the question form on his face: **What about me? Did he talk about me?**

"Your teas are ready!" calls Emma.

Sam carries the tray as I push the BMW into the courtyard. We take the lift up to the publishing offices. It used to be the goods lift, and it's decorated with painted tulip leaves, flowers, and bulbs. It stops at the fourth floor, where Ralph, Andrea, and Poppy work. From here a spiral staircase leads up to my flat.

Next to their messy desks stand a sofa (Ralph), several chairs (Poppy), and a farm bench scattered with embroidered cushions (Andrea). Ralph likes to surround himself with oriental furniture. Alongside his light table is a layout table where he occasionally does watercolors for our covers or makes copperplate prints with a hand-operated press. Poppy decorates her workplace with gothic objects and insignia, while Andrea stores manuscripts in scrupulously labeled Plexiglas containers surrounded by piles of books.

In the center of the room is the "atrium," as we've named the large production table where the four of us work together on a book during the important prepublication stages, such as deciding on the cover, writing the blurb, and making the final adjustments before going to print. This is where Blue, our proofreader, sits when she comes in to check the galleys—the printouts of the type-set manuscript she must scan for any spelling and grammar mistakes. She plows through the pages while listening to Metallica or Berlioz at full volume on a gigantic pair of headphones.

Sam prowls around the office until he comes to the "trophy cabinet." There, on shelves running along the big room's long side wall, their covers facing outward, are all the books Realitycrash has published over the past twenty years. First editions, translations, special editions, reprints, and paper-backs.

Sam's face lights up with delight and wonder. I catch myself blushing with pride. "We only publish speculative fiction. We aren't big, but we are highly specialized. Two of our most success-ful titles are **Schrödinger's Cat** and **The House with a Thousand Doors**. I founded Realitycrash at the age of twenty-four. I was a huge Michael Moorcock fan."

Sam whispers, "**The Lives and Times of Jerry Cornelius**."

"**A Nomad of the Time Streams!**" I shoot back.

Obviously enjoying our little joust, Sam counters with another Moorcock title, "**The Eternal Champion**."

"I loved the Eternal Champions because—"

"They keep the multiverse in balance and make sure the parallel worlds don't merge."

We stare at each other, happy and surprised, and for a moment I'm thirteen again, a bookworm with a proclivity for subjects that remain largely obscure to others of my age. They read romantic novels, I read steampunk; they read **Smash Hits** and **Just Seventeen**, I read books by Ursula K. Le Guin about superluminal speeds and time theories. She gave me my maxim for life: "Truth is a matter of the imagination." I had no one to share my exotic hobby with and would have given my right arm for a fellow reader like Sam.

We pick up our cups of tea from the tray and clink them gently, but alerted by the approaching click of lacquered high-heeled pumps, Sam spins around to be greeted by an incredible sight.

"Winnie darling, you haven't given me any feedback on the cover design."

Poppy blows her gleaming black, meticulously styled Bettie Page fringe out of her eyes. My press officer and marketing director is a practicing rockabilly girl with a bit of the pinup about her. Today she's wearing a black dress with white polka dots and a red hem over seamed stockings and patent-leather Mary Jane shoes.

"Poppy, let me introduce Sam. Sam, this is Poppy. Sam's into speculative fiction."

"Oh, that's lucky. It's the only genre I like," says my secret weapon, stretching out a delicate white hand in fingerless black lace gloves.

I don't tell Sam that Poppy can do anything. She can spoil authors and take care of PR, have the press eating out of the palm of her hand, and compose amazing tweets even after seven Hendrick's gin and tonics. I've known her for as long as I've run Realitycrash, which is to say twenty years, and we both love alternative realities, as do Ralph, the graphic designer, and Andrea, my chief editor.

Poppy is famous in the industry for the tattoo on her back. It depicts an open book in which she collects her favorite quotes by asking an artist to inscribe them in ink under her skin. Some authors would rather be immortalized on Poppy's skin than win the Man Booker Prize.

She hands me a printout. We're publishing a special tenth-anniversary edition of **Thousand Doors**.

"What's it about?" Sam asks.

"It's a multiworld scenario," Andrea replies, having also left her corner with the Plexiglas-boxed manuscripts. "One day an anxious young criminal barrister discovers a door in his office that he's never seen before. He steps through it and finds himself back in his office, only the parameters of his life have shifted ever so slightly. He has—"

"A fling with his boss's wife," Ralph completes the sentence after noticing the gathering by the trophy cabinet. "One hell of a moody diva, but what can you do?"

"He escapes, but doesn't notice that he's left through the hidden door of the **second** office," Andrea explains, taking up the story again.

"And as he searches for the 'best' possible life, he becomes hopelessly confused by the thousand doors and the many thousands of different ways of living one's life," Poppy concludes.

What I haven't revealed to Sam is that this was the unedited manuscript I read to my dead father over ten years ago as I kept my vigil beside his corpse. I know it practically by heart, and every time I see it I think of the silence in that room and of how empty life seemed without him. I think it took me four years to learn to laugh again without bursting into tears.

"What do you think of the cover?" I ask Sam.

He puts down his cup of tea, takes the design from my hands extremely earnestly, and studies it. The cover is very conventional—a blue door floating over a sea that turns out on closer inspection to be composed of dozens of similar doors. Covers are like faces: none ever pleases everybody, and they don't always convey the full complexity of what's behind them.

I wish there were a door I could walk through into a new life in which Henri and I had never met. Or else were a couple. With a little girl. And he wasn't in a coma.

Sam says, "The cover's for girls, whereas the story's for boys. It sounds interesting, but the picture's lame."

Andrea groans, "Ouch!" Ralph says, "I told you so!," and Poppy lays her arm around Sam's shoulders and makes a suggestion. "Hey, Samuel, how about coming to all our cover presentations from now on? I think that having a genuine reader's perspective would buck up our ideas. What do you say?"

He glances at her bashfully before looking her squarely in the face and whispering almost inaudibly, "Okay!" He seems ready to explode with joy.

I did say that Poppy can do anything, even turn unhappy boys into young men—and very happy men at that.

"I think it's a great idea, Sam," Ralph agrees, "and if you know someone else who reads speculative fiction and—"

"My friend Scott!"

Oh, I do like you, little guy, I think. **Your first thought is to share your good fortune rather than keep it all for yourself.** My heart goes out to him.

The boy's eyes alight on the large clock hanging

on the wall of the corner kitchenette next to the stylized Doctor Who TARDIS. "I've got to go," he says cheerlessly. "The SIG's meeting at Forbidden Planet and then later at Kister Jones's house."

"SIG?" I ask. We're all familiar with Forbidden Planet, London's largest and best bookshop for science fiction, speculative fiction, and niche literature like our own.

"Special interest group," Poppy says quickly, then adds, to Sam: "So you're a Mensa member? Wow. How old are you—fifteen?"

"I'm thirteen. Well, almost fourteen, actually," he replies, drawing himself up to his full height. Another sprinkle of magic from Poppy.

"You're going to Kister's?" says Ralph. "Well, say hi to him and tell him he still owes me a drink and a manuscript."

"When did we start publishing Kister Jones?" I wonder aloud. Our budget doesn't really stretch that far.

"He lost a bet, but I'll say no more. Gentleman's agreement."

"Can you at least tell me what the book's about, or is that also under embargo until publication?"

"Oh, the working title's **Slackline**. It's about people being put into induced comas so that they can travel through time in the dreams of the dead."

There's no need to look at Sam to know that Ralph's words have punctured the sense of childish frivolity that has slowly returned to his demeanor over the past few hours. That's how it is with pain: it responds to particular words the way a circus animal reacts to commands. **Coma** is the word that saps our courage and rekindles our dread.

"I'll drop you at Forbidden Planet," I whisper as Poppy admonishes Ralph with a punch on the arm and Andrea says, "Okay, I'll come up with an alternative cover brief for **Thousand Doors**."

SAM LETS ME take him to the tube station and no farther. Cracks have appeared in our fragile relationship. We're standing close to the stairs, and a gust of air comes surging up from the Underground. It's heavy with the typical smells of diesel and too many people, coupled with the heat generated by the trains. He looks me briefly in the eye as we say goodbye.

"We have a SIG group, organized by Mensa, that meets weekly" he whispers. "We always meet at Forbidden Planet and then go on to Kister Jones's. My mother picks me up from there. She thinks I've been hanging out with Scott all day. She doesn't want me to see my father, even though I'd never met him before all this happened. Thanks for the tea, and, well . . . bye."

And with those cryptic comments, he leaves me standing there and runs down the steps.

"Hey!" I call after him. "Bring Scott with you next time!"

He turns round on the stairs and lifts his hand in a Vulcan salute.

I'd have loved to have had a child with Henri. I'd have loved to have had everything with Henri.

IT'S DARK by the time I feel too weary to drink any more Talisker. Its slight tang of amputation anesthetic has numbed my senses. I keep asking myself the same questions, but they are swirling around my head more slowly now.

Do I want this? Can I do this? Can I take care of Henri as Dr. Saul expects? Can I ask Wilder to put up with this? Can I ask myself to leave Henri alone? Will I be able to fetch him back? And what if I turn on him one day, if I feel like taking revenge or letting him die? And why, for hell's sake, did Sam never see his father?

Dr. Saul advised me to consult other people to see if I wasn't taking on too much, "biting off more than I could chew." Sure, but the only person who knew me well enough, intimately, is dead. I still ask him, though. Silently I inquire, **What should I do? Will I be able to do it? Should I do it?**

My father was a lighthouse inspector. He didn't just check the ones dotted along the Cornish coast but also those on the other side of the Channel, from Cherbourg to Saint Mathieu, just north of the roadstead of Brest. The sea around there was chock-full of lighthouses. He was able to hear if there was too little air in the bottles that heated the revolving lights. He could also hear if a storm was brewing by the whistling of the wind through the tower and open windows. And he would always steel himself before climbing a tower, especially during the winter months, when it felt as if he were ascending a fragile finger that rose mischievously from the foaming waves, while the waters crashed again and again around him, billowing up against the sides of the beacon like a giant collar of spray and rage.

My father told me to forget about the height of the staircase when I entered a lighthouse and to concentrate instead on the first step, taking it step by step from there.

"That's how you confront a challenge that seems overwhelming at first. That's how you manage." Shrink the world, be precise; pay no heed to the long night before you but only to the next moment. That's what he told me. "You must follow the path to the very end to get an overview of the whole journey, Edwina."

I throw my arms around the pillow and press my face into it. It seems like an age before I finally doze off, and then Henri's there, kissing my tummy. I can feel his lips and his breath. I feel him kissing the sides of my rib cage and up my neck, his mouth brushing mine and his lips on my eyelids, kissing me the way only he could and nobody else.

When I open my eyes to look at Henri and tell him I've had a dream, a terrible dream in which I chased him away and he fell into a coma after a mysterious accident, he isn't there. Only my eyelids are cool, as if they've been kissed, really kissed, because the wind blowing in through the open window has dried the fine film of moisture on my delicate skin.

I'm forty-four. Henri rejected me long ago. I owe him nothing, let alone to sacrifice my life for his! No, I feel neither guilt nor any willingness to make sacrifices. I sense that any decision I make will be wrong.

I can decide against Wilder. Or Henri. Or myself.

Sam

⸺ // ⸺

Every evening my mother showers before she goes to bed. She applies a body lotion she orders from Paris that smells like pastry, and then sits in the kitchen in her knickers and bra until her skin has absorbed the cream. In the meantime she reads one of those pastel-colored novels that are on special offer at the supermarket.

She checks the last page of every new book first to make sure it has a happy ending; if not, she won't even start the "stupid thing." She sips a small glass of sparkling wine as she reads. No one's allowed to speak to Marie-France during this ritual. Not Steve nor me, and even my younger brother, Malcolm, who used to be able to interrupt her when he was small, mustn't disturb her.

I now know why she does this—it's the only time she feels safe. The only time she knows that everything will turn out fine. My mother's most urgent need is for everything to turn out fine after spending too long in parts of the world where life will never, ever be safe again. She's seen every gate to hell.

I go into the back garden and sit there in the dark. I gaze at the house, the cube we live in. A small terrace house in Putney, with a bathroom whose light you turn off by tugging on a cord. My mother bought the brick-faced sandstone house because of this so-called garden, which consists of a patch of lawn and an evergreen hedge. Through the lit windows I can see Maman in the kitchen and Steve sitting in front of the television. There's a football match on.

A small, safe cubic life.

I play a game called "If my father were here." Here's how it goes: I shut my eyes and imagine what it might be like and every idea comes true when I reopen my eyes. There would be a huge bookcase, crammed with novels. We'd have a dog called Winterfell or Lobsang. I'd wear a pointy black hat like Sir Terry Pratchett, and on Towel Day my father would quote Douglas Adams and spend all day in a striped dressing gown. My father would demonstrate how to cross a minefield on your own using a chopstick and a graffiti spray can. Eddie would come by on her motorbike. And Maddie would be there too.

I keep my eyes closed while I imagine Eddie

climbing off her BMW and going into the house. My father would kiss her.

But what about Maddie? She'd come toward me with her hands covering her eyes, as in blind-man's buff, and yet she'd know exactly where I was. Suddenly she would be facing me, very close, and then she'd lower her hands and look at me.

When I open my eyes, the only books in the house other than my mother's supermarket potboilers are still the ones in my room. Steve's watching football, and Malcolm's playing on his console.

"Super-Sander" is how Scott once described Steve. Steve's a floor layer and works at a DIY superstore. He's not such a bad guy, even if he does insist on calling me "Fanman," as if he can't remember my name. Scott's usual name for my stepfather is "Fanman Steve."

I count to five, swallow hard once, twice, count again, and then force myself to go inside.

"Have you done your homework, Sam?" my mother shouts out. Her glass is empty.

When did I have time? I want to call back. **When?** I go to my room without answering.

A few minutes later she's standing by my door, her body shrouded in a dressing gown. She smells of pancakes, with a whiff of alcohol. "Have you practiced your French vocab?"

"Hmm."

"The tests are in three weeks."

"Yes."

"You know what that means, don't you, Sam?"

"Yes, Maman."

It's the same dialogue every day, and we already had this conversation earlier in the car when she picked me up from Kister Jones's. My mother is terrified that I might lead an unstructured life.

"Sam, those tests are really important if you want to make something of yourself and have a good career."

"So Steve didn't pass the tests back in his day?"

A sharp intake of breath from my mother. I have no idea why I said that. It wasn't fair, and she can't help the fact that I'd rather be somewhere else—anywhere but here. Anywhere but living this square life with Steve calling me Fanman.

"I know you missed school this afternoon, Samuel."

"No, I didn't!"

"Where were you?" My mother looms over me.

"Here and there," I mumble. "I was at Forbidden Planet. The new Pratchett just came out."

"Samuel," she says, "you skipped school. And you weren't at Forbidden Planet because I rang them. They know you there. So . . . where were you?"

My mother would feel betrayed if I told her the truth and said that I was at the hospital, as I have been every day for the last two and a half weeks. It's always been this way. Every time I suggested I had any hint of love for my father, my mother would act hurt and say nothing for days on end.

That's why I keep lying to her now. "Scott and I were smoking."

Scott would laugh his head off at this, as the only time I took a drag on one of his Lucky Strikes I felt dizzy and had to lie down for half an hour.

The volley of abuse that rains down on me now is infinitely better than the inevitable gloomy, disappointed silence that would have met an admission that I'd been visiting my father at the hospital. Her tirade is followed by a strict ban on buying any more of those dreadful fantasy books and ends with an announcement that there'll be no pocket money or television for a while.

My mother looks around one more time before leaving the room. "You're ruining your life, Sam!"

She shuts the door behind her and I sit there, longing to shout after her, **Nothing's the way you think it is! My father rescued a child and he's wearing the scoobie and was dead and is in a coma. And there's a girl at the hospital called Maddie whom I want to be with me forever. My life can never be as ruined as hers. She'll never sit any tests and never have any opportunities.** But instead I sit silently at my desk and press my fists into the tabletop.

My mother's a wounded woman. Ever since I came into the world, I've been aware of a shadow hanging over her soul. There's no need to hurt her. Sometimes I want to protect her from everything.

I want to tell her I love her, but I don't know how to go about it.

I hear Steve zapping through the channels and then my mother calls to him to come to bed. A short while later I hear a rhythmic scraping from their bedroom. It's the head of their bed rubbing against the wallpaper as Steve and my mother make love. Nine minutes every time, followed by the sound of the toilet flushing.

Malcolm comes into my room. He doesn't yet understand the cause of these noises. He gets into my bed, studies my face, and says quietly, "You don't smell of smoke at all, Sammy."

I don't immediately answer. Malcolm is on their "side"—a member of the happy family. That's nonsense, of course, but every time I look at him I see myself as an intruder in this family. A nuisance. Yet I also know that I'd do anything for my brother. He's one of those people who can never understand why other people might lie or be nasty.

Malcolm sits down on my bed. "You weren't smoking, Sammy. Where were you?"

Where was I? Good question. My life has been hacked and reformatted. Into the life I "really" ought to lead. With a father who's lost his entire family.

Or what happens when everything changes? If your life isn't being hacked but the world is seriously out of kilter? Maybe I'm like the barrister who steps through a secret door in his office and roams through his different lives until he can't be sure which is the real one.

I stop chasing my thoughts through this labyrinth and count to five hundred. My brother has fallen asleep, and I'm trying to figure out if I'm still in the real world or not.

I quietly fetch two ski-boot boxes from my wardrobe to help me decide. They contain two heavy files. I open the first one and flick through the headlines of the newspaper articles inside.

```
LOST IN EUROPE: THE FORGOTTEN
    CHILDREN OF THE BALKAN WAR

THE GIRL WITH A BOMB IN HER
    RUCKSACK

THE PHONY WAR: HOW THE US ARMY
    CENSORS JOURNALISTS

KIDNAPPED BY REBELS: REPORTERS
    AS BARGAINING CHIPS
```

And so forth. Frontline reports, essays, photos. Until my birth thirteen years ago my father was a war correspondent, and I have virtually every article he ever published. I printed them off the Internet or cut them out of old magazines I found at flea markets or on eBay. I also wrote to newspaper offices from school with requests for back issues.

The second file contains a portrait piece published in **Time** in 2002. My father's face is on the front cover, surrounded by the famous red frame. The headline below the photo is "Mr. Fearless." My father's staring past the camera. His blue eyes suggest he's probably gazing at something in the distance. His skin is deeply tanned and cracked, and his square chin is dotted with silvery stubble. A scar slashes across his left eyebrow, and no hair grows there. He says in the interview that he sustained the wound from a knife belonging to a drunken soldier in Vukovar. My father had to kneel in front of the soldier for two hours, being peed on and beaten, before being allowed to continue his journey. He'd hidden a Serbian orphan in his car and smuggled the boy across the border.

I once told Scott that story. He was silent for a long time and then something unusual happened: tears welled up in his eyes.

"Your father's a real mensch, **mon ami**. Not showing off, not playing along with all that shit, like 'I own this, I do this, I can afford such-and-such a watch.' Your dad, my little smart-ass sidekick, is someone who lives life to the full."

Time magazine had named Henri M. Skinner its "Person of the Year" to represent all the war correspondents worldwide who risk their lives to report on grim events.

My father stopped reporting from war zones when I was born. My mother said it had nothing to do with me, but it might have. She hasn't read the interview in **Time**. I have. I can recite it by heart, including the passage in which my father says, "No war correspondent should have a family."

I flick back a few pages to a report about child soldiers in South Sudan. There's a photo of a man slumped forward in a jeep. In the background my father is crouching down beside a boy with a rifle in his hands. In the foreground lies a shattered cowrie necklace. My mother took this photo before she began to fear for her life.

I've calculated. That would be about right. It might have happened out in Africa. My mother never talks about when she met my father and what happened afterward. Nor does she say why she came here from Paris when I was four.

Malcolm asks drowsily from the bed, "What are you reading?"

I pick up the file, sit down on the edge of the bed, and show him the **Time** cover with my father's face on it.

"Is that Daniel Craig?" he asks.

"Close," I answer. It's true that my father does slightly resemble Daniel Craig, a serious loner who gives the impression that he doesn't know how to laugh, but his hair is darker than Craig's.

"What's he doing?"

"He's sleeping, like you." Malcolm obediently closes his eyes and within seconds he's asleep.

When, in my state between waking and sleep, the letters start to blur before my eyes, I carefully replace the files in their boxes and push them to the very back of the wardrobe.

Write about the world to understand it. Write about people to make them visible. Write down my thoughts to stop myself from going mad. I bought myself a notebook last year to do all those things, but there it lies, unopened, as if to suggest, **What have you got to say anyway?**

I gently roll Malcolm a little closer to the wall and lie down on the narrow strip of bed beside him.

What would have happened if my father and my mother had stayed together? I imagine that he wouldn't be in a coma now. I don't know how Eddie fits into this picture, but maybe, somehow, she'd be here regardless.

Still attempting to cram my father, my mother, Malcolm, Maddie, and Eddie into one picture, I fall asleep and dream of the little comatose girl. Her face is floating under a thick layer of river ice, staring up at me against a backdrop of black sea. The sea parts, and I fall into a dream I used to have even before I went to school—a dream that the pediatrician said was a **pavor nocturnus,** a night terror, and that the child psychologist described as a stress reaction to a traumatic experience.

But I've never experienced what happens in my dream. A train approaches from a long, black tunnel, and I'm terribly scared because someone's lying on the track bed below and the train's going to run him over. I have this dream over and over again, and when the train arrives and its headlights shine in my face, I wake up and lie there in the dark with blood pounding in my ears.

DAY TWENTY

Henri

I tumble out of the moving jeep and cover Marie-France's body with mine, shielding her head with my hands. She's screaming beneath me, and the sand is hot and burns my knee through my trousers.

The jeep rolls a few yards farther and crashes into a wall. Nelson, our driver, is slumped over the steering wheel. The two Blue Helmets lie dead, their faces turned to the sun, on the scorched grass beside the road through Wau in the Bahr el-Ghazal region.

The boy with the machine gun staggers out of the hole where he was crouching when he shot Nelson. A hole with a strip of cardboard over it.

Marie-France is whimpering now.

The gunman is young, perhaps thirteen, but his eyes are as old as death. He is just as scared as I am.

The boy crouches down, cradling the rifle loosely in front of him, and shuts his eyes.

"Don't go! Don't go!" Marie-France yells as she notices my weight lifting from her body.

I stand up and walk slowly toward the boy, displaying the palms of my hands. He doesn't even glance at me and offers no resistance when I relieve him of the rifle. I empty the magazine and toss it as far away as I can, then squat down beside him. His upper body is rocking back and forth, back and forth, and all around us is silence. Sudan is paralyzed by horror and heat, and I'm thirty-one and have spent far too long in war zones. I've also seen far too many of these aged children. UNICEF flew two thousand five hundred of them out of here last week, and others are congregating in hastily erected SOS Children's Villages in the savannah. The objective is to disarm them and provide them with new papers and identities. They would no longer be known by the weekday on which they were born. But what, after all, is in a name? You're nothing without your community.

At the SOS children's camp we would like to talk to the demobilized child soldiers who can neither read nor write but are capable of aiming a gun, pulling a trigger, and locating mines. None of the laws we know apply here; the only law is the law of the gun.

Marie-France rolls herself into a ball behind the jeep, from which I pushed her at the sound of the first gunshots. Our newspapers in London and Paris teamed us up, but we don't get on.

At some point I see her grab the strap of her green camera bag and pull it over the sandy, dusty ground toward her. She lies on her side and holds up the camera to create some distance between herself and the horror she sees. She takes a photo of the bodies of Nelson and the Blue Helmets, with me crouching beside the child killer with one hand on his trembling shoulder.

I have the impression that I've seen this picture before, as if I've seen myself from the outside in the photo Marie-France is currently taking. Nelson's cowrie necklace lying bloodied in the foreground, the child soldier and me in the background.

The heat flickers before my eyes, and the momentary déjà vu—a certainty that I have lived through these seconds before and know exactly how the photo is going to turn out—fades.

"What's your name?" I ask.

He looks at me, quietly says, "Boy," and averts his gaze again.

I crouch beside him as the shadows shift and Marie-France takes photographs. Otherwise, nothing moves in this street, as if we were the last living people in this corner of Africa. In the whole world even. Flies and goats, gutted vehicles, plastic bottles, rubbish, and nothing else.

Sometime later Boy tells me that his father used to call him Akol. His father is dead and so are his mother and younger sister, but his elder sister's still alive. She cooks for the commanders. At night she's allowed to sleep in the leaders' huts while he curls up under a plastic sheet suspended from two dead tree trunks.

I ask him if he knows that UNICEF helps boys like him.

"But what happens to her?" he asks. "What happens to her?" He's scared that the militias that trained him will sell his sister to Italy if he doesn't fight.

I can't do this any longer, I think. Over and over again I have tried to take realities like this home with me and to expose them to people who have only ever seen war on the television. They avert their eyes, as they always do when they've seen their fill of life's atrocities.

I can see why.

I let Akol run away, and now have an unloaded rifle; Marie-France, whose heart seems to have partially turned to stone; and a two-hour trek back to the camp. Marie-France refuses to take off her heavy protective vest printed with the word "Press" and let me carry it, but she's grateful when I shoulder her green camera bag.

Fear grips us and drives us out into this all-too-real world. The only thing we have in common in this lawless warring environment is our horror, like a terrible disease from which neither of us will recover.

THAT NIGHT Marie-France doesn't want to sleep alone under a camel-hair blanket on the camp bed in the press tent lit by two thin candles.

"I want to make love one last time before I die," she says.

"You're not going to die here," I reply.

"So don't you want me, you arrogant prick?"

I don't know why love is so important to people that it comes to their minds when they're in mortal fear. I'd rather have a bulletproof vest and a bottle of whiskey. I say that, and Marie-France hits me. She slaps me in the face and punches me in the chest until I grab her wrists and clasp her body to mine. Marie-France starts to weep. There's so much misery and hatred in the look she gives me that I end up kissing her.

It's one of those moments. What moments?

The thought fades as Marie-France's lips respond to mine. She kisses me, and it seems as if every kiss makes it easier for her to breathe. I answer her kiss and take her in my arms. I stroke her back and it begins to relax at my touch. I put my mouth to her ear and hum into it, and I kiss her neck. Just as I'm about to stop because her sobbing has ceased, her hands seize me and pull me closer.

"Make love to me," she whispers.

And because her caresses tear open my loneliness and communicate hers to me, because I don't want to hurt her and humiliate her again, and because I have the same furious urge to live, I obey.

I feel her body relax, feel her relent and forget herself in lust. I kiss away her fear, I move very gently inside her, I hum and, cheek to cheek, sing "Somewhere over the Rainbow" to her. She lets go. Sensing this softness, the enticing, inviting lust between her legs, I glimpse Marie-France's soul. For a second I am ineffably close to her.

"Don't go!" she says when she feels my body pulling away from hers after no more than a minute. Her hot hands push on my lower back to bring our bodies together again. There's something comforting about resting inside her like this, but I nevertheless feel an urge to withdraw before I lose myself completely. It's a reflex and we're unprotected in three senses: we're naked, we're young, and . . .

"Come," she whispers. "Come inside me!"

This is one step further than we planned. Only one. **This time**, I think, **I'll do things differently**. Then I stop thinking. I stay inside her as I come, and it's like a long, profound, cathartic exhalation.

"I still hate you," Marie-France moans in despair, clinging to me, and I know that we've never loved each other and never will.

For a few moments, snuggled against Marie-France's back, I fall into as deep a sleep as is possible in this heat and the constant oppressive vigilance of the camp, and I dream that we have a son. He asks me if I'll come to the Fathers' and Sons' Day at his school. Because he's never met me. I say yes, and after that I die, drowned in a river whose waters taste of the sea.

I don't tell Marie-France about this absurd dream or my previous déjà vu, that strange sensation of having reached a fork in the road. As if I already lay on this camp bed and had the option of kissing Marie-France or not, of coming inside Marie-France or not.

Two days later we fly to Paris via Cairo. Marie-France nods off against my shoulder as we cruise over the Mediterranean. She's embarrassed when she wakes up and huddles against the misted-up window for the rest of the journey.

Standing facing each other in the blue-gray light of Charles de Gaulle Airport among the holiday-makers, suits, trolley cases, and Air France steward-esses in their short pencil skirts, I ask her, "Do you want to see me again?"

She shrugs, which could mean "I don't know" or "Ask me once more." I don't know much about her. She's twenty-seven, doesn't like children, loves painting, and refuses to drink rosé wine.

"Not necessary," Marie-France drawls. She has a particular way of tucking her hair behind her ear while she fixes me with those big, insecure, girlish eyes.

I think of the murderer who was once called Akol until he lost his identity and became Boy.

There are some women, I think, who say no because they'd like to be persuaded and because they don't want to be the one who said yes, the sign that they've lost.

I think of a path that only becomes apparent when you take it, as in **Indiana Jones**.

I shift my heavy bag onto my other shoulder. I feel my flight instinct urging me to turn on my heel and walk away, fast. Part of me doesn't want to explore the path that's opening up among the arrivals and departures in the long airport halls. This part of me simply wants to return to London, do the washing, go to the pub, get drunk until I feel like sleeping, and then sleep for a month and then set off for somewhere new. Anywhere but home.

That's what always happens. No sooner have I slept with a woman than I'm already on my way out of the door.

I imagine what it'd be like not to see each other again, ever. The first hours would be a mixture of relief and shame. It would be forgivable: most journalists sleep with one another on overseas trips. But Marie-France might be pregnant with our son. She'd probably have an abortion because I jumped on the next British Airways flight with sufficient stocks of gin on board, rather than agreeing to stay and start a family.

I must be mad!

"Okay then," says Marie-France, bending down to pick up her camera bag and her rucksack.

Now, I think. **Say it, Henri! Do things differently this time.**

That same old "this time"!

"Take care," she mumbles, and leans forward for the obligatory kiss on each cheek. Air-kiss left, air-kiss right.

Go? Or stay?

I'm overcome with curiosity at the completely fresh possibilities I might discover by staying in Paris with Marie-France instead of returning to London or flying on to Kabul. A jolt inside me. **Come on! Be an adult for once!**

And yet . . . I don't know where this contrariness comes from. It's accompanied by a sense of "this time, this way."

As we touch cheeks for an extra kiss, I whisper, "I'd like to stay with you," but even as I speak the words I know it isn't true. I dismiss my shock, thinking that this must be normal and every man feels this way the first time he stays.

She hugs me tightly and whispers, "I still hate you, but not as much as I did," and clings to me.

I skip my onward flight to London, don't take my other flight to Kabul, and stay in Paris instead. Three months later, Marie-France shows me the ultrasound scan. "I want the child, but I don't want you," she says.

"Of course you don't want me. You're always saying that. But I don't believe you, so I'm going to stay on regardless."

She throws her arms around my neck and says, "You're right." But she never says "I love you" because she can't and neither can I. I do know Marie-France well enough, though, to realize that she's continually testing my affection for her. She's looking for proof that I want her. She keeps sending me away so that then I can come back to her. This is the only way for it **almost** to be love, because we both know that it isn't really.

It's the miracle of that night. Our son, Samuel Noam, is a child of fear. Speechless at the idea of how we might deal with this miracle if we don't stay together, we stay together. Marie-France sets only one condition. "If the child is born, don't go off to war again. I don't want him to be scared for you."

I keep my promise.

I SPEND three and a half years reassuring Marie-France that I'm going to stay with her, even when she says she doesn't want that. She wins a prize for her photo of Nelson's cowrie necklace, and I get a part-time job at **Le Monde**. I don't go to war again.

Samuel's a delicate child. Marie-France often despairs when our little darling suddenly refuses to continue walking or begins to wail when he's forced to enter an unfamiliar room. She never tires of getting up at night when the little chap is plagued by dreams, pointing at shadows and huddling in the farthest corner of his crib. She carries him, she consoles him, but she doesn't know what I know about those dreams. I soon move into Samuel's room. Marie-France is jealous and at the same time grateful that I find it so easy to care for our son. Her gratitude is sincere and tender, and we spend some wonderful times together. I never find Sam too hard to handle—not for one second. For ages he can't talk properly and when he does speak, the nursery school teachers report that he says strange things. The speech therapist is also concerned. I'm the only one who doesn't find the things he says weird. The words sound a bit like Tibetan or as if he learned words in his dreams that may well be logical descriptions of the things he sees during his nighttime adventures. It's just that no one in the real world understands his language.

Marie-France sleeps with her boss. Her boss's wife tells me this one day and even suggests we should have an affair—"To balance things out, **mon cher**." However, I think of Sam and the fact that he already reacts quite violently to his mother's efforts to keep her liaison secret from us—something that is both good and a cause of terrible worry for her. Yes, Sam can feel and empathize with his mother, and that might be another reason I don't hold it against her, for my son learns to feel what I feel. When Marie-France treats him with indifference, he isn't spiteful toward her but loving. He runs over to her on those chubby little legs and climbs onto her chair to stroke her cheek. I sometimes have the impression that he catches her moods as he might a cold.

I turn down Marie-France's boss's wife's offer.

I watch Marie-France for a while, listening to the excuses she invents and her lies about where she is and when. Like many women, she commits the cardinal mistake of wanting to make love with me more often than ever before, as if every legitimate hour with me offsets a forbidden hour with him. I'm touched by her inner turmoil. Sometimes I'd like her to feel ashamed, but ultimately I wish, for all our sakes, that we could simply be honest with each other.

I usually decline to have sex with her, and she's relieved and simultaneously restless and suspicious. "Who are you sleeping with if not with me?" she asks one day when we haven't held each other's naked bodies for three or four months.

"How about you?" I retort. "Still sleeping with Claude?"

"I hate you," she whispers, and I can see why. We hate people who don't show any hurt when they're being cheated on. Yet I genuinely don't feel aggrieved. I don't really care. I even hope she loves him: it'd do her a lot of good to love someone.

She suffers from the knowledge that I don't love her, but the miracle that came into our lives is still powerful enough to bind us together—our miracle child, even if Sam is more foreign to her than to me.

I reckon that if her boss, Claude, were to separate from his wife, Chantal, tomorrow morning, Marie-France would have moved in with him by the evening. However, Chantal doesn't make things as easy for her husband as I do for my wife.

I love Sam infinitely. He's the miracle of the lack of love between Marie-France and myself, and occasionally when she comes home exhausted and relaxed from their tryst, reeking of white wine, Claude's aftershave, and freshly laundered hotel bed linen, I quietly get out of bed and watch Sam sleeping.

So this is the meaning of life.

For the first time I understand men who don't leave their families, even when they've fallen out of love with their wives. It's because of these little people. These pure little people. Loving them is so simple and incurable.

Sam's extremely sensitive to the outside world, for his only means of resistance to it are wailing, sleeping, or crawling away. I watch his tiny head swivel when he hears a pleasant voice or sound, but he turns away when he detects a tone of voice that he doesn't like. He can hear lies, for example, and exaggeration and grief. He finds them practically unbearable, and so he cries.

Being with Sam seems to improve my perception of the world. He also reacts to spaces and places. We mustn't walk along certain streets, and he once had a fit of crying outside the entrance to a building. I later discovered that someone had been mugged and killed there.

He's my little seismograph of invisible worlds. He observes me and everything else around him with an outlandish, almost primeval sensitivity. He's capable of perceiving the fifth dimension of reality so many modern people cannot see in our digital age.

The fifth dimension was the name given to it by a spirit investigator who had had a first career as a physicist and biologist and now, in his second life, was conducting research into the irrational. "The sphere between heaven and earth. You know, strange coincidences. Somebody dies and a child is born. You're thinking about a friend you last saw thirty years ago when the phone rings and he's on the line. Odd sensations that take hold of you in a ruined building or when you drive through countryside that was once plagued by war. The coast of Normandy still has a bloody pall over it. Have you ever been there?"

Yes, I did go once, with Malo and Yvan, and what the man said is true: the sky was more gray, the grass more tired, and the centuries-old houses seemed lower and sadder than elsewhere. The land lay defeated on all sides. At the time I thought the fault lay with me and attributed it to my knowledge of the tens of thousands of people who had died there, not to the fact that the land had its own memory. A bloody pall.

The spirit investigator explained that there were many things that people could not perceive through reason or with their limited senses tamed by civilization, either because they aren't physically or mentally capable of it, or because they no longer want to do so.

"Children, dogs, and cats see and sense things whose existence we deny. Growing up doesn't always make you smarter. It usually makes you more stupid."

My son, on the other hand, can still see all these things. His senses have thousands more eyes and ears than mine or, presumably, anyone else's. A funny thing happened one day. He pointed to a corner and said, "Grandpa! Grandpa!" He could have meant either Malo or Yvan. I couldn't see anything, but Sam started laughing and giggling. Can he see my father or grandfather? Can children see the dead?

One day in May, when I'm trying to teach Sam to count, repeatedly attempting to represent the number four—four fingers, four shoes, four blades of grass—he shouts out, loud and clear, "Yellow."

"No, Sam. Four—not yellow."

He shakes his little head, taps my fingers, and repeats forcefully, "Yellow." He points to the list of numbers I've drawn with a long twig in the sand by the side of the Bassin de la Villette, not far from some old men playing **pétanque.** Then Sam points to the eight and says, "Gleen," his word for **green,** and to the five and says, "Plue." The six is red, the seven light green, the three bluish-yellow, and the two gray-red. He doesn't like the figure one at all.

"Aha. So what is yellow plus yellow?"

"Gleen," he answers straightaway, pointing to the figure eight. He loves eights. He loves dark green.

All that day we play the "numbers are colors" game, and by that evening, I've realized that not only does my son see numbers in color, but he also assigns sounds to colors and numbers, or character-istics such as friendliness or strength or nastiness. The sound of an Underground train arriving in a station—"wy-elv," meaning "white eleven"—or of your blood pounding inside your head when you put your hands over your ears—"Plue-dweam, Daddy!," meaning a blue dream. I also know that Sam assigns colors to the emotions he detects in other people. Objects too, although he cannot tell me which objects. He points to shadows and puddles, and I reckon I'd be happy to spend my entire life learning his language.

He's very pale and quiet as we walk across the Place de la Bastille, clutching my hand and trun-dling along on his little chubby legs. I can feel the sun's warmth on my back.

"It's red and white here," says Sam, although he doesn't just say it, he gestures at walls and columns that have stood for a hundred years or more. "Ow, loud!" he says, his wise old eyes filling with tears.

That's the day I finally begin to understand him properly. My son has more sensory receptors than other people, and so he suffers a constant bombardment of impressions that normal people don't even notice on the edges of their perception. He's a synesthete. I decide to break the news to Marie-France as gently as possible. However, Sam's going to need a lot of courage and determination to cope with this gift and this "extra world."

I search for a route home that I'm pretty sure doesn't take us past too many corners, squares, and windowsills where attacks, murders, riots, suicides, or lynchings have taken place. Along the way, I buy Sam a large salted-butter caramel ice cream of the kind we used to eat back home in Finistère, at the tip of Brittany. As he licks at it, I promise him and myself that I'll do everything I can to help him to survive in this extra world.

I'm overwhelmed with a feeling of such tenderness for my son that I have to bite the inside of my cheek. It hurts, but at least it stops me from bursting into tears.

All of a sudden Sam peers at me and says, "Daddy ouch?"

I nod. **Daddy ouch, but a good kind of ouch.**

I don't get around to telling Marie-France. Sam and I are waiting for the metro, and as the "wy-elv" sound approaches, so does the sad, drunken accordion player. He trips over a strap dangling from his instrument and barges into me with his shoulder, knocking me off balance and tearing my hand from Sam's. I fall onto the tracks directly in front of the oncoming train.

Not yet! Please! It's too . . .

DAY TWENTY-FIVE

Henri

I tumble out of the moving jeep and cover Marie-France's body with mine, shielding her head with my hands. The jeep rolls forward a few yards and crashes into a wall. Nelson, our driver, slumps forward over the steering wheel. He dies on the edge of the road through Wau in the Bahr el-Ghazal region.

The boy with the machine gun is young, perhaps thirteen, but his eyes are as old as death. I've seen many of these old, tired children. Too many. We stare at each other until he lowers his gaze and lets the rifle slip from his thin fingers, as if he's awfully tired of always doing the same thing, killing and more killing and yet more killing. It must be hell to keep living the same life over and over again, repeating every hour, every mistake, every wasted moment.

Marie-France rolls into a ball behind the jeep. I see her grab her green camera bag. **Ever the pro,** I think, **even now.**

The heat flickers before my eyes, and for a moment I think I know how the picture is going to turn out. For a further second I also know that Marie-France will sit alongside the editor in chief at the light table, going through the slides and contact sheets. Their bodies will touch and negotiate something. At the end of these negotiations, after a few weeks and glances, the two of them will be naked, moaning and writhing around inside each other. Years later, there will be more tears.

I see all this in the blink of an eye. My eyes are running, my head's throbbing, and I feel an insatiable thirst.

One of the company doctors to whom my editor in chief Gregory sent me told me that I had no more room in my brain. It was crammed with images, hyperrealistic footage and polytraumatic emotions that I'd absorbed over the years as if I were a sheet of blotting paper. They'd never been processed, "in therapy, for example, Mr. Skinner." But can therapy ever drive the war from your mind?

I crouch beside the boy as the shadows shift and Marie-France takes photographs. The murderous boy tells me that his father used to call him Akol. His father is dead, so are his mother and younger sister, but his elder sister is alive, for now, cooking for the commanders.

"Nahia," I whisper, and he nods. Only I realize that Akol hasn't mentioned his sister's name. **How then do I know it? What is this? What's going on? I've got malaria,** I think. **I'm hallucinating. I'm going to die. Am I going to die?**

Reality topples over the edge. Boy and Nahia and Nelson's blood dripping onto the car seat, onto his shattered cowrie necklace. And Marie-France, who will sleep with her boss one day.

I'm dying and I feel a sense of bitterness that there are so, so many things I haven't done.

Akol jumps to his feet and runs away. The rifle lies where it fell.

We walk back to the camp. Marie-France gives me her protective vest with a label saying "Press" on it, but she carries her bag herself.

"I can't do this anymore," she says at one point. "I don't think I can take a picture of anyone ever again."

That night on the camp bed lit by two thin candles I take a swig of whiskey and pass the bottle to Marie-France. I keep passing it to her, again and again, as if it were milk to help her sleep.

"I want to make love one more time before I die," she says. Her consonants are slurred.

"You will," I reply, thinking of her boss Claude, whom I've never met.

"So, don't you want me, you arrogant prick?"

She waits for me to answer. If my limbs weren't so heavy from the whiskey, I'd already be embracing

169

Marie-France. I can hear her loneliness calling, begging me. I can see the gentleness and goodness through her rage. I fight the urge to console her because I don't want to; it's only pity.

"I don't know why people find love so important that it only comes to their minds when they're in mortal fear. I'd rather have a bulletproof vest and a bottle of whiskey."

Marie-France's hand lurches forward as if she's going to slap me. She's too tired, though, and instead makes a dismissive gesture in the freezing air, topples back onto the bed, and nearly falls asleep.

"Kiss me at least," she mumbles, slurring the words.

I lean over her. Her mouth is a fruit. She's a beautiful woman and she craves what I too so desperately miss—life. Such thirst for life. I could drink life straight from her lips!

It's one of those moments. What moments?

The thought fades as I pull the camel-hair blanket a little higher and cover Marie-France with it. The nights are very chilly in Wau. My desire to kiss her has passed. I vaguely regret not making love to her but also feel relieved.

Two days later we fly to Paris, where our ways part in transit. I feel another surge of wistfulness as I watch Marie-France cross the large, bright marble slabs of the terminal floor with quick strides and then stop at baggage claim. Lost in thought, she runs her hand over her flat stomach.

I feel discontented, empty, cheated of something beautiful and bright. I don't understand my mood but put it down to the difference in temperature and to Wau.

I think of Nelson. The Blue Helmets recovered his body and took it to his family. How quickly life can end, and how mysterious are the paths leading to death and life. An accumulation of tiny decisions. A few small gestures and life will take a very different course from the one it would have taken an hour or a day ago.

And what about me? Should I have kissed Marie-France? Slept with her? Would that decision have brought me closer to death or distanced me from it? I try to shake these thoughts out of my head, but they cling on, like fear-sucking leeches.

Survive, from one moment to the next. Do everything right. But how do you know what's right?

I look around for Marie-France once more, but what would I do with her? I don't particularly like her or her cruelty, born of a vulnerable ego, which unleashes her aggressive libido. Nor do I like the feeling of having to console her, as though consolation would make her a good person.

Nevertheless . . . My feeling intensifies that our brief encounter might have opened a door through which I could have stepped, and that by slamming that door I have missed out on something.

I go to the Hilton bar, get drunk, and then, out of anger and spite, board the next plane to Kabul with a sickening feeling that I'm wasting my life for no good reason.

I fall asleep. My dreams are aggressive and confused. I dream that I'm lying silent and numb in a hospital bed. Nobody will meet my eye. I want to scream but discover I have no tongue.

I resurface briefly from my slumbers and press my forehead to the cool window of the plane. I'm thirsty. My head is aching. My throat too. I doze off again, and just below the threshold of waking, I find myself back at the hospital, with strange faces bending over me but not looking at me. One of them belongs to a woman with piercing eyes. She seems vaguely familiar, but then she disappears and I have an unmistakable feeling that I'm going mad.

Ten years ago my editor in chief Gregory gave me a piece of advice that was supposed to serve as a sort of psychological life jacket. "You have to know who you are or else you'll go missing in action. Do you know who you are? Do you have a mantra? What's your headline, Henri? What reminds you of who you are?"

I'm still thinking about that.

I know Greg's wife, Monica. On his birthday, every birthday, she brought a New York cheesecake with strawberry topping to the editorial office, and

Gregory would cut it very seriously and share it. Very calmly and coolly, Greg would stare down all the old, cynical, smart-ass hacks who viewed any show of emotion with contempt and might be tempted to make some derogatory comment about this ritual, saying, "Family saves you. Every man needs a family to save his soul."

I don't have a family. It feels as if the wounds of my forefathers are also in my blood and determine my direction in life.

I no longer have a mother; she died shortly after I was born. No grandmother either: she went missing after going out alone in a storm, and for years afterward Malo would stand on the cliffs, waiting for her to return.

Greg also told me, "Henri, give up this job before it's too late. You should start a family **after** your wars but not **during** them. You must never make your wife and children watch you walk out of the house with your helmet, your bulletproof vest, and your passport, numb with despair that you might never come back. Wait until you've had your fill of war and really trust yourself to live life, then look for someone who loves you and can cope with the fact that all the warfare inside your head prevents you from sleeping at night. But don't wait until you're thirty-five to wean yourself off war. It's your only chance of breaking free."

—— // ——

I HAVE a headache when the plane touches down. On the way from the German military airfield to the US camp in Kabul I swig some water from a canteen. I've made many trips to the devastated city, as the Afghans call Kabul. Some people say that if you come here too often, one day you won't come back.

I think back to the tea merchant who came to Camp Holland last time I was here and took me along to an opium den in Kabul to introduce me to an alleged jihadi who was undergoing reform. We drank. We smoked opium. Mud houses in Afghanistan might not have toilets or windows, but they always have a Kalashnikov in a cupboard and a poppy patch out the back.

Maybe I should go back to smoking opium and find some peace. No more dreams ever again. I'm fed up with dreaming. I've been dreaming my whole life, and I feel weary, so weary.

"YOU'RE EARLY," the commander of the American camp snaps. "We were expecting you three days from now."

"That's the problem with a free press," I reply. I can understand his annoyance. The army is only able to keep an eye—in both senses of the term—on a limited number of journalists. The Americans would love to have more reporters they can keep under control by embedding them with their troops because then they can't file unbiased accounts.

To get out from under the commander's feet, I hitch a ride to Kabul on a mule cart. Greg has left me a voicemail message to announce that **Time** would like to ask me a few questions on my return from Afghanistan.

The scorching heat here is different from the heat in South Sudan. It's dry and smells of fire, exhaust fumes, sweet tea, and curry. I walk along dusty dirt tracks, past stalls selling chickpeas from gray sacks, most of them old German army mailbags marked **Deutsche Bundespost**.

There's an aroma of lamb sprinkled with Persian spices roasting on skewers over open fires. Vendors shout loud advertisements for the wares—figs, dates, or melons—in baskets hanging from the flanks of their donkeys. Merchants sit in the open-fronted shops among piles of silk wedding robes, European-style secondhand clothing, and electronic waste, relating dirty jokes and headlines from the **Anis** daily newspaper to one another. Some women stroll around the market in light-blue floor-length burqas, others in black niqabs with a slit for the eyes, but many women wear fashionable dupatta shawls that leave their faces uncovered, more reminiscent of Grace Kelly's head scarf than forced marriage.

I'm thirsty.

I see soldiers with machine guns and legless beggars on low carts. Paper kites soar through the flickering blue air alongside a minaret. Splinters of glass on their lines, designed to cut through their competitors' strings in midair, sparkle in the sunlight. In the distance are the snowcapped peaks of the Hindu Kush, as white as the **perahan tunban**—flowing trousers and knee-length shirts—worn by two passing men. I look for my confidential informant from my last visit. I steer my way through the crowds, past fat moneychangers and vendors whipping up interest for camels' heads in wheelbarrows, past sheep intestines going gray in the sun, surrounded by clouds of buzzing black flies.

I buy some fresh peppermint tea and drink it with small, greedy sips. It soothes my mouth and throat.

I have no idea how the little boy suddenly pops up in front of me. He blocks my path, shakes his head, waves his hands, and chatters away insistently at me.

What? I want to ask him, scouring my brain for the Persian words, then ask him the same thing in the Dari dialect I've picked up from the soldiers. "What do you want?"

He points to his water bottle. Yes, I'm thirsty too. I'm constantly thirsty because my thirst is only ever stilled momentarily. But the boy keeps staring at me, his eyes restless, wavering, hypnotic. Like the candles on the floor beside the bed in Wau, the night I slept with Marie-France.

I glance over my shoulder. Is someone following me?

I never slept with Marie-France. In the plane, just before I fell asleep, I did imagine doing it, but I didn't sleep with her.

My head is spinning from the heat, alcohol, and thirst.

The boy tugs at my sleeve. He's about twelve years old and looks like a chai boy in one of Kabul's ruling households. Servants and errand runners—they keep boys for every single task. **Were this boy mine, I'd shoot his master,** I think as violent, irrational anger comes boiling up inside me.

The boy doesn't have his hair cropped short like pupils at a Koranic school. His reddish-brown locks are longer and peek out from under an embroidered purple cap. His eyes are two shiny green marbles in his emaciated yet beautiful face. The boy grabs my hand.

"Ibrahim," he says. "I am Ibrahim. They told me to bring you."

I let him pull me along. It is easier to be pulled along, and I feel lighter with every step. I shouldn't let the boy lead me anywhere. I should take him by the hand, but something tells me that it won't work any other way. Not now. Because I didn't kiss her. That was the start of this other life. If I'd kissed her I would now be in Paris.

I spit out this absurd thought. I must have caught something in Africa. Dengue fever? I'm hallucinating. I must talk the army doctor into giving me some medicine later.

We wend our way past the bazaar stalls, the shops, the wheelbarrows, and the birdcages, through the swirling fug of colors and fragrances. It's as if we're sliding down a never-ending pipe. I catch a passing glimpse of a pink rucksack.

A deep female voice shouts inside my head, "Don't go!"

But I can't do otherwise. I'm losing touch with myself and I can't do otherwise.

Soon after that absurd thought, the air smells of singed cables and hair, and someone screams, "Adrenaline!" My heart contracts into a stone, and the pain takes my breath away. Then there's a massive explosion, the detonation of a huge bomb only a few yards away. The pink patch fragments. I'm hurled backward and smash into a stone wall, my mind a mass of pain and blackness. Ibrahim's hand is torn from mine.

The world goes dark, night encroaching from all sides, from above and below, and beyond this blackness shadows jostle me, grope for me, stab me, clasp their hands around my heart.

A boy screams, and I hear him yelling, "Dad! Dad!," his voice cracking with panic. Then the darkness recedes, and it's Ibrahim who is screaming, on and on, until all at once the screaming stops.

The camel-head seller is staring helplessly at his missing lower legs. An embroidered purple cap lies discarded on the ground, alongside scraps of silk and chunks of melon.

My father emerges from the fog of blood and dust. He walks calmly toward me. He's wearing faded jeans and a striped Breton fisherman's sweater, just as he was on that day when we both went to sea but only I came home. He kneels down beside me and whispers, "Oh, Henri. You're still caught in between everything, between different times and different paths."

A sheet of newspaper wafts past, and I glimpse the headline. THE GIRL WITH A BOMB IN HER RUCKSACK. My name is printed underneath. I don't understand.

Ibrahim's lying there, unmoving. Blood is running from his eyes.

I'm sorry, I want to tell my father. **I'm sorry that I don't know which path is the correct one, but I have no courage or strength left.**

There is a tear in reality. Through the tear I spot women and men in blue smocks, bending over me, and beyond them I see a boy staring at me. I had it before. I had it but it was too big for me to cling to.

The "in-between" zone. The hospital. The girl in the river, and this woman. To her, always to her, to tell her something very, very important.

This world is dying. I'm falling into the silence beyond the void. I'm falling and . . .

DAY TWENTY-SEVEN

Sam

"Is that ballet you're watching, **mon ami**?" Scott asks. I can't pause the YouTube video fast enough and am forced to turn off my smartphone screen. "Maybe," I lie.

"Maybe? Or was that one of those videos my father always turns off when my mother knocks on the door of his study?"

"I don't know what your father turns off."

"And you don't **want** to know." Scott's voice turns bright yellow. It doesn't suit his look. He's posing as the playground tough guy at the moment by wearing things like studded belts with his school uniform. Geeks are out.

Scott plops down onto the immaculately tended lawn on the far side of the hockey pitch and digs out a packet of Lucky Strikes. Smoking is one of the habits he indulges in purely to annoy his father.

Last month he was planning to become a synchro-
nized swimmer, and before that he was learning to
knit and to crochet. His dad hates his guts.

He lights a cigarette and takes a drag, but the
smoke soon filters out of his mouth again. Then he
lies back on the grass and takes some more languor-
ous puffs. He tries to blow smoke rings. I know it
gives him a head rush, but I also know he'd never
admit it.

"Coming to Forbidden Planet this afternoon,
mon ami? There's a SIG."

I shake my head.

Scott blows an unsuccessful ball of smoke.
"Going back to the veg compartment?"

"Uh-huh."

For almost four weeks now I've skipped not only
lessons but also most of the Mensa SIGs to go to
the hospital.

"And your mum seriously hasn't noticed anything?"

I shrug.

"So what was that video?"

"I thought you could tell your dad you're going
to be the next Billy Elliot, only in a tutu."

"With my smoker's lungs? Who'd want to see a
smoked swan?"

I don't tell Scott that the dance videos I was
watching feature a girl who can see every world but
this one with her eyes open. In the videos she dances

and laughs and fools around and is the most beautiful and fabulous girl in the world. She tells stories with her body. Her eyes and her movements paint feelings and forests and laughter in the air. Her blue eyes stare out at me when the camera zooms in on her face. They glow like sparks of sunlight on the surface of the sea, like a glorious summer day.

There's also an interview with her on YouTube. I must have watched the video a hundred times, and, seeing it, my chest first expanded and then contracted.

"Hey! So what do you reckon, **mon ami?**"

I didn't even hear Scott's question.

"Are you at least coming to Kister Jones's later?" he repeats. "He wants to do a reading at his house today. He's invited a few fellow writers—Joanne, Dave, and some others—and he's going to read some extracts from his as-yet-unpublished novel **Slackline.**"

Instead of answering, I hold up my smartphone so that Scott can see the video.

"Wow," he says after a while. "So that's her." He looks at me with the cigarette stub dangling from the corner of his mouth and arches his eyebrows theatrically. "Got you there, eh? You thought Brainman didn't realize what was going on? Didn't notice that you were watching dance videos even in English lit? Well, who is she, when are you going to see each other again, and how come you haven't introduced me to her? Scared she'll immediately swoon for Brainman?"

I tell him all about Maddie. Almost everything. Not what I do when I leave her room. Every time I glance back to see if I can catch her eyes brightening, focusing, and boring a secret grin into my back. But I'm never quick enough.

"Have you noticed, Valentiner?" asks Scott after a while.

"What?"

"That life's being good to you."

"Good? You call this good?"

"Yes, you moron. It is. Listen to me. The life you're leading is probably the most interesting of anyone at this school. I know it may not be an easy or comfortable life, where the only things that matter are eating and sleeping enough and making sure your phone's charged. But it's a real life, and you can be what you are and who you are. When else, other than in a crisis, does a man have a chance to show his mettle?" He squints at me, says, "My God, where did I get my gift of gab?" and gives me a wry smile. I know Scott's right. He's right about everything. I also know that he is actually the more brilliant of the two of us. He has real flair, greater talent, a quicker wit, and more courage.

"You look as if you'd love to give me a hug or something disgusting like that. I'm warning you, I won't stand for any of that," he says boorishly.

I nod and say something like, "Hug you? Dream on!" Instead I tell him about Realitycrash and insist that he meet Poppy.

The school bell rings once. We stand up. We've often had this kind of conversation, but something's different this time. We are. It's as if we have changed for good between the moment we sat down on the grass on the other side of the hockey pitch and the moment we got up again. It feels as if something has happened, as if we're no longer children and know, for the very first time, who we might be in the future.

"One day, **mon ami**," says Scott, "we'll look back and wonder what happened to those boys. Let's make an oath: if ever one of us becomes an asshole, trapped in his own little caged life like a hamster, the other one swears to rescue him. Okay? Rescue me if I ever become like my father. Rescue me if I marry the wrong woman, or if I ever stop being Brainman."

I nod; he says, "No hugs, please"; I punch him on the shoulder; and we hug all the same.

Scott then presses a parcel of new excuse letters with my mother's faked signature into my hand. I run to the main building, slip one of them into the secretary's pigeonhole, and then I'm out of there.

———— // ————

FORTY-FIVE MINUTES LATER I'm taking the lift to the fifth floor of the Wellington. Passing the nurses' common room, I hear a woman I've never seen before pronounce Madelyn's name. I stop and pretend to tie my shoelace.

"All psychogenic noncompliance of the kind Madelyn is exhibiting is a form of protest. It's all about finding the sensory channel they are trying to transmit on and the one on which they wish to receive. It's easier if someone loves them. Along with fear and hatred, loving and being loved are the strongest stimuli." God stares at the woman and then turns round, as if he has sensed my presence. I think God's synesthetic too.

"Samuel," he says. "Allow me to introduce Angela. She's an . . . empathy therapist." She actually seems very nice, although I guess God would still dearly love to kick her out.

Every week brings a new group of pilgrims to Madelyn's bedside. Doctors from all over the country and even from as far afield as America and France. She's been described as a "fascinating case," because her brain damage isn't necessarily the reason for her vegetative state or, as some people call it, "minimal consciousness." God used his disc diagram once more to explain this to me. Around "Awake" there are places just below the surface of life, as if a disc or an impenetrable film lies between the person and the outside world. They can hear everything and occasionally feel things, but they don't understand the information and cannot express themselves.

He then cut out the circles and laid them on top of one another. Maddie is simultaneously numb and in a coma, although that isn't actually possible. She rises and falls between the discs without touching "Asleep" or "Unconscious." Her open eyes prove that part of her is "here," but a more significant part is elsewhere, and between us lies not a pane of glass or a film, but a layer of ice and solitude.

Nurse Marion said she'd definitely prefer to see me than the "luminosities"—she means the luminaries—who take turns to inspect this "extraordinary case" and release her from her "condition."

Marion is convinced that the experts who call Maddie a "condition" are of no use anyway. "Sam, darling, whenever doctors think nobody's listening, they talk about people as if they're cars. But what Maddie needs aren't some hotshot luminosities publishing self-important articles with her photo in the **Journal of High-Brain Medicine**." She shows me the scrapbook she's keeping. "What Maddie needs are things that make her happy. It's always the little things, those precious little things that keep people in a coma closer to 'Awake.'"

Unfortunately, there's no one left to tell us what Maddie likes. Does she like **Gilmore Girls**? **Diary of** a **Wimpy Kid,** perhaps? Does she like Taylor Swift or Bartók? Does she prefer literature or painting, the sea or the mountains? Cats or dogs? Spaghetti or sushi? If someone talks a lot or a little?

Nurse Marion calls the coma treatment unit the "bottom rung of heaven." And that's where God and the empathy therapist are sitting now. She's telling him something about the "organ clock" and "daily cycles" when God briefly interrupts her to tell me, "You can't visit Maddie now. Angela wants to see her first."

"May I have her book then?" I ask.

Dr. Saul digs it out for me.

Marion keeps a record of all those "sitting on the bottom rung." She has shown me these logbooks, which she produces with the help of their relatives, carers, and doctors. They document the patients' favorite meals, hobbies, everyday rituals, and favorite words. The nurses start to keep the records in the intensive care unit, then they follow patients throughout their stay.

There is not much in Maddie's book. Her former dance teacher, Mrs. Parker, knew little about her, due not to any disinterest but to a focus on dancing, her main preoccupation, combined with age-related forgetfulness.

Maddie doesn't like:

• Mozart

Maddie does like:

- Russian composers

- Anything blue with polka dots

- The odor of an empty stage before the lights go up: this she told Mrs. Parker one day

Also:

- Jane Austen (very probably)

THEY FOUND **Pride and Prejudice** in Maddie's rucksack after the accident. I dip into it while I'm waiting for the empathologist to leave, and I don't really understand what's going on. I think they all get married at the end, though.

The card in the pocket attached to the inside front cover shows that she borrowed the novel from her local library in Oxford. It's overdue.

I feel an intense flush come over me. Perhaps I can take it back, and maybe the librarian can tell me something about her? But I have no idea how to get to Oxford. By train? Yes, by train. But then how am I supposed to disappear for a whole day without my mother's finding out? I hate being only thirteen. You're nobody at my age.

I put the book in my bag, then start to flick through Maddie's logbook. Nurse Marion, Liz, and the doctors all note something in it every day, either about the tests they do with her, the world in general, or the weather, as naturally no Brit would feel properly alive without a little meteorological discussion. There's also the occasional human-interest story, such as "Kate Middleton is allergic to horses" or "Donald Trump wants to be president." Entries about the noise in the unit, the angle of Maddie's bed, the rhythm of the ventilator—anything that might someday explain what happened while she was away.

I take a pen from my school rucksack and write under today's date: "Samuel Noam Valentiner (13) was here again." I can't think of anything else to say, and I imagine her reading it one day and asking me, "Why did you write that? 'Was here again.' You can find more original entries on a calendar!"

I give it another go. "It was normal in ancient Egypt for a cat owner to shave off his pet's eyebrows when it died. Cats were buried with mummified mice. There is no record of the mice having their eyebrows shaved too."

Good—or better at least. Now, something about her perhaps. "You keep your eyes open most of the time. Sometimes they're closed, but no one knows if you're asleep or not. You're in a place where no one's supposed to find you. I will shave off my eyebrows for the rest of my life if you never wake up again."

I felt like writing "die" but chose not to, because you can't be sure that the universe isn't eavesdropping and might misunderstand. I have palpitations by the time I add a full stop. I can hear Scott saying, "Your whole life is a pretty long time, **mon ami**. Is this your new policy then? Promising to permanently disfigure yourself for girls you don't even know?"

THE WOMAN who reads emotions just won't leave. Quietly and dispiritedly, I slink away from the fifth and take the emergency staircase down to the second and my father.

Will Eddie be there? Eddie always brings along books to give me or leave for me. She sometimes comes in figure-hugging leathers, sometimes in a cocktail dress, and a few days ago I saw her on-line with the famous author Wilder Glass. They were walking arm in arm along a red carpet some-where, he in a tuxedo and she in the dress she'd been wearing at the hospital that afternoon when she washed my father's feet.

Dad is alone now, though. The lung machine is doing his breathing for him, and his face is impas-sive. I nod to the nurse who checks up on him every fifteen minutes. His name's Dmitry and he's Russian. When he turns my father over, he seems to do so with great ease. Dmitry has explained all the different devices assembled beside my father's bed. My father is surrounded by catheter stands, recording devices, and other machines that almost appear to be feeding off him.

Dmitry has also told me about the various doctors. There are some who only check the depth of my father's induced coma: the anesthetists. He calls them the "gas men." Typically, his nickname for others responsible for urine, blood, and the like is "plumbers." Then there are people like God and Dr. Foss, who keep an eye on the brain, and doctors who monitor my dad's circulation.

I don't bother asking who's taking care of his emotions because I know. Nobody. Nobody watches out for his worry or morale or loneliness.

I try not to think about any of the things I now know about comas. Some patients are lucky and can go into rehabilitation after two weeks without a stay in the veg compartment. Seven percent, or seven in a hundred.

Fifteen percent go straight into the freezer compartment, as the pathology department is known. And the rest live in a coma and stay there. Expressed as a number: forty thousand people in Britain every year.

The ones who wake up remember what people have said to them while they were in a coma.

"**Salut, Papa,**" I say. Ever since I found out he's from Brittany and that both my parents are therefore from France, I try to skip French lessons less often. I rummage in my rucksack for the book I've planned to read to him, then wheel over the roller stool, bend down to his ear, and whisper so that my voice doesn't crack, "**Salut.** It's the thirteenth of June 2016. This is Sam, your son, speaking. I'm thirteen, going on fourteen. You are Henri M. Skinner. **M** for **Malo,** and **Skinner** as in . . . no idea. I don't know very much about you. You used to be called Le Goff. You're forty-five years old and a war correspondent. **Were,** before my birth. Almost four weeks ago you had an accident. You've been in a coma for the past twelve days and have had a cardiac arrest. You are at the Wellington Hospital, which is pretty expensive, and the director is called God. Outside it's warm, and girls are wearing red feathers in their hair. Scott's currently in his second rebel phase. He hasn't stopped smoking, but he does still want to study psychology. And I was just with Eddie at her publishing house. Today, for starters, I'm going to read you a passage from **A Song of Ice and Fire,** volume one."

My father's very far away. I can make out the black aura of pain that's always hanging around him like a fine mist. Nonetheless, I continue.

"It must be time for tea soon. You'll be fed something tasty through the tube into your tummy, probably blended cucumber sandwiches and electrolytes with a drop of milk. I'm going to eat my school sandwich. Oh yeah, I bunked off school again. If you don't agree with that, I suggest you wake up and tell me yourself."

I peer at my father. Do I sense some tension in him? He's exhausted and seems a little blurred, that's it.

"Okay, if you think so. Mum would probably beg to differ. Her name's Marie-France. She's a photographer and you slept with each other once, but then something happened. You didn't stay together. I don't think you were even there for my birth. She told me shortly before I started school that Steve wasn't my real father. He's not too bad, though. He's a floor layer and works in a DIY superstore. Anyway, I'm going to read to you now, if you agree."

I open the book and begin to read aloud.

DAY THIRTY

Henri

I fall until I hit the ground. It's hard and cold. The candles have burned down and gone out.

Marie-France has pushed me off the camp bed we were sharing. I was cradling her naked body in my arms, and turning over in her sleep she pushed me out.

Images of the attack are still swirling around my head, and my heart is pumping. A war correspondent's mind is a machine that's always overheating and needing to be patched up.

I gaze at Marie-France. It wasn't mutual seduction—we simply devoured each other in our hunger for life. I ought to go and see the company doctor Greg's always talking about. So far I've refused to do so, but I barely ever sleep through the night now. During the daytime I'm assaulted by recollections so blurred and vague that I can identify them neither as elements from the past nor as illusions. It's as if, when I doze off, I hover just below the threshold of waking, losing my way in a half-light of thoughts and images.

Marie-France doesn't look me in the eye later as I hand her a metal cup of steaming coffee.

We fly to Wau and from there back to Paris via Cairo. Marie-France nods off against my shoulder as we cruise over the Mediterranean. She's embarrassed when she wakes up and huddles against the misted-up window for the rest of the journey.

As we're standing facing each other at Charles de Gaulle Airport I ask her, "Do you want to see me again?"

She shrugs her shoulders. They're narrow and delicate, but they can bear a good deal—apart, perhaps, from the knowledge that I've seen into her soul.

"Not necessary," Marie-France drawls.

When I say nothing she adds, with deliberate nonchalance, "Okay then," and bends down to pick up her green camera bag.

Air-kiss left, air-kiss right. One last quick, searching look from her dark eyes. There's a glimpse of wounded vanity there because I don't insist on staying, but I can also catch a hint of surprise that **she** isn't urging me to stay.

Go? Or stay?

As we touch cheeks for an extra kiss, I whisper, "Thank you," and even as I pronounce those two words I'm flooded with relief. Relief that she genuinely doesn't want me to stay and that I don't have to lie and say I do.

"I think it's better this way," replies Marie-France, and shakes her head again, as if these words too have caught her off guard.

As I take a couple of steps away from the baggage conveyor belt where she stands, rubbing her stomach absentmindedly with one hand, she calls, "Henri!" and when I turn around, she asks, "Do you sometimes think, **I've already had this experience** or **I've stood on this exact spot before?**"

"Yes," I say.

"Like now?" she asks.

"No," I lie, although it's true. I have an intense feeling of having already been here.

She shrugs again and walks away.

I fly back to London. My editor in chief Gregory wants me to be one of twelve reporters interviewed by **Time** magazine to represent war correspondents worldwide. I know the other eleven, and all of us are familiar with the rules of our profession as messengers of horror.

1. Do not take sides, simply observe.
2. You cannot save anyone.
3. Get out of this business before it's too late.

The interviews take place one after the other at Claridge's hotel in a suite hired specially for the occasion. I find this both fascinating and repulsive because all I can see are Akol's frail hands clinging to the hot barrel of a gun.

Time asks each of us to say something about the others. Sia of the **Washington Post** calls me "Mr. Fearless." If she only knew that the sole reason I jet from one war zone to the next is to escape. I'd rather not survive and that's why I'm so cruel to myself. What would she call me if she knew? "Mr. Lifeless"?

One day later a bomb goes off in a street in Kabul. A seven-year-old girl is suspected of carrying it. Greg immediately sends me out to investigate. I try to establish the facts and in the process I make the acquaintance of a chai boy called Ibrahim, an orphan who was searching for his sister when the explosion happened. Ibrahim's twelve, and his younger sister had been kidnapped.

The Taliban forbade her from going to school, and instead the girl blew herself up with a bomb in a Hello Kitty rucksack, killing twenty-four other people.

Ibrahim doesn't have his hair cropped short like pupils at a Koranic school. His reddish-brown locks are longer and peek out from under an embroidered purple cap. His eyes are two shiny green marbles in his emaciated yet beautiful face.

He wants to show me absolutely everything. He wants to betray the Taliban. He wants revenge because nothing was more precious to him than his little sister—neither religion nor fear nor money. The Taliban commanders are frequent guests at the house where he works as a servant. I break the first rule of every war correspondent: I take sides. I want to save Ibrahim, for if he acts alone he will die.

I stay in Kabul for a few weeks, and during that time Greg sends me the cover of **Time** with my photo on it, and Marie-France sends me a Polaroid of her positive pregnancy test at the pharmacy. "I want the baby, but I don't want you," she writes.

I beg her to let me meet our child, but she replies, "Please don't go to war again after the child is born. I don't want him to be scared for you." She doesn't respond to my request to see the baby, though. That's the moment I decide to quit my job. I'm almost thirty-two.

I keep my promise and never report from war zones again. Yet Marie-France only lets me see our child once, shortly after his birth. She sends a photo of him—it's a boy—sleeping with his little thumb tucked into his clenched hand. She calls him Samuel Noam, meaning "God has heard" and "joy, delight." I write back to say that I can think of no better names for the boy.

Marie-France never sends me another photo. Every month I mail a check that she never cashes. Initially I ask once a month, then twice a year, if I may come to Paris. She won't let me. It seems Marie-France still resents the fact that I didn't ask her at the airport if I should stay with her.

The story of Ibrahim's sister is the first portrait of my career as a non-war-correspondent. From then on, I only write about people, what they go on to do and who they are.

The man who reads stories without pause to keep humanity alive.

The actress who decides to spend the rest of her life in a tree.

The eighteen-year-old boy who'd rather meet his maker than have a heart implant.

I travel around the world to listen to people, and gradually my obsession with never allowing a single war to go unwitnessed wanes.

At my request, Greg manages to bring Ibrahim to London. Greg and his wife, Monica, take the boy in and a few years later they ask him if he'd let them adopt him.

One day I hear from a female colleague that Marie-France had an affair for a few years with Claude, the editor in chief of her newspaper, but he wouldn't divorce his wife for her.

Sam is four when his mother moves to London. She still denies me any contact with the boy. Greg and Monica say I could sue her for access, but is that really the proper way to deal with such problems? By suing one another? I slept with the woman when she was lost and petrified. There's no way I'm going to take her to court. Then again, perhaps I'm giving up too easily. Maybe I should keep on asking Marie-France, over and over again. Knowing my son is in the same city, my ignorance of his appearance fills me with a numbing pain. I see my son in a thousand boys' faces in the street.

When I do manage to sleep, I dream of seas without coastlines, of long, dark Underground train carriages hurtling over me. Again and again, I dream about war.

Out of sheer force of habit, I continue to see the company doctor, Dr. Christesen. Alongside Greg, Monica, and Ibrahim, he's the only constant in my life. He prescribes pills, but he'd rather prescribe me a different life. "Your sleeplessness, Mr. Skinner, is a sign of profound trauma. Your brain is full. You get lost because there's no room left in your head for yourself."

Ibrahim is now sixteen, going on seventeen. With his green eyes and reddish-brown hair he looks more like an Irishman than a former Afghan refugee. He explains to me that a father is the most important thing in a man's life. I'm like a "little father" to him, and Greg is his "second father."

"Little father, you too need someone who's important to you."

"That's you, Ibrahim. I have you."

"I'm not your flesh and blood."

He still has the purple cap he wore in Kabul, back when he was a chai boy. Monica has put it away in a cupboard somewhere. It dates back to another time and a different life. If only life were as easy to discard as a cap.

It took Ibrahim three years to inquire about my father. He asked as we were setting off for his end-of-year speech. Every year the best pupil in the class had the honor of making the concluding speech in the school chapel. I told him how incredibly proud I was of him, and as the taxi drove through London, past houses glowing in the early spring sunshine, he asked me whether my father had ever told me he was proud of me.

"Yes, Ibrahim, when I was very small."

"How about later on?"

"Later, it was my grandfather Malo who said it."

Ibrahim senses that he really shouldn't push the matter any further, but he's excited and so he presses ahead.

"But why didn't your father—"

"Because he was no longer alive when I was your age, Ibrahim."

The young Afghan says nothing for a minute. He bends his head and says, "Please forgive me!"

I'm in no position to grant forgiveness, I want to say, but I remain silent. I've only ever told one person that I was to blame for my father's death. Only Malo knows what happened off the coast of Brittany when I was thirteen years old and why I came home alone without my father, Grandpa Malo's only son. The look Malo gave me—a mixture of loathing and compassion, grief and horror. I don't know how Grandpa got over that and consoled me. Me, of all people. That's why I detest the sea, Brittany, and myself.

DAY THIRTY-ONE

Eddie
//

The fourteenth day since I was asked to sign to say, "Yes, I will."

I've got into the habit of going to the small hospital chapel before my dates with Henri. Not because I have accidentally found religion. No, because the basement chapel, three corridors from the pathology department and the freezers, is one of the least visited places in the labyrinthine Wellington Hospital.

I sit on the floor and don my courage like a mask. I dissect my competing, struggling, mutually obstructive instincts until only three essential ones remain. I focus entirely on keeping them in my mind and preventing any other emotions from approaching them. Self-pity? Doubt? Resignation? Away with you! Out! I think of Henri with all the tenderness I can muster and weed out my feelings of guilt toward Wilder, who isn't aware of what I'm really doing when I claim to be meeting new authors.

I breathe in and out and think: **Affection.**

I take a deeper breath and pray: **Courage.**

I breathe in and beg: **Be like Sam.**

Sam responds intuitively to Henri. He talks to him—and he listens to him too. I, on the other hand, struggle to cast off the self-censorship imposed by my unwaveringly rational mind. Unlike Sam, I don't see Henri. I can't hear him. It's like attempting to communicate with a deserted corpse, but I mustn't show my desperation, ever, because there's nothing more toxic than a relative's resignation.

I close my eyes and gather my thoughts. **Courage. Affection. Be like Sam.**

Listen. See. Sense. No doubts, damn it!

It's hard not to doubt. Thirty-one days unconscious. Fifteen days under heavy anesthetic, then clinically dead. Eight minutes of eternity, then sixteen days in a coma.

The passing time takes Henri further and further away from hope, and closer and closer to being one of the statistics I've come to hate. The longer a person lies in a coma, the lower their chances of ever again resembling the person they used to be.

The doctors make a great effort to measure Henri's consciousness, letting down soul echo-sounders inside him to listen out in the remote darkness for what might separate him from us. They use scanners and measuring devices. They tap on his knees and elbows, shine a flashlight in his eyes, carry out smell and hearing tests, and change the lighting, the temperature, and the angle of his torso. They don't leave him in peace for even an hour. And still the waters do not stir.

My father used to say that when you're sitting in a lighthouse, the fear doesn't hit you during the storm but the moment a strange silence settles over the sea.

The next plateau of hope comes after three months. If by that time an estranged soul still hasn't given any sign of life, Dr. Saul explained to me, the struggle is only just beginning. He spares me no bad news.

"Your arguments with the health insurance company will intensify, Mrs. Tomlin, and you'll get a bewildering glimpse of the empathy-free zone that exists in their administration. After two years, the insurer will refuse to pay and try to persuade you to pawn everything you own. After you've taken a battering, various reports by well-meaning experts will advise you in soothing tones to let your friend pass away peacefully—that is, allow him to starve or die of thirst or turn off his air supply. If you show the remotest interest in shortening his life, people will push an organ-donor contract under your nose, naturally only for the most heartbreaking cases who are dependent on Mr. Skinner dying as soon as possible. And you, of course, because you can't sleep at night from all these worries, will look up all you can find about coma patients online."

I was already doing that, every night and every day.

He went on. "You'll criticize us, stand accusingly in our way, and rightfully and angrily point to the disastrous care and staff shortages here. Yes, rightfully! Finally, you'll cast about with grim determination for answers and outside help. Incidentally, I'll respect your right to turn up here every week with a different specialist—one of the new brain whisperers. Just please don't light an open fire beside his bed."

Here too, he's right, and I hate him for it. I'm planning, for example, to meet a "body reader"— a neurologist who specializes in pain therapy and alternative medicine. For if coma is the symptom, what is the cause? I imagine that I might be able to save Henri if I can find out the cause of his reclusion. I've read somewhere that it's normal to drift from hope to hope, from remote treatment to empathy therapy, constantly searching for a way out and suppressing the thought that it might not exist. I still know far too little.

Every day I get used to having a date with a man in a coma. I so want to touch him, and I'm so scared of doing something wrong.

"You don't need to have studied to be important to him. You have two legs, two hands, and a brave heart. You've got everything it takes," Dr. Foss told me.

"Replace the word **visit** with **date**," was Nurse Marion's contrasting advice. "Visiting is a duty; going on a date is pleasurable. Try to see him less as an invalid and more as a person with whom you have a date, even if it's an unusual one." She's the one who teaches me to use my legs, my hands, and my heart, and also to divide up my despair into portions. "Don't cry all your tears at once. You'll often be so desperate that you'll want to weep but your ducts will be empty. That emptiness is the worst, when you can no longer express your sorrow because you've used up all your despair.

"My wanderers more frequently return at night than during the day," the nurse says with conviction. Wandering—that's what she calls being in a coma. Wandering souls.

Marion teaches me how to treat Henri's skin as it becomes ever more tender. **Thin-skinned** is not a metaphor here. She also shows me how to dab his mouth with water. Having spent thousands of nights with thousands of deep sleepers and patients with "passage syndrome," a state of unresponsive waking midway between here and the other side, she knows that thirst is the most unbearable aspect of being in a coma. When patients are able to speak again, they all report that the worst aspect was the thirst—that and the noises. So she taught me to arrange ice cubes containing peppermint or frozen Orangina into "cocktails on sticks."

I learn to call Henri by his name, repeatedly,

because a person's name is the "longest fishing line," as Nurse Marion puts it, to reel them back from whichever depths they're swimming in. I imagine throwing him a rope ladder consisting of five letters.

In the chapel I whisper, "Henri." **Courage. Affection. Be like Sam.**

I also apply a little Chanel No. 5 body lotion. I unscrew the top of the bottle and rub some cream into my neck and wrists, immediately filling the chapel with scents of jasmine, cinnamon, shortbread, flowers, and my own skin.

An aroma is the most effective voice in the wilderness of wandering souls. Fragrances can apparently reach the level where the comatose reside. All sensory impressions pass through the thalamus—the gateway to the self—before they are processed. If the thalamus is damaged, then comatose patients can neither hear nor feel. Fragrances, on the other hand, take a secret and direct path into the limbic system—something they have in common with emotions. Fragrances trigger memories, and memories are identity.

So I bring Henri aromas of things we used to eat and drink. Items from the past: newspaper, moist sand, rosemary, and fresh pancakes. Once I dig up a bit of rain-soaked soil, redolent with summer, from outside the Wellington. I bring him fresh sheets. I scour my memory for his everyday pleasures.

Today I'm bringing him the scent I was wearing

when we made love and my skin grew warm. The scent of a woman and love and us.

I MAY BE forewarned, but I am still shocked by how haggard Henri looks when I reach his bedside. The pneumonia he contracted ten days ago has really drained him. His fever has finally broken, but the night has hollowed him out. I notice that they've attached more electrolytes to the portacath under his collarbone.

Dr. Foss is testing Henri's reactions. He nods, and I can tell from his expression that he isn't happy. Silence at sea. No news of ships. Fozzie Bear notes this in Henri's file.

Sam is standing over by the wall with a shy smile on his face. He packs up his things; the lesson he skipped has nearly finished. I take a novel from my bag. I bring along a new one for him every three or four days, and this time it's **The Bone Season**.

"I'll leave it here, Dad," he mutters in a completely natural tone of voice, as if Henri might feel like reading a few pages tonight. I envy Sam. He doesn't look at me as he says quietly, "If I were to request that we take a trip to Oxford together, would you ask me why?"

"Give it a try."

This time he doesn't avert his gaze. "Can we take a trip to Oxford?"

I nod. He's visibly relieved that I don't ask him why.

I recognize more and more of Henri in him. His father was also very reluctant to explain his motives and always kept his life tightly sealed. I'd like to meet Sam's mother, but I know it's too early for that.

"May I stay for a little longer?" Sam asks.

I nod.

Henri's lying on his side today. His back is uncovered.

You can gauge a person's self-confidence from their back posture. If it's curved, it shows that they are unwilling to bear their own weight, bear themselves, knowing that they have flaws, sensing that other people are observing them. Anxiety and anger influence the poise and stiffness of the body between the nape and the lower back. That's from my correspondence with the body reader. I don't know how much to expect.

"Hi, Henri," I say, slowly moving closer to him and warming my hands by rubbing and blowing on them. I place my palms between his shoulder blades. Beneath my fingers I can feel his muscles and his pulse, which accelerates very slightly at my touch.

"I'm here, Henri," I whisper as I concentrate on attuning my breathing to his—or rather to the beat set by the oxygen machine. Eight inhalations and eight exhalations per minute. I close my eyes and breathe and hope that a little of my courage, affection, and warmth is being transmitted to Henri.

Next, I take Henri's hand and stroke it, along

the sides of the fingers where the skin is particularly sensitive. "I'm here," I whisper, thinking over and over again to myself: **Courage, damn it! Please give me courage!**

I wait until Fozzie has left before leaning over Henri and conducting our usual introductory ritual. Our everyday ritual. I place my iPod and the boxy wireless speaker on the table and select a playlist of songs I know Henri likes, including the tango to which I taught him to walk and hold me: "Sólo por hoy" by Carlos Libedinsky. "Only for Today."

Back then I had short hair and never wore dresses. I danced the tango every night, with hundreds and hundreds of men. Every day, only for one day. But I stopped when Henri came along.

The music streams out into the room, bathing us in an illusion. I put my lips very close to his ear and whisper, "Hello, Henri. I'm Edwina Tomlin. Eddie. We danced together once. We spent two and a half wonderful years together. I'm here at your request . . . and my own. I'm here with you. You are Henri Malo Skinner. You're living in a coma, and I'm begging you to wake up."

I can smell the Chanel scent rising from between my breasts.

"I'm here," I repeat in a whisper.

The tango washes over us. I feel like being silent, as we were the first time we faced each other and were silent all night and all the next morning. The way we gazed at each other, caressing each other softly with our eyes and our gestures. That first night only our hands touched.

The way he left. And then came back.

Henri is the personification of tango: closeness, distance, passion, tenderness, trust, estrangement. He doesn't stay, but he always comes back. I knew it at the time, and it offers encouragement now.

He's only in a coma for today. Only for today.

He probably cannot hear or understand us. That's what Dr. Saul and Dr. Foss and all those stupid brain scans suggest. I want to caress his face, his arms, and his stomach, to do all I can to tell him with my hands that he is not alone. That's the clearest language I have, and using my fingers I try to hear if Henri is still inside this strange mannequin that bears his name.

I touch him, but Henri's face remains waxen, his lips silent, and his fingers do not close around mine. Not this time. Not yet. Perhaps. Never before have I derived such comfort from a lack of certainty. As long as nothing is sure, nothing is lost.

Next song: "Assassin's Tango" by John Powell. We used to dance to this. We made love to it too. Sometimes we danced and made love at the same time. Sometimes we merely lay on the roof to this song, my hand touching his, and said nothing. I've never talked to a man less than to Henri, and yet I've rarely felt so close to anybody.

My fingers glide slowly down his back and along his legs to his feet. I can feel his pulse, his warmth, and the latent tension in his muscles. Is he running or flying, dancing or diving? Is he making love?

"Dance with me," I whisper. **Where are you, Henri? Oh, where are you?**

Sam glances back and forth between our faces. It's the first time he's been here when I do what I do every day. I carefully wash the soles of Henri's feet and massage them with warm oil. I'm like a maid, the devoted Magdalena. I wash him. I speak his name. I dance with him. I maneuver his legs, his arms, and his hands in the hope that, one day, he'll be able to stand upright again—even if it's only to walk away from me. I must reckon with that, for his nature is not to stay.

I focus entirely on the task of relaxing his battered body. The first minutes of daily awkwardness soon pass. My hand on his chest, his hand on mine, our eyes closed, united as we once were when we danced. I feel as if I've never lived as intensely as in this moment. My life expands every time I caress Henri's body. I'm feeling, I'm loving, I'm fighting. All the beautiful aspects of existence are more beautiful than ever, and all the trivial things have never seemed more remote. I feel as if I'm in the right place here.

DAY THIRTY-THREE

Henri

I only ever spend a few days in London to visit Ibrahim, Greg, and Monica. I can never stand it here for very long. I need to move on, because it's only in airport transit lounges, hotels near railway stations, and guesthouses on the harbor's edge that I can sleep. I can sleep in places that resound with the noise and hustle of departures and arrivals, but nowhere else.

If I don't sleep, I'm seized by an unspeakable fear of dying. What soothes me in those moments is the memory of Marie-France and how we conceived Sam. Conception: two such inept people created new life—proof of how incredibly benevolent and lavish creation can sometimes be. Like a rose blooming in the desert, or love emerging from solitude, and death from life.

When I'm in London or whenever I have to stay

in a large city for more than three days, I make it through the dark nights by walking and drinking. Occasionally I drive out to the airport to watch the human tide ebbing and flowing as many lives mingle, touch, and then go their separate ways. Afterward, I walk through the streets for hours, through streets unknown or familiar, dirty and dark, peering into lit windows, seeing how life goes on inside, whereas mine has been on pause ever since that day in my childhood, when I came home with the blue boat, leaving my father behind. Time has held its breath, and I'm caught in the middle, between no end and no beginning.

During one of those restless nights in London, my turmoil drives me into a concrete ruin in the East End, somewhere between Hackney and Columbia Road. Outside, the temperature is still in the nineties, but inside it is cool, a summer cave. In the corners and behind the pillars are shadows as deep as black water. The only light comes from lanterns, candles, and torches.

Old wooden chairs with curved legs and broken backs have been arranged against the unrendered walls, and between them are sofas and armchairs that might have been stolen from a hotel storeroom. Planks, old blackboards, and doors have been laid across overturned fruit boxes and wooden crates to form tables, which are strewn with bottles and glasses, ashtrays, and a few pairs of gloves that lie there on top of one another like empty, abandoned hands. Each table also has a red rose in a crystal vase. Individual women are leaning against the sofas or the pillars, all of them alone. Men—soloists too—roam in the semidarkness. Bats dart across the high, unfinished hall, as inquiring and evasive as the eyes of the men and women below.

Halfway along one of the long brick walls stand two bandoneon players, a third man with a bass, and a violinist with a guitar leaning against a closed suitcase at his side. The men's white shirts glow in the light produced by the flames. Here, in this place where everyone appears to be alone, slowly, imperceptibly at first, time starts to breathe again.

The two bandoneon players glance at each other. One of them has gleaming black hair and his biceps ripple darkly under the thin fabric of his tight white shirt. The other man, who has a moustache, stares at his colleague with such intensity that it seems as if he might dive into his eyes. They are intensely, erotically, almost furiously virile. The bassist and the violinist have their eyes closed. They have surrendered, and their abandon fills the room with an erotic charge.

The first bandoneon player's foot taps the rhythm, and the second falls in with the beat, soon joined by the bassist and the violinist, whose eyes are still closed. They are music incarnate. I'm addicted from the very first note.

A man in a suit steps out of the shadows into the flickering light. His eyes too are closed as his arms embrace an invisible woman. Thus he dances, but he is not alone.

Women detach themselves from the scattered sofas, pillars, and walls; men begin to stir. They resemble wild beasts circling each other in a cage or prowling under the open sky, and although I cannot figure out how it happens, the first couples come together, catch hold of each other for an instant, dance, and then release each other again. Their changeovers appear to symbolize my unrest in recent years as I hastened from one war to the next, from one person to the next, and then back to my solitude. Like the man still dancing on his own with his eyes closed, as if that is the only way he can visualize the woman in his embrace, I clasp at empty air and do not know who is in that space.

Eschewing grand gestures, the couples spin wordlessly across the concrete floor. They stride, they fuse, they continue on their twisting paths. Their eyes flash with menace and hope. **One more step and you're mine!** Inhibition lurks just beneath a veneer of restraint.

The woman emerges from the depths of the darkness, as if she were surfacing from the waters of the night. I don't know her, and yet I've seen her a thousand times before. I have no idea who she is, but I've been calling her name forever.

At first I cannot see how she does it. Does she

grab the men as she passes? Does her hand say, **Take me**? Is her body emitting secret signals that you can only detect from up close?

Then I realize she does it with her gaze. It does not ask, it does not invite; it simply says, **Come!** and the men obey. Only when she melds herself to a man does she close her eyes.

Her body is slender. Not curvaceous, not full. Hers is an androgynous figure, the physique of an Amazon whose beauty isn't immediately apparent to most. When she moves her warrior's limbs, I see myself. Her dancing expresses my unrest and my anxiety; she dances as if she doesn't wish to carry on living—not like this—and yet she's fighting to survive. Her dancing gives voice to my emotions and every shade of my life, the grays and the whites, the blazing fires that consume all color, and the endlessly forlorn melodies too.

She dances, and I watch her for hours and hours, dreaming thousands of different lives. Her movements are harbors, and I'm a castaway. What might be possible with this woman of whom I know less than any other?

I see this unknown woman dancing and in parallel I watch our daughter climbing onto her mother's feet to learn the waltz, foot on foot and hand in hand.

I see this stranger as I take her to Ty Kerk, unlock the blue door, and take out everything I've kept stored away for so long. She'll inhabit the rooms, and her bright eyes will banish all the shadows. That's how it will be.

I see myself kissing this stranger's delicate yet proud neck.

I see her in a white dress in the eight-hundred-year-old chapel by the sea, goose pimples on her arms because she senses that time has a different consistency here. There are places where time is thinner, where yesterday, today, and tomorrow converge and we can feel the presence of the dead and the echo of the future.

It is then that the stranger spots me, and her eyes say simply, **Come!**

I nod.

After so many hours she strides toward me, her piercing blue eyes as clear and deep as the sun-drenched waters of the Iroise Sea. Her eyes are awash with the ocean, and for the very first time I don't hate the sea.

I want to go home.

Take me with you. She doesn't say a word or touch me. She steps very close to me, and I can see her chest rising and falling. She's so close that her mouth and nose are level with my collarbone. I can feel the air between us being warmed by the heat from her body. She looks up at me, and I breathe out as if it is my very first exhalation and as if time has finally snapped back into place.

—— // ——

THAT NIGHT we lie facing each other on a fresh white sheet on a low, wide bed in her flat in an old tulip warehouse in the East End. Immediately above the loft is a roof garden where my dancing Amazon lives among silvery grasses swaying in the night breeze, bougainvillea flowers reach for the stars, and a flower bed blooms like a Breton meadow in summer.

By the light of countless candles we gaze silently at each other and explore each other's bodies with our eyes. Both of us long for affection, but we are unable to bridge the distance between us because with affection comes anxiety. A hankering for distance. A shared desire not to be "we." And yet this irresolvable yearning binds us closer to each other than to anyone else.

At one point she closes her eyes, smiles, and lays her hand on the sheet between us. I put mine on hers. That night I sleep soundly in the knowledge that I'm in the safest place in the world.

THAT NIGHT we lie being seen when on a
treasure sheet on a long voyage, and I take the lined
old ship's cabin out into the still. And immediately
above the bed was week garden where the dancing
Amelia lives among silvery graces anywhere in the
night being divided. I know each for the pas—
and a flower-bed thermal like a thicket meadow in
summer.

By the different coupled candles we gaze silently
at each other and explore somebody's bodies with
our eyes. I cannot, us long for attention, but we are
unable to bridge the distance between us, because
with affection unnecessary, I am aching for the
name. A silent desire not to be near, and yet this
impossible sleeping holds us closer to each other
than to anyone else.

As one point she closes her eyes, smiles, and
is her hand on the sheet between us. I am quite
on her. That night, I sleep soundly in the knowledge that I am the safest place in the world.

DAY THIRTY-FOUR

Henri

//

I wake up as the plane from Vancouver touches
down at Heathrow five minutes ahead of schedule. My hand feels numb, and yet I have pins and
needles. It sounds as if the plane engine is wheezing
as we taxi toward the gate. I'm thirsty, but there's
no flight attendant in sight.

London is shrouded in a morning fog that
divides the world of the nightwalkers—I used to
be one of these people who restlessly pace the dark
streets—from the world of those who rise early to
go to work. Two parallel worlds that ignore each
other on the buses and in the tube and the steaming
early-morning bakeries where they rub shoulders.

The nightwalkers dare not entertain the thought
that another day of their lives is already over, and
so they extend it into the dark hours so they never

have to stop. Early risers, on the other hand, want to make the most of the day that lies ahead.

I know where to find the key to Eddie's flat, which is the same one that unlocks the doors to the goods lift and her offices. It's in the cavity behind a half brick in a wall in the yard, in the left cheek of a graffiti Bugs Bunny.

I'm always afraid that the key won't be there waiting for me as a sign that I'm no longer welcome. I don't know why I'm so scared, for Eddie would never do anything like that—or at least not in that fashion. She would meet my eye and tell me. She is the most reliable, most candid person I know.

I know lots of people, and she is different in many ways. There's never a "maybe" with her. Yes means yes, no means no, and both are categorical and nonnegotiable. Maybe that's what I'm afraid of: if Edwina Tomlin ever says no to me, there'll be no way back into her life.

But there is one thing I have kept a secret since we met: Sam. I have kept my own son a secret from her.

Ibrahim knows her. We took him to the airport with Greg and Monica. He's studying law in Washington, specializing in human rights.

IT IS SHORTLY after seven when the taxi drops me off in Columbia Road. Is she still asleep? Eddie usually reads manuscripts until three or four in the morning.

I walk into the yard and carefully pull out the half brick. My fingers explore the cavity. Where's the key? Panic grips me, but then I find it. I unlock the door, tiptoe through the office and up the spiral staircase, and sit down on the bedroom floor, leaning back against the wall that separates it from the rest of the loft space. Eddie looks as fresh as a young girl in her sleep. Her lips are pursed, as if she's just finished chatting to someone.

I sit there watching her as she sleeps and I feel at peace. Her flat is the only place where I can settle down and resist the urge to flee.

Forgive me, I think. **How am I now supposed to explain to you how it came to this? How Sam came about, and why I'm not allowed to see him? How can I tell this to your face without making you disappointed in me?** I know that the longer I conceal this from her, the more appalled she'll be.

She wakes up and life floods into her body, like summer and all the laughter and desire and fragrances it brings flowing into a house that has been empty throughout the winter. Her eyes are wide awake and say, **Come to me!**

I undress before those eyes and this body, as inviting as a beach in summer. I don't know how Eddie does it, but her lingering eyes make me feel handsome. I exist because those eyes see me.

"Take your time," she whispers. "I don't want to miss a single detail."

I unbutton my shirt, unbuckle my belt, and slip out of my trousers. I never wear socks. Just like my father, whom I remember differently when I'm with Eddie.

In fact, I can only ever think of him when I'm with Eddie, and it is only now that I'm in my forties that I notice all the things I've inherited from him. The shape of my fingers: just like his. My love of going barefoot—being able to feel the world with my feet instead of simply trampling all over it.

I lie down alongside Eddie. She smells of pancakes and sugar and salt and freedom, like a beautiful ripe fruit—an apricot—and a flower: jasmine, I think. She is the whole world.

I take her face between my hands, framing it with my fingers. She smiles, keeping her eyes open as I explore the warmth between her thighs until we nestle seamlessly inside each other. The boundary between us has dissolved.

My darling, I think. **My darling, darling Eddie, how can I even breathe without you?**

THAT FIRST SUMMER we often made love on the top of the world—my name for Eddie's magic garden above the rooftops of London. One night when the stars appeared to breathe more freely in spite of the light pollution, she told me why she had planted the meadow. She was lying in the crook of my arm on the raised bed as the bats wheeled overhead and a blue moon—the second full moon of the month—rode high in the dark sky.

"When I was a little girl, I always longed for the grass behind our house to grow tall enough for a unicorn to be able to hide in it. At dawn it would emerge from the half darkness, lift its nose toward my room, sniff the air, and then wait for me to come to the window. For a brief instant we would look at each other and it would send me a thought like **I know I'm safe with you** before lying down in the grass and slowly lowering its head to rest at last. It would be safe from the world, safe from being caught and killed and tortured. Because humans always destroy what is miraculous, and the unique makes people uncomfortable."

I stroked her head, whose form was so familiar, so perfectly matched to the curve of my arm. The texture of her skin was already part of me. My hands, fingers, lips, chest, and thighs all knew the feel of her.

"My father would cut the grass on our lawn with a scythe and later with a battery-powered lawn mower. One day when I was five I tried to stop him by standing in front of the mower."

I was touched by this image of a small girl standing in the path of revolving blades to save a unicorn.

"And when he asked me why, I told him about

the unicorn. My father never mowed that lawn again, and when my mother brought in a gardener to cut the grass with a scythe, he paid him to leave it be. My mother didn't speak to us for weeks, but the lawn stayed just the way it was. Because of me and the unicorn."

She paused before going on quietly. "The unicorn never came. That's when I stopped believing in inexplicable miracles and contented myself with wonders that could be explained. When my father died, the unicorn died with him."

I realize how much fathers are capable of loving when they're loved, how much my father loved me, and how much I miss him.

Then my heart crashes to the floor with shame.

Sam. Does anybody love him? Does he have a father who loves him when I'm not there? The mere idea drives me mad—mad with guilt and shame. I cling to Eddie and don't move. Can she read my mind?

I've never lied to her. We owe each other nothing but honesty, but still I say nothing.

"What was your father's name?" I ask, and my voice doesn't crack, although it ought to break, as should my silence and my heart.

"Edward," she replies. "Actually, he was always Ed, and I was always Eddie. I was a smaller version of him, and sometimes I still feel that way: as if my larger ego—the more intelligent and more loving part of me—were dead." She takes my hand and places it on her chest above her beating heart. Her kind, loving, great big heart. How can someone like her stand being with someone like me?

"I occasionally feel like ringing him to tell him something. It's a painful reflex, like moving an unsplinted broken leg. On occasion I close my eyes and try to listen for his advice."

She twists in my arms to face me. It only lasts for a few seconds, but she represents everything I've ever needed to embrace.

"How about you, stranger? Have you ever dreamed of your father?" she asks. Straight out. No scruples. Without shame or fear of causing pain. That's Eddie through and through.

Never, I want to say. **Please don't ever ask me that question again.**

I exhale and nod. The urge to flee is always with me, requiring only the smallest encouragement to kick into action. "Yes. In my dreams my father doesn't usually know he's dead," I confess, "and I don't tell him. I relish those moments with him and savor an opportunity to chat to him, share a room with him, or go for a drive together."

Or sail out to sea, the last remaining freedom, but I can't bring myself to bring up that scene. How often I have had that dream! Over and over again, and each time my father is unaware that the wave is about to hit us, and I'm never quick enough. I never see it early enough or grab hold of my father fast enough.

I've told Eddie that he drowned while he was out fishing, but I've never mentioned the fact that I was with him. Nor have I told her that I'm losing all sense of what is true and what isn't. **Did he let go of me, or I of him?**

THAT FIRST SUMMER gave way to a first autumn, winter, and spring; became a year, followed by a second; and then began the final summer.

Eddie never said, "Stay!" or "Don't go!" and so I kept coming. I often spent the first days and nights at her place sleeping as if I were half-dead because the naps I grabbed in airport transit, lounges, trains, and long-distance buses were never sufficient, and in any case I never slept for very long or very deeply anywhere. I sometimes imagined how it might be to spend the rest of my life with Eddie. One thing was for sure: I would never sleep badly again. Was that love, or merely gratitude?

I had absolutely no trust in my capacity for love. My love was powerless and fainthearted.

Sometimes I'd be in London after an interview tour but wouldn't tell Eddie. She didn't deserve to be used as a pillow. During those nights I wouldn't go home, as I used to, and I avoided the light and the echoing emptiness of my flat. Only when I could barely stand for fatigue, and the days and outlines of objects grew hazy, did I give in and go to her place. The key was always in the cavity.

THE LAST DAY begins with faint sunshine. An October day.

I watch Eddie dip her forefinger into the pan of milk on the stove to test if it's already hot enough for her coffee. She has been doing this for so long that it's now completely automatic, and she would check the temperature even if the milk were already boiling.

She turns around, and I quickly close my eyes. I've no idea why I do this because I could spend hours ogling her bare legs below her shirt, her furrowed brow, and her mouth as she blows on the milk. We often watch each other across the room, holding a conversation with our eyes, but this time I hide the fact that I've been observing her.

I'm scared of her expression today and what it might signal. Today.

I sense her shadow as she comes over to the bed and the slight cooling effect as it falls on my face. I can feel myself sliding into trouble, as if the bed were a grassy slope. It's one of those days when life could go either way. I feel like throwing back the covers and inviting her to lie down beside me with her back against my tummy so that she won't look at me or speak.

Eddie does speak, though. "I love you," she says.

"I want you forever and beyond, in this life and every other."

I open my eyes and answer, "I don't want you."

Eddie scowls at me as if I've just slapped her for no reason. That same moment I know that it's a lie, but in my shame and confusion I stay stubbornly silent rather than immediately taking back what I've said. I should cry, **I love you! I panicked. I'm sorry. There are reasons. They might not be real, but . . .**

The opportunity is gone, and I see that the door Eddie has held open to me for three summers has now slammed shut, and the life I might have begun sweeps away from me like a tree trunk caught in the rapids.

"No," I beg, meaning this sight of the future drifting away, but her voice quivers with controlled rage as she orders, "Out! Clear off! Get out!"

My voice fails me in the light of my knowledge that I've just broken Eddie's heart. I can hear it screaming, even as she orders in a faint but controlled voice, "Out, Henri. Clear off!"

I get up and dress. She doesn't watch. I can feel myself fading and diminishing because those eyes are no longer trained on me. But still I don't manage to say anything or take the three steps toward the spot where I can hear her breathing. She is not weeping. **Oh my God, what have I done?** I pick up my bag and walk over to the door. **What am I doing?** I turn round and stare straight into her chill eyes, longing—no, pleading for her to say something. Something like, "Stay!" or "Don't go!" or "You were lying just now, weren't you?"

I was.

I can feel my growing pain and only now do I recognize the feeling behind it. **So this is love?**

I'm incapable of saying anything. My life silently shrinks, as if I've denied myself a lifetime of opportunities. Love, children, and nights when I might finally have slept. No more dread of death.

Seven days later I reach into the cavity for the key, and it's gone.

Sam

———//———

"**O**h man!" shouts Scott as we cross the bridge to Hammersmith station. He cannot hide his excitement that we're actually on our way to Eddie's publishing house, Realitycrash. He's tried his best to act cool by twiddling an unlit cigarette in his fingers, wearing shades, dressing in a black rollneck sweater and gray trousers, and turning up his jacket collar like one of those French existentialists you see in photos from the seventies.

"Oh man!" Scott exclaims again. "We're totally unprepared for real life, **mon ami**. I mean, rent, insurance, death and that. We have **no** idea." He is holding the cigarette between his thumb and forefinger, sketching shapes in the air. "And instead they send us into exams about vector geometry and amino acids. You, my accidental rebel, are the only one they can't force to go. Are you planning to take the tests sometime soon, or are you going to whistle while your immediate future disappears down the drain?"

I don't answer. I haven't missed all the entrance tests for St. Paul's. Only the ones I don't consider essential—although my mother would presumably have a different opinion. I couldn't care less, though. I can't stay at school while my father is fighting for his life and Maddie is perhaps only waiting for someone to discover what she likes.

"Wait a second," I mumble. We stop on Hammersmith Bridge. I'm standing on the very spot where my father was rammed by a car. Not far away, a man in a threadbare tuxedo is sitting on a piece of cardboard and leaning back against the railings. He's the beggar in the video.

There are thousands of places in the world like this strip of asphalt. Thousands of places where something ends—a life, a belief, a feeling—and none of them resembles a graveyard.

The man in the tuxedo is keeping a close eye on us.

Scott leans on the green cast-iron railings next to me. They're warm with stored-up heat from the sun. My thoughts turn to Maddie, and the resulting sensation is exactly like this spot: full of warmth and fear.

I peer over the railing. It's a hell of a long way down to the water.

Scott is still talking. "Everything they teach us is

one huge distraction. Binomial formulae, the citric acid cycle, French grammar, perspective drawing, ovulation, triple jump, continental drift, haplotype analysis . . . all so that none of us gets it into his head to ask, 'So what's it like to die?' 'How do you find a flat?' 'How do you find the right woman?' 'What's the meaning of life?' or 'Would you jump from here if it really mattered, and how do we know when it really matters?'" Scott removes his shades and looks at me earnestly. "You know, **mon ami,** they never mention the most important thing in life."

"And what might that be?" I ask.

"How to be happy."

I screw up my eyes against the sun and feel the railing against my back and simultaneous convulsions all over the world. I study the Thames, which doesn't seem to be a mixture of the Atlantic and the North Sea, just as it isn't clear what most things and most people consist of. Worry, nostalgia, grief, desire, childishness, or tenderness.

They don't teach you that at school either. How's it even possible that all these different worlds can exist simultaneously? School. The city. My father in a coma. This bridge, from which my father jumped to save a girl's life. This street, where a car crashed into him. All over the world there are places where people's lives are ripped apart.

"Are the very places to blame? Do they hurl

you into a different dimension if you happen to walk past them? Or might it be that you read or think some words one day and all at once you've left your own life, as if you'd stepped off a bus at an unscheduled stop?"

"Wow," says Scott. "I have absolutely no idea, but thanks all the same for answering. Maybe next time your answers will bear some relation to my questions and existential reflections."

Both of us gaze down at the river in silence.

I have nothing of my father's. No coffee cups, no watches, not even any memories. I don't know what I should cling to.

It's unfair to be thirteen. It's unnecessary. It's the moment when life reveals its fifth and sixth cardinal points—error and despair. How am I supposed to know what's right and what's important?

I'm no longer a boy, but I'm not yet a man. I'm in between. I don't know what makes you wake up one morning, see some girls, and suddenly not find them quite so bad. Well, one particular girl anyway. I don't know why I've begun to worry about my appearance and what I should do with my life. I'm quite sure that I'll never be able to kiss another girl without thinking of Maddie. I press my lips together; I know it looks stupid, but it's always been my way to stop myself from crying.

The torment, the joy, and the pounding heart. The happiness of thinking of a girl and missing her without really knowing her. The pain of not knowing if she even notices I'm there. The sweet tickle in my heart when I think of her. All of those things, simultaneously.

"No," I say, finally responding to Scott's remarks about how teachers, grown-ups, and the whole world keep quiet about the most important issue there is—how to be happy. "No, that's not it. What they keep secret is how we **notice** we're happy."

Here and now I'm happy, and at the same time I'm not. Fear and warmth. Happiness and despair.

We came onto this bridge as inquirers, but we're leaving it as something else, taking our first steps toward finding answers, knowing that we'll no longer accept what other people say as we once did. We must now learn to recognize things on our own.

AN HOUR LATER we reach the East End. Scott tries to pretend he's not overawed by Realitycrash. Eddie was expecting us, but I can see how tense and tired she is. She leads us to the bookshelf containing all the books her company has ever published, and here Scott's cool facade finally cracks.

"Ray Bradbury!" he lets slip, as jittery as a five-year-old in a sweet shop. "Isaac Asimov! Kurt Vonnegut!"

"Well, we did once have the paperback rights," Poppy says behind us. Scott spins around, and I witness a strange scene. I can feel Scott's heart initially swell, as if unfolding like a paper kite, and then crash to the floor. He changes—forever. He looks at Poppy and his world will never be the same again, and I see it all and yet I don't know why or if it is of any use.

Andrea brings some mugs of steaming tea, a plate of scones, some cucumber canapés, and a bag of incredible-smelling Cornish pasties. But Scott can't eat a bite of it. Who could when his whole inner life is being rearranged, brick by brick?

We learn about blurbs and cover designs. "We argue over the front and back covers for longer than we discuss the four hundred pages in between," Poppy explains, and I catch Scott staring in rapture at her black-painted lips as she speaks. "Most people pick up a book because the cover or specific words on the back appeal to them."

"Which ones?" Scott asks.

"Unfortunately, we have almost no idea, Master Scott," Ralph says curtly. "The truth is that nobody knows why people buy the books they do."

Poppy asks Scott what he's reading at the moment, and naturally his answer—**The King of Dreams** by Robert Silverberg—makes an impression. When Poppy puts the same question to me, Scott answers for me, "He's always carrying Jane Austen with him," before pulling **Pride and Prejudice** from my bag.

"Hands off!" I hiss.

"Oh," says Eddie. "A library edition. It's lovely. May I?"

It's hard to watch somebody else hold something that Madelyn has touched and that contains her experiences and thoughts and dreams. However, Eddie handles Madelyn's book with great care, as if it were a small animal. She opens it and reads the slip stuck to the inside front cover, studying the various entries and the date and the name of the most recent borrower.

Quietly she says to me, "Madelyn Zeidler. The ice maiden."

I stare at her quizzically. Why does she call Madelyn the ice maiden? It's true, though: Madelyn is trapped behind a transparent wall of frozen memories and ice-encrusted hopes.

I hear that the others are still discussing cover designs and blurbs.

"The girl on the fifth floor," Eddie says.

I nod. The pressure in my heart grows until I think it is going to turn inside out. I'd dearly love to tell Eddie everything, but when I try to put into words how thinking of Maddie makes me feel, nothing comes out. It's a wound that consumes me, like laughter waiting to be heard. It is my rampant hope of being with her and the terrible fear of having to endure a lifetime without her.

"Excuse me, I need the toilet," I mumble.

When I come back after what feels like five thousand years, Eddie's standing in the kitchenette, still clasping the book.

"It's Maddie's birthday in three days," I say.

"And nobody knows what she likes. It's important to know, just as important as with Dad."

She waits, nods, and replies, "I know what he likes—and I hope he likes it so much it'll bring him back."

"Nobody knows Maddie, apart, maybe, from—"

"The librarian."

I shrug my shoulders. It suddenly strikes me as a stupid idea.

"Maybe we should go to Oxford," Eddie suggests, "and take the book back."

"Yes, maybe. I could go in the holidays if—"

"No, Sam, I don't mean in the holidays, I mean now. Let's drive to Oxford now and visit Madelyn's library. Let's set off straightaway and find out what else she enjoyed reading."

My mouth must be hanging open like a cow's as I stare at her, but she's being completely serious. I think of Maddie's birthday in three days' time and I realize that there's practically nothing in her coma book and that my heart is still attempting to turn itself inside out and scream and sing its emotions when I think of her.

"Straightaway? Really?" I ask. Perhaps she's only putting me on. Maybe this is all a cruel joke.

Eddie puts her hands on her hips. "Yeah, straightaway," she replies. "Let's do it. Let's look for Maddie."

As she says this, it's as if a door has been opened in my life and the sunshine comes pouring in.

I call to Scott, "Eddie and I are off to Oxford. See you this evening, okay?"

Scott takes a peep at Poppy, shrugs, and remarks with all the self-assurance of an almost-fourteen-year-old, "Sure. I'm still needed here."

Sunlight is flooding through every window in my day.

TWENTY MINUTES LATER Eddie is getting in the lane to take the main road to Oxford. The weather's living up to every cliché about England: it's drizzling.

"Your father was never like a British shower," Eddie remarks out of the blue. Her hands on the steering wheel are relaxed, but she has her eyes firmly trained on the road ahead. "If people were weather, your father would be an Atlantic storm."

My tummy suddenly feels hot, and a deep, hungry hole forms in my chest. **Carry on,** I silently plead. **Please tell me more about him.**

The corners of her mouth twitch. "We didn't talk very much when we first met, as if words would have spoiled everything. Words are the sandpaper that scratches away at a feeling until there's nothing left. I first saw your father in one of the huge ruined buildings around here. They still hold tango nights there to this day, and back then I used to tango almost every night." She smiles, and her face takes on a beautiful, unfettered glow. "When I saw him standing there, in the near-darkness, with all that loneliness and longing in eyes that were concentrating so intensely on me, it seemed as if I could see everything he had ever been and everything he would become. And he was staring at me as if he'd glimpsed something that had shaken his life to the core—and that something was me."

She shakes her head, seemingly incapable of comprehending this fact, and stares ahead at the street rather than at me, refusing to glance back so as not to burst her fragile bubble.

"I was agitated, as if it were a performance, and I felt sick, as if before a flight. Dizzy with my desire to be close to him and feel his eyes on me. I couldn't have said anything even if I'd wanted to. I was paralyzed by joy and anxiety."

She overtakes a shuttle bus from Heathrow to Oxford.

"Henri always sat in the same chair in my flat—an old Eames a publisher friend gave me as a housewarming present twenty years ago. From time to time, I stare at that chair and chat to your father as if he were still sitting on it. But it all happened a very long time ago, even though it feels like only yesterday." Her eyes are glistening now, and it has nothing to do with the oncoming headlights.

"What happened?" I ask. There's so much I want to know. Why didn't they stay together? I don't know my father and I don't know Eddie either, but it sounds as if they are two nuances of the same word.

"He didn't love me the way I loved him, that's all." A single tear trickles down her cheek. "It can happen, Sam. It unleashes a war in your heart. You're fighting against yourself, and you always lose." She glances across at me. "Sometimes it's the other way around and the other person thinks of you more often than you think of him, or loves you more. Love's such a stupid cow!"

I have to laugh.

"It's true!" she adds, flicking the windscreen wipers onto full power.

We drive for a few miles in silence. I think of Maddie. If she were a form of weather, then she'd be a summer breeze. I also reflect that we may not come away with any discoveries. Perhaps we should try to meet Maddie's friends or her teachers. But how are we supposed to find them? My thoughts drift to my father. Did he have any friends? Did they like him? Did he ever mention me to them?

"What was my father good at?" I ask.

She replies without a second's hesitation. "He was free of prejudice, Sam. That was one of his great strengths. He never thought of anybody as a 'foreigner.' He took a far more candid approach to the world and to others than all but a handful of people are able, or even want, to do. But he still had some blind spots. Have you heard of the blind spots of the soul? It's when you're unaware of some of your own characteristics, either unconsciously or deliberately. They might be weaknesses you refuse to accept or strengths you find unpleasant or creepy. Your father couldn't see that he was wrong about himself. He thought he was incapable of love. I've figured out over time, Sam, that even the cleverest people are fools when it comes to love."

I take a deep breath and decide to run an emotional gauntlet. "Did he ever talk to you about me?" My voice is walking a thin line between yellow and fear. It catches, but cracks only a little.

Eddie shakes her head.

I knew it, but I'd hoped it wasn't true.

We fall silent, and an hour later we reach Oxford.

OXFORD IS a little like Dr. Saul's disc world. On its outer edges, where the countryside rubs up against the outskirts, the city comes across as cool and dull, but then the city condenses into something altogether more substantial. We drive past ruins and neat little town houses, past pubs adorned with advertisements for the TV series **Inspector Morse,** and along streets that could have been lifted from the film **Billy Elliot.** The city center is wide awake, its thirty-eight colleges a combination of Harry Potter's Hogwarts and a botanical garden. I spy punts drifting along the lazy side arms of the river Thames.

The streets in the center are packed with tourists and buskers, steeped in stories and emitting a gentle hum I can only hear in my mind. Is it the hum of thought and knowledge?

I've never seen so many church spires and battlements in one place, and of so many colors—copper, slate gray, white, and sandstone gold.

"The city of dreaming spires," says Eddie, as if she's read my mind. "That's the common name for Oxford, but to me it's the city of slumbering stories. There are more authors per square foot here than in any other spot on this earth—well, apart from Ireland maybe. Novels are born here, Sam, and some people even say that stories lurk in the shadows of the parks and houses and streets until someone walks past whom they trust to tell them properly. Then they attach themselves to that person and don't let them go until the person has written them down. Many people only discovered here in this city that they could—or had to—be writers. You cannot decide to become a writer. You either are one or you aren't, and those who didn't make it either went mad or lived unhappy and restless lives."

Her words tug at my emotions in the oddly familiar manner that I've always felt when I study the scrapbook or read my father's articles. At the same time I'm assailed by a growing whirlwind of sensations: the city's streets are full of questions, answers, and restless energy.

I contemplate writing something about my father or other things most people can't detect because they're on the outer edges of their sensory spectrum.

Eddie steers the car skillfully through the narrow lanes that wind around the high walls shielding the many colleges. She parks in a street behind the Bodleian Library, not far from the Museum of Natural History.

Maddie's library is in a side street near Christ Church College and Balliol College. Most people are familiar with these institutions without knowing it: the dining hall scenes in the Harry Potter films were shot in their formal halls.

I imagine how Maddie might have left her imprint on this city. She must have passed Ben's Cookies in the covered market and smelled the heady aroma of caramel. She's bound to have looked up at the high college walls and seen the statues staring back at her. She surely skipped and danced along these streets.

We reach the small library.

"Would you like me to come in with you?" Eddie asks.

The library is nestled snugly between two residential buildings and has probably been here for eight hundred years. The windows sit in pointed arches, and the floorboards in the entrance creak. The tops of the outside walls are crenellated, of course.

Behind the counter sits a petite woman in a

white-and-purple-striped jacket with a dark page-boy haircut and a kind expression behind enormous glasses.

"Hello, dear, what can I do for you?" she asks me in a friendly voice. The sign on the counter indicates that her name is Myfanwy Cook.

"I'd like to return a book. It was borrowed by a . . . friend."

Much as I'd love to keep the book forever, I nevertheless push it over the wooden counter. The librarian studies the card and then me, her eyes wide with surprise.

"Oh, it's Madelyn's!"

"You know her?"

Myfanwy nods. "Of course. Madelyn has . . . ," she says, gently stroking the book, "hasn't come to the library for a long time. I did wonder, because she usually drops in once a fortnight to borrow some books. Where's she been? Is she on tour? Is she dancing with a famous singer again?"

She can see from my face that this isn't the case.

"Perhaps we could go somewhere to talk about Madelyn?" suggests Eddie, who has appeared out of nowhere. Mrs. Cook turns pale. "You may be able to help us."

"Me? To do what?"

"To wake Madelyn up," I say.

———— // ————

MYFANWY FINISHES WORK two hours from now. She's jotted down two addresses for us. The first is Maddie's home—"I take it that you're familiar with the concept of data protection, so I never gave you this address"—and the second is New College, where "Maddie would always sit under the large oak in the college cloister. She once said that that tree was her best friend, along with music."

MADDIE'S FAMILY lived on the outskirts of the city. It doesn't appear to be a rich area and reminds me of Putney.

"Can you manage?" asks Eddie as we approach the house.

I immediately recognized Maddie's house as we were driving along the road, scanning the house numbers for the right one: it is the bleakest house in the whole area. We pull over to the curb.

The windows look as if they haven't been opened for ages, the front lawn is overgrown, and the entire front of the house makes a miserable impression. Houses shrink when they aren't lived in. As we stand gazing at the building, unsure what to do next, someone appears from the house next door.

"Can I help you?" the woman asks. She's wearing an apron and wiping her hands on a tea towel.

"Almost certainly," says Eddie, walking up the

garden path toward her. I cannot hear what she says to the lady, but she points to Maddie's house, then to me, and the lady claps her hands to her mouth, nods, and vanishes into her house.

Thirty seconds later she returns, having removed her apron, with a key in her hand. "Come with me," she says. "There won't be anything left in there soon. The owner sold the property, and the house clearance specialists are bringing their skips next week."

I feel slightly queasy. If we hadn't come today, they'd have emptied Madelyn's home. Just like that.

Linda—that's the neighbor's name—unlocks the front door and says, "Please, go on in."

Maddie, I think, and it's the last thought I have because soon I'm not capable of thinking, only feeling. The whole house is full of her presence. It's well lit with lots of light-colored furniture. The walls are plastered with pictures of Maddie dancing, smiling, and reading, sometimes alone, sometimes with her parents. Her parents are always holding hands and leaning toward each other.

Is this how fate strikes, so cruelly? This house used to be filled with laughter, kindness, trust, countless plans—and love. The loss of this love lingers on in the rooms like a plaintive echo.

"I'll wait in the kitchen, okay? Take your time. All the time you need." Eddie lets me explore Maddie's world on my own. I feel half thief, half archaeologist.

There are pictures of dancers hanging on the wall above the stairs. They're twirling onstage, on tightropes, in the street, everywhere.

I hear a loud clatter downstairs. "What are you doing?" I ask.

"I'm packing some pictures for Maddie. Pictures and a few other things she's sure to want to have. We'll let Linda know what we're taking with us. Okay?"

I have no idea if it's okay or if it might land us in jail. I couldn't care less if it did.

There's a silence in the room of the kind you only find in places where people no longer sleep or laugh or hold hands. My mother and Steve's bedroom is sometimes this quiet.

There's a pile of books beside her bed. A mirror and a bar run along the whole of one wall, and a carefully rolled-up yoga mat stands nearby. A metal gull is attached to the papered wall above her bed. It has a gently curved yellow beak, outspread silvery-gray, black-tipped wings, and a structure of fine, delicate bones is visible on the gull's underside. A herring gull that's common in Brittany. A powerful bird. Not one you would expect to find in a girl's bedroom, but so typical of Maddie.

My heart is hanging by a thread. I sit down gently on the bed, pull back the covers, bury my face in her pillow, and weep. I miss her, I miss myself, I miss my father. The pillow smells of coconut shampoo, washing powder, and, very faintly, past warmth.

I lie down on the edge of the bed. What could Maddie see from this position? Shirley MacLaine. A complete collection of **Famous Five** books. Her ballet shoes. A picture of the pianist Clara Schumann. A Rolling Stones poster. And a few jars containing sand and soil. I go over to examine them. There's a slip of paper under each jar. The contents are from various places she has visited.

I take a sheet of light-blue writing paper from Maddie's desk and hastily note down everything I can see in her room. I hear footsteps, and Eddie appears in the door with an empty fruit crate in her hand.

"What do you think? Shall we take her back a little piece of herself?"

We put into the crate books and the jars of soil from Scotland, Australia, New York's Central Park, and Paris. I carefully unstick the Shirley MacLaine poster. I add CDs and her ballet shoes to the other items in the crate and, on top of it all, the mobile made of shells, leaves, and bits of wood and glass that was hanging by the window. Lastly, I take her pillow with us.

"She obviously likes piano music and beautiful little pieces of nature, and clearly she loves the color blue," Eddie says as she leans against the doorjamb.

"She also values friendships, even if she has very few of her own," I reply. I feel both close to and distant from Maddie, but I now know that she likes coconut and used to read John Irving, prefers

Russian to Italian composers, likes the color blue, and arranges her books but not items she's picked up outdoors. She loves every part of a tree: leaves, bark, branches, and knotholes. There's a picture of her looking at herself in the mirror, and in that photo I see the woman she might one day be. I want to be there when she becomes every Maddie she can possibly be. I want to see every woman she becomes, until my time comes.

By her side, I will become the best man I can be. Without her I am nothing.

"Congratulations, **mon ami!**" I imagine Scott saying. "You have now taken your place in a long line of men who could only offer their lives in return for love."

Eddie and I carry seven crates out of the house and then the car is full. Linda shakes Eddie's hand and gives me a hug. "They were a team, Samuel. They were all different, but for all their differences they fit together and they watched out for one another. Some people are best protected in a family, while others . . ." She doesn't finish her thought.

Maddie's house watches us drive away.

WE HAVE only fifteen minutes remaining to explore New College. The cloister is cool and shady. The large oak gleams silver in the afternoon light. I imagine Maddie talking to it or sitting among its roots to think. I sit down there too.

"Maddie?" I ask. "What are you searching for?" I shut my eyes and rest my hand on the trunk of the tree.

Is she searching for something? Yes. For an exit? Where to? From her solitude into the solitude she imagines life to hold, or does she want to leave this world and be reunited with her family in the place we all hope exists but cannot be sure?

I gather up some large oak leaves that lie scattered on the ground. I'll take them with me for Maddie and then maybe the tree can tempt her back.

We go to the Eagle and Child, a pub in a white building on St. Giles' Street with cavernlike booths and a surprisingly small bar. Myfanwy Cook is already there and orders tea for three. I tell her about Maddie, her accident, the coma, and the idea that people find it easier to come back if they're surrounded by their favorite things.

The librarian takes a long sip of tea and then waves to the barman. "A gin please, Oliver," she says. "No, make it a double." She wrings her hands before commencing her story. "Madelyn was a little girl when she started coming to the library. She loved stories, especially books such as **The Hunger Games** and **Pippi Longstocking** about girls who escape from sticky situations, not stories about princesses and stuff like that."

Mrs. Cook tells us that Maddie prefers cats to dogs and blue to green. She also says that her parents love her very much—"loved," she corrects herself, then she weeps, but in such a way that the tears flow inward, while on the outside she dabs at her eyes and drains her double gin in one long swig.

Mrs. Cook also mentions that Maddie loves tarte tatin. "She read about it once in a French cookbook. It's made with cinnamon and caramel from Brittany sea-salted butter and baked facedown." She really does say "sea-salted" and "baked facedown," and it's at that moment that I decide I never want to be without Maddie again in my whole life.

"Can I come and see her in London?" Mrs. Cook asks.

I nod and glance at Eddie, for none of this would have been possible without her. "Yes," I say. "Please come as soon as possible. Maddie's so lonely."

"No, my dear, she has you!" she says.

I don't know which way to look in my happiness and vulnerability. However, I do still have one last question. "Can you tell me if there was anything in particular that Maddie really loved or would really like?"

She considers this for a second and then says, "A pajama party."

DAY THIRTY-FIVE

Henri

I was once at the beginning of my life. I was once immortal, but now I'm dead, or as good as. That's right. It's the truth. I'm as good as dead.

I'm lying on my back under a streetlamp, and my heart is bleeding out underneath me in great spurts of blood.

I grope along the asphalt and then I beg the young man, who is staring at me in disbelief, to take off my wristwatch and hold it up in front of my eyes. I want to see my final hour. I want to know the time of my death at the end of this gray day.

Without Eddie, all color has seeped out of life, its very pulse has gone, as if that final bright October day has been followed by one very long, gray day. I spent that long, gray day looking for what was real. Many times the world has seemed shaky, as if it were flickering and behind the flickering there were something else. Mind you, that might have been caused by alcohol.

When I was in London without a new assignment to rescue me, I felt as if I were in a great urban cage. I drank too much and if on those hazy nights I met a woman who suggested, either forthrightly or subtly, that I might spend a night with her to recover, I didn't take up her offer. What was I supposed to do when I kissed her, embraced her, undressed her? If she wanted me to watch her? Me, a man who never manages to hold on to what he loves.

I was always roaming, continually inebriated to dull the pain, but not drunk enough to be able to sleep at last without being plagued by dreams. And then, as I reached a stretch of road where some of the streetlights were broken, Carl was waiting for me in the dark.

"Hey, mate, I need help, you know," he said. "Name's Carl. What's yours?"

"Henri."

"I've got two kids, see, but me wife tells me she don't wanna see me shooting up no more, so I'm out on the street. Can you help me out?"

I realized that this wasn't some uplifting message or a plea for a place in rehab. I gave him all the money I had.

"Ain't you got no mobile, mate?"

I gave him my mobile.

"Shit, it's fucking ancient." He threw my Motorola Razr into the bushes. He really did look like a stressed-out father of two, but in the dull glow of night his face had twisted into a junkie's.

"I sniff, I do pills. I'll take anything that'll get me high. What's the time, by the way?" he asked slyly.

I glanced at my watch. "Just before three."

"Gimme yer watch!"

"We can go to a cash machine instead."

"Forget it. Too many people." He scratched himself. His eyes were red. "Go on, gimme yer watch. Now!"

"There are derivatives now that ease the withdrawal symptoms and—"

"Shut up and gimme that watch!"

"No. It was my father's."

"So what? Did he croak or something? Gimme the fucking watch or I'll chop yer arm off!"

I refused to hand over the watch and aimed an uppercut at his chin, but Carl struck back with a swift stab between my left armpit and my chest. The knife was cold, but the pain only hit me when he pulled out the blade.

I staggered a short distance to a pool of light cast by a streetlamp, and that's where a young couple from Sussex found me and called an ambulance.

The young man shows me the dial of my watch so that I can register the time of my death. The last thing I see before my heart empties of blood is my father's watch. It has stopped at five to three. Then my heart fails for lack of blood.

DAY THIRTY-SIX

Henri

I grope along the asphalt with my left hand and ask the young man to help me to my feet and call an ambulance. He stares at me in disbelief.

As always, I was out and about. I swim through the nights as I used to in the period of suspended time before I met Eddie. When I meet a woman in these hazy, drunken, wandering nights I let her go her own way. What am I supposed to do if I enter the unknown realms of her being and don't find the same riches as I found in Eddie? Her goodness and magnanimity.

I reached a stretch of road where some of the streetlights were broken, and there Carl was waiting for me in the dark.

"Hey, mate, I need help, you know," he said. "Name's Carl. What's yours?"

"Henri."

275

"Okay, Henri, I've got two kids, see, but—"

"No need to explain. I guess you want money?"

"You guessed right, mate."

He really did look like a stressed-out father of two, but his face had twisted into a junkie's. I gave him all the money in my pockets.

"I sniff, I do pills. I'll take anything that'll get me high. What's the time, by the way?" he asked slyly.

I glanced at my watch. "Just before three."

"Gimme yer watch!"

"We can go to a cash machine instead."

"Forget it. Too many people." He scratched himself. His eyes were red. "Go on, gimme yer watch. Now!"

"There are derivatives now that ease the withdrawal symptoms and—"

"Shut up and gimme that watch!"

"No. It was my father's."

"So what? Did he croak or something? Gimme the fucking watch or I'll chop yer arm off!"

I refused to hand over the watch, although his knife was hovering level with my stomach.

"My father and I were out at sea," I said, gazing into Carl's inflamed eyes.

"So what?"

"Give me a minute to say goodbye to it, please. Would you do that for me? I tell the story and then you get the watch?"

He nodded nervously. "Okay, but make it quick."

Slowly I slipped the watch from my wrist while continuing to talk.

"It was one morning when there was more sun than clouds, and the sea was as smooth as oil. Shrimping and lobster season. The mussels were still too small. My father always took off his watch and put it away in his jacket pocket. The jacket was lying on the bench as a cushion. Then came the wave, building up just below the smooth surface until it hit a submerged reef on the sea bottom and started rising. After another line of rocks it grew to a height of a dozen feet above the sea level, loomed over us, and then crashed down on the boat so fast that my father, who was reaching over the side to pull up a lobster pot, was swept overboard."

Carl had lowered his knife an inch or two. I was still holding the watch in my palm, and his eyes darted back and forth between it and my face.

"He knocked his head against the hull. I grabbed his hand and clung on to it for hours and hours. My father was floating on the waves, drifting in and out of consciousness. Blood was running from his ear. His other arm was broken. I was thirteen. And then the tide started to come in again. An hour before sunset I was too tired to hold on to him any longer." Here I paused, as my memories circled like vultures.

MY FINGERS were cold and had turned blue, and my neck was as stiff as ironwood.

That awful feeling as my father's beloved and powerful fingers started to slip from my grasp.

Watching him sink into the sea, his open eyes staring up at me as the dark deep swallowed him up.

Thinking about jumping into the water after him.

But I couldn't follow him and save him. I wasn't capable of diving into the sea.

My father's eyes, still peering up at me out of the darkness.

Me, sitting there, holding my breath with the horror of it all—and then letting go of him.

And in losing my grip on him, I lost my grip on myself. I became a mere breathless, passive creature who wasn't strong enough to save him and wasn't quick enough to rescue him from the deep.

WHEN I'D RECOVERED my voice, I said to Carl, "This watch is his only possession I brought home with me that day. This watch . . . and his jacket." And with those words I held the watch out to Carl, adding only, "Remember to wind it up before you adjust the time."

Carl stared at me with his runny eyes and then batted my hand away. "You idiot," he roared, and half staggered, half ran into the shadows, leaving the watch dangling from my fingers.

When he had covered some distance in the dark, his final words came drifting back to me through the night. "Maybe **he** let go, mate, not you. Fathers sometimes have to let go of their kids to save them."

I fastened my watch strap to my wrist. My fingers were shaking. I glanced at the dial. Shortly after three in the morning. My legs were wobbly, but I managed to make it to the pool of light under a streetlamp. There, I vomited and was suddenly so dizzy that I had to crouch there until a young couple from Sussex stumbled across me and called an ambulance.

THE DOCTOR who's treating me at the hospital now, a few hours later, has recommended that I draw up a living will for the future.

"For the future? Just in case I get mugged again and the guy stabs me? Do you really think it's worthwhile?"

"Of course. Just in case you don't get off so lightly next time or are so badly injured that—"

"Or in case someone shoots me on the tube."

She doesn't pick up my sarcasm. "Possibly, yes. If you're so badly injured you need to be connected to a life-support machine or fall into a deep coma and can no longer express whether you want to die or be kept alive. Everyone is entitled to be left in peace if he or she has no wish to continue. You shouldn't leave that decision to overworked trainee doctors, especially if you're an organ donor."

And so that very night I put Eddie's name on

the living will to cover just such an eventuality. I can't think of anyone I trust more than her to know what ought to happen to me.

She only needs to sign it. **Only.**

I'm flirting with the idea of sending her the living will to ask her . . . Ask her what? **Will you be my medical carer and decide if I'm to live or die?** How romantic. How morbidly romantic.

Instead, I leave London and run away. I never send Eddie the living will, even though I always carry it with me. Her "no" erected a barrier between us.

I only go to London once every few months and when I'm there, I drift from one person to the next.

But then I receive an email that changes everything.

Dear Dad,

We don't know each other, and I think we should do something about that. If you agree, come to Fathers' and Sons' Day on 18 May at Colet Court. That's part of St. Paul's School for boys in Barnes. It's on the banks of the Thames. I'll be waiting for you outside.

Samuel Noam Valentiner

My son wants to see me.

———— // ————

THE EIGHTEENTH of May is a warm day, and so I walk. Sam's school is on the inside of a bend in the river Thames five miles west of the center. Four Underground lines converge at Hammersmith, and from there I walk past some of the places Dickens mentions in novels, although they are now occupied by office buildings and old brick houses.

I've been up all night, beseeching the hours to pass more quickly, for I have vowed to live a different life. I'm going to tell Eddie that I've loved her since the very first time I saw her dance, and I'm not going to be late for today's meeting with my son. I'm never going to make either of those two people wait for me again. Ever again.

I feel like running!

Everything takes on greater clarity as I step through the magnificent arch onto Hammersmith Bridge: the warmth of the sun, the waves sparkling and winking as if the summer were already beaming at us, and the delicate, sweet scent of the trees.

I breathe in deeply. Will Eddie take me back? Will Sam like me?

I can already spy the pink blossom of the Japanese cherry trees, reaching out toward the honey-colored sun, along the riverbank by St. Paul's School.

I smile when I see the young couple kissing. A few yards farther on, a beggar is leaning against the green railings. He's wearing a threadbare tuxedo and appears to be setting up shop by laying out some sheets of cardboard in a patch of sunlight.

Nearing the other side of Hammersmith Bridge, I pause for a moment to savor the warm, silky air. I'm about to see my son. Life's so beautiful. Why didn't I come to this realization earlier?

A pleasure craft is forging up the Thames toward me. A girl is standing on the second railing from the top with her face tilted to catch the May sunshine when a chance wave slaps against the hull, raising the stern and throwing the girl forward. She doesn't utter a sound, but her eyes are brimming with boundless curiosity.

We watch her fall—the kissing couple, the beggar in the threadbare tuxedo, and I. The beggar whispers, "Oh my God!" The couple stare at me. None of them moves a muscle as the child floats downriver, away from the bridge and its four crenellated towers.

It's a matter of life and death, so I clamber over the green cast-iron railing, wait until the small figure surfaces below me, and jump.

DAY THIRTY-SEVEN

Sam

Today is Maddie's birthday. I've baked a cake for her in the school kitchens. My French teacher, Madame Lupion, gave me the recipe for tarte tatin and lent me a special pan from home. First I put a large knob of sea-salt butter into the pan before adding some sugar and heating the pan until the mixture turned to liquid caramel. I then arranged the sliced apples on top, having left them to cool—this, said Madame Lupion, was "**très important**"; it was even better to put the chopped apples in the freezer for a few minutes and then briefly heat them up. I covered all of this with short-crust pastry and baked the tart in the oven for twenty minutes, left it to cool, and turned it "facedown." Now I know what Myfanwy Cook meant. Finally, I wrapped the tart in apricot-colored paper and hid it in my locker in the corridor at school.

The hardest thing, though, was asking Madame Lupion what girls' pajama parties are like.

"What age? Eighteen, fourteen, twelve?" When I couldn't immediately give an answer, she added, "There's a massive difference. They still eat cake at twelve, but at sixteen they want vegan smoothies and by eighteen they're drinking gallons of Bacardi and Coke or some other revolting drink."

I told her that my (nonexistent) cousin was turning twelve.

"Oh! My daughter and her friends sang along to a romantic dance film when they were twelve. They put pink candles on the birthday cake and blew them out. Some of the girls had makeup parties too."

"Hmm." This was starting to feel a bit weird.

"Why do you want to know, Samuel?"

"Oh, no particular reason," I lied. "Just to make sure I give her the right present."

"You're a very wise lad."

LUCKILY, NONE of the shop assistants at the pharmacy next to Hammersmith Underground station asked why I was buying blue eye shadow, strawberry-flavored lip gloss, pink candles, and a toy microphone.

I scanned the "romantic movies" section of the iTunes Store for a film that contains some dancing and kissing. There's one called **Dirty Dancing** or something. I've never heard of it, but it seems to be popular. With girls, in any case.

TIME HAS STOOD still at the Wellington. I nod to Sheila at reception, and she gives me a quick smile before returning to her bubble. First I take the lift to the second floor.

I can see it from a distance: the pain is black and pungent, and my father is lying on his front. Why is he on his front?

Dr. Foss intercepts me and presses a mask into my hand. "Only two minutes today, Sam. Your father has pneumonia again."

I can sense the floor giving way beneath me. I feel dizzy with worry, but I stifle the flare of panic. "Hey, Dad," I whisper, kneeling down beside him and staring into his face. It's as impassive and empty as ever, a haunted house full of sinister torments.

"Dad? I'm going up to see Maddie. It's her birthday today. Any message you'd like me to pass on?" I tell him about my plans for a pajama party to liven up her day. Either that or Pippi Longstocking. My father doesn't raise any objections, and I take this for his blessing. "Wish me luck, okay?"

My father's ventilator makes a rattling noise, but there's nothing more. Not a thing. He shows no emotion, not even when I tell him what I have in my pocket for Maddie.

"Samuel Valentiner." God's voice catches me

completely off guard. "Is that a tart you've brought with you?"

I nod and stammer, "T-today's Maddie's birthday."

God gives me a wink. "Sing her a song for me, lad."

If only you knew, I think.

"By the way, your dad's had two visitors today. A young man called Ibrahim, and Greg, a very old friend of your father's and his former boss. Do you know them?"

I shake my head. I don't know anyone. My life and my father's never touched before his accident. I feel a brief but wild surge of anger toward my father. Because he's ill. Because he tried to sneak away. Because I miss him.

God hands me a card. "Here, this is Greg's number. He's a journalist. Call him. Ask him about your father. Bug him. Promise me you will?"

I nod, slip my rucksack onto my shoulder, take the lift to the fifth floor, walk along the corridor, and ease open the door of Maddie's room with my toe.

"Hi, it's me, Sam."

She's lying in bed with her eyes open. I wave the tart in front of her nose. "It's your birthday today," I say stupidly. **She knows that, you twerp.**

I gather my courage to do something I really, really hate. "Happy birthday to you, happy birthday to you," I start, and as there's no one else but me there on her birthday, I sing with rising volume and cheer. "Happy birthday, dear Maddie, happy birthday to you."

She stares at me without seeing me, and I glance at her schedule for the day. Ah, it'll soon be time for her eye drops.

"Okay," I say. "This is apple tart, or rather tarte tatin. It was invented by two sisters, Stéphanie and Caroline Tatin, who lived near Orléans, where Joan of Arc comes from. It's my first ever attempt at baking, so don't get your hopes up too high. But I did find some French sea-salt butter, even though the apples are from Sussex. Should I cut the tart?"

Maddie doesn't answer so I make a suggestion: "Maybe we should watch a film and then taste the tart? I've got everything we need."

I dig out the iPad I nicked from my mother's bedside table, followed by a set of peach-colored pajamas—also my mother's—and a pair of slippers with pictures of Batman's face on them that Malcolm was desperate to own. I hurriedly don my outfit.

"Ta-da!" I exclaim, giving her a little whirl. My heart is pounding in my ears. I feel like a complete dork, but who cares. I would do anything to make her smile or roll her eyes.

"You're already in your nightie, so I'd say this is going to be one hell of a birthday pajama party! Do you want to dance or play karaoke first? Or open your present?" I pull the small parcel from my trouser pocket. "No? Okay, I'll just put it down here on your bedside table. What's that you say? We should make ourselves pretty? Luckily, I've brought something along."

I pull out the makeup kit I bought at the pharmacy. "Can you give me a hand?" I ask her. "You can? Great, then hold this mirror for me." I lean the mirror against her pillow and try my best to apply the crumbly blue stuff to my eyelids. I miss and it stings like hell; I really don't understand why women put themselves through this. You end up like the scary clown in Stephen King's horror story. Also, strawberry-flavored lip gloss really does taste like litmus paper.

I seek Maddie's opinion. "How do I look? As gorgeous as Kate Winslet, right?"

I listen out and I'm pretty sure that I hear her giggle. Somewhere, perhaps. Inside my head, Scott is most definitely chortling.

"Want some too? No? Not your color? What? Lip gloss? It doesn't taste anything like strawberry, I swear."

She wants some anyway.

"Did you know they make strawberry aroma from sawdust? Well, they do!"

With the utmost care I use the little stick to apply some gloss to her lips. She holds still so I can trace the curve of her mouth, then I hold up the mirror so that she can admire my work.

"You don't actually need this kind of thing, Maddie." **Because you're beautiful as you are,** I think, but I don't say it. I'm pretty sure that she would now say, "Thank you, Sam." That's what I imagine anyway, and I blush.

"Good? What next?" I ask her.

Now I would love to watch a film, Sam.

"With pleasure, Maddie. How about a dance movie?"

Is it romantic?

"I think so. Yes, I guess so. Why, is that a problem?"

No! I'm so happy you thought of it, but I do hope it isn't soppy.

"Do you know this film, **Dirty Dancing**? I've no idea if it's soppy, but we can give it a go."

I sit down gently on the bed beside her. I search the iPad, start the film, and hold up the screen so that we both have a good view.

"Can you see properly?"

She says nothing, but she's watching with rapt attention.

Okay, here we go. Oh my God. "What's she doing? Are those melons? Maddie?"

Girls are like that, Sam. We're shy.

"Maybe, but **that** shy?"

The plot is really peculiar.

"The guy isn't too bad, is he? He wears strange clothes, and what have they done to his hair? Do girls like that look? Is 'Baby' a real name?"

Most girls I know—and, to be honest, there aren't very many—always talk in such an affected fashion and roll their eyes at this and say, "Oh, come on!" But that's what I like about Maddie: she stays completely cool.

Then the dancing starts. **Okay. Whoa.** This

291

is the kind of thing girls like? What would Scott say? "You don't have to understand women to like them. We don't understand cats or hippos, but we still think they're great."

"I'm sorry, I didn't realize it was this romantic."

Well, Sam, I guess you're going to have to make up for your mistake. Can you dance the way they just did?

"No."

Oh, please!

"Maddie, I can't sing. And I can't dance either."

Please, Sam!

I gaze into Maddie's gorgeous, expressionless eyes. I'm sure she's with me right now and is merely keeping still so as not to spoil the moment. Yes, that must be it. But I've decided she's not going to be able to keep this up for much longer.

"Okay, I'll do it, but don't you dare laugh." **Oh, please do laugh! I would gladly make a total fool of myself if you would only laugh, just once.**

I place the iPad on the small table next to the bed, pivot it so that Maddie has a good view, and replay the scene in which Baby walks up the steps, practicing her dance steps and waggling her behind. Then I try to do the same.

"Like that, Maddie?"

I put my hands on my hips and wiggle my bottom. At least, that's what I try to do. I dance to **Dirty Dancing** in my peach pajamas, Batman slippers, and blue eye shadow. I think Maddie is cracking up with laughter.

I'm really getting into the swing of this now. As I dance, moving more stupidly and more freely than I've ever done before, I fall in love with Maddie. I fall in love with her as if she were the song of my life, which I will hear over and over again. She'll be the soundtrack to my life.

It's no wonder I don't notice the door open.

"Hi, Sam? Or should I say: 'Hi, boy-who-looks-a-bit-like-Sam?' Have you got blue eye shadow on?"

Nurse Marion comes into the room. I trip over my Batman shoes and go all red in the face. Again.

"Think green might suit me better?" I ask breathlessly.

"Now, don't be cheeky. What are you doing in here?"

"We're celebrating Maddie's birthday."

"Oh yeah?"

"This is how girls like to party."

"Oh, sure. Yeah. Right." She eyes me up and down, and I take a peek at the wardrobe mirror to my left and am amazed at how ridiculous you can make yourself if you're willing to put a little thought and effort into it.

Marion points at the iPad. "What are you watching?"

"**Dirty Dancing**. It's a film about melons."

"Is that so? Did you tread on Batman?"

"Hmm."

Nurse Marion picks up the eye drop bottle, moistens Maddie's pupils with a practiced gesture, and sits down on the other side of the bed to watch the film with us. I take up my former position on the bed and hold up the screen, even if it'll make my arms go numb. It doesn't matter.

I notice that I blush from time to time when they start snogging.

"It's healthy," Marion explains. "Exchanging bacteria is good for the immune system."

"Yuck," I exclaim.

Maddie giggles. Well, I think she does.

Dramatic twists and turns come thick and fast.

"Hey, why doesn't he tell Baby's dad he didn't make her pregnant?"

Because then the film would be over.

"Oh right! Wow!" I'm thrilled because Maddie continues to talk to me despite Marion's presence. Only in my head, of course, but I don't think anyone can really object to a little bit of craziness.

Don't you think Johnny's cute? Maddie asks.

"Me? No. Why, do you?"

No, I don't either. I think you're **cute, Sam.**

"Knock, knock. A little bird told us you were serving tart in here." Two female doctors come in with Liz the physiotherapist. They're all wearing the kind of tiny, ridiculous paper hats you only usually find in Christmas crackers. Liz hands Marion one, and as cool as a cucumber, she puts it on. I no longer feel like the only idiot.

"What are you up to? Sam, are you wearing—"

"Yeah, it's Batman. You can get Superman ones too."

"I'm sure you can," says one of the two doctors in a deep voice, and the other women, including Marion, burst into giggles. Women can be really weird.

Now there are five of us sitting with Maddie on the bed watching **Dirty Dancing,** and everyone, apart from Maddie and me, is soon sniveling.

Okay, I do admit it's a bit moving.

"Did you bake that tart yourself, Sam?" Marion asks after the closing credits.

I nod.

"That's a tarte tatin!" Liz shouts excitedly. "But where are the candles?"

"Not yet. Karaoke first," I explain, taking the pink toy microphone out of my rucksack.

"Oh no, just as things are really heating up I have to go," says one of the doctors, peeping at her pager. Liz also says goodbye, casting a longing glance over her shoulder at the tart.

"Well, I'm off duty now and I **love** karaoke," says the other doctor.

Nurse Marion checks her patient's monitors and after a couple of minutes, she mutters, "Oh all right then, but only because it's you. Maddie's fine, although she's sweating a little. Are you enjoying yourself, darling?"

"What's on your playlist?" the doctor asks. Her badge reads, BEN. **Sheerin**. Ben? She studies the iPad. "Oh, by the way, my name's Benny," she says. "It's short for Benedicta. My full name wouldn't fit on the badge."

"Oh. I'm Sam. Samuel Noam Valentiner. That wouldn't fit on a badge either."

"No, it wouldn't," says Dr. Benny, scrolling through the songs on my mother's iPad. "Oh wow, 'Dancing Queen'!" she squeals. "Do you know that one, Marion?"

"I'm fifty-one, not **a hundred** and one. Of course I know Abba!"

Benny fumbles with the iPad, turns up the volume, and announces, "All right, Maddie. This is especially for you."

She takes the pink microphone from my hand, and the two women line up at the end of Maddie's bed and give a cringeworthy yet completely awesome performance of "Dancing Queen," with Benny singing the tune and Marion on backing vocals.

I dance to it like the woman from **Dirty Dancing** and try to style my hair like Patrick What's-His-Name, the guy who played Johnny. I'm pretty sure Maddie's almost peeing her knickers with laughter. I hop around a little more, and the girl with the ice-blue eyes lies there in her bed as we dance and sing for her.

After the song has finished, Marion gets out a lighter, sticks the twelve candles into the tart, and lights them. I also have a sparkler shaped like the figure 12. It tingles and sparkles and makes crackling noises as if a star has fallen into the room.

Maddie's present is still lying, fully wrapped, on the table.

"Let's sing something else," Nurse Marion says, laughing, her ginger curls clinging to her lovely, kindly face.

"Let's sing 'For She's a Jolly Good Fellow,'" Benny suggests.

So we sing and Nurse Marion turns off the bright ceiling light, leaving only the tart with twelve candles on it, the crackling of a little sparkler, the three of us, and Maddie. That's how we celebrate her twelfth birthday.

"You have to blow them out, Maddie," I whisper when we've finished singing the song and hold up my apple tart with the little flame on top in front of her face. "And make a wish. Wish hard, and then it'll come true."

For one crazy instant I think I glimpse the fleeing raven and its black feathers swooping across her eyes. But she doesn't blow out the candles, of course she doesn't. Her ventilator is breathing for her, but her pulse does seem to accelerate slightly.

"Okay," I say, surprised by my profound, exhausted disappointment. "Well, in that case I'll blow them out for you and make a wish."

I fill my lungs and as I blow out the candles, I reflect that I'd like to argue with Maddie one day—argue and then make up. I can't imagine anything more wonderful than having her glare at me and then hugging her until she has to laugh.

She doesn't look at me, though. Not even her greatest wish has been sufficient to bring her back.

I place the two oak leaves on the table beside her bed.

DAY THIRTY-EIGHT

Henri

//

Day breaks with mild sunshine, which gently tempts me from sleep.

I see Eddie dip her forefinger into the pan of milk on the stove to test if it is hot enough for her coffee. She's been doing this for so long that it's now completely automatic. She would do it even if the milk were already boiling.

She turns, and I hold her gaze, her bright wintry eyes. Her bare legs below her shirt, her furrowed brow, and her mouth as she blows on the milk. I never want to be without her.

I can feel myself sliding into trouble, as if the bed were a grassy slope. I feel such an overwhelming urge to throw back the covers and invite her to lie down beside me with her back against my tummy that I say to her, quite simply, "Come!"

I sense her shadow as she comes over to the bed

in her bare feet, the slight cooling effect as it falls on my face. It's one of those days when life could tip either way.

"I love you," she says. "I love you and I want you forever and beyond, in this life and every other."

"And I love you, Edwina Tomlin."

I feel growing relief, and now I recognize the feeling that causes this relief. **So this is love!**

Seven days later, we know that we shall get married in Brittany later in the summer.

EDDIE HAS BENT over to drink from the fairy-tale spring. That's what we called it when we were kids, the point on the D127 to Trémazan near Saint Samson's chapel. The water flows directly out of the rock. An old stone tub and a sculpted standing stone stand beside the old spring, which is said to have made children's wishes come true. The gorse blazes yellow nearby.

"Let's have a baby, Henri," she says to me. She's beautiful in her white dress. A little earlier, as we stood in the eight-hundred-year-old chapel of Saint Samson, the goose pimples formed a magnificent pattern on her skin.

"Time weighs less here," she whispers.

"Time is thinner here," I reply. "Places like this have a greater concentration of miracles than anywhere else in the world."

"If we ever get lost between different dimensions of time, let's meet up again here," Eddie whispers into my ear. "Deal?"

"Yes," I answer. "I love you. Please forgive me if I don't always get everything right."

"Stop thinking in terms of right and wrong," she says. "Those categories don't exist. Just live your life, won't you? Just live your life."

We take another sip from the spring. Today the sea is dressed in a dark turquoise robe embroidered with little white foaming crests. The wind is driving the Atlantic and the Channel into headlong collision, and the Iroise Sea swells and froths between the two. It is the world's most beautiful sea, and I'm with the world's most beautiful woman.

Tomorrow we shall drive on along the coast. I want to show Eddie everything: Le Conquet, the Pointe Saint Mathieu, the Baie des Trépassés, and the Île de Sein, where time is at its most permeable and all unlived lives meet with virtually nothing to separate them.

We walk hand in hand along the cliff-top path trodden into the bumpy fields hundreds of years ago by customs officials and smugglers. We climb down from the cliffs.

We're alone. It's lunchtime, and everyone else is sitting down to their meals, relishing the pleasures of being alive and the chance to eat such wonderful things as **moules marinières,** lobster, wrasse, and cod.

I touch my lips to hers, and the tip of her tongue feels soft and flirtatious. I embrace my bride and whisper into her ear that I know some spots along this steep coast where nobody but diving black-backed gulls will be able to see us.

We seek out a smooth, flat, warm stone. Eddie half lies, half leans against it and opens her sun-kissed legs to me. I turn my back to the sea. The sun is shining warmly on my shoulders and the back of my neck. And then I'm fully inside her, so deeply that I can no longer feel where her body begins and mine ends. I taste salt and the thirst comes. I lean forward to kiss Eddie, and she holds me tightly inside her. She's soft and warm and slippery, and I begin to make love to her in time to the waves breaking against the cliffs below us, firmly and not too fast.

"I love you," I say to her open eyes. "I love you and I want you forever and beyond, in this life and every other."

She merely gazes at me as if it were not me taking her, but she taking me. She takes me, takes me in, takes me into her life and molds it around me. She pulls me into her and receives me, and it feels as if my entire soul is streaming into her.

As I release myself into her, I suddenly sense a great, cold wall looming behind me, and then the shadow comes crashing down on me like a giant hand, swiping me into the sea.

I'm falling, I'm being washed away, lights and colors and voices envelop me. I'm sliding down a pipe, I'm dissolving, I'm falling ever faster. I'm falling and . . .

DAY THIRTY-NINE

Eddie

///

Henri!
I awake as the final ripples of the orgasm shake my body. I'm lying on my back, my hands up beside my head. Arousal built up slowly in me like an invisible wave gliding along the bottom of the sea and then rising gradually to the surface, up and up, before something exploded in my body. I don't know what it was—it's the only orgasm I've ever had while I've been asleep. I'm forty-four and for the first time ever I've fallen out of an erotic dream into reality.

Wilder is lying alongside me. He's sleeping, while between my legs a soft fist of desire is clenching and relaxing, clenching and relaxing. The muscles of my upper thighs are taut. I can taste salt on my lips. I've been making love with Henri. That's what my body tells me, and it also says, "This isn't a dream. This is real." I can still feel Henri's weight on me and inside me. I feel loved.

Is Wilder still sleeping, or did I wake him?

I cried Henri's name. I know it from the sensation in my mouth. It's as if I can still feel him. The warmth his lips have left on mine, their pressure and his breath. He was always so warm, like an oven or a fire. Certain stones are also capable of storing up the heat of millennia.

The images from my dream fade, leaving an abrupt feeling that he was torn from me and washed away.

What a ridiculous thought!

This is the real world, where Henri is lying in a coma, contracting repeated bouts of pneumonia that are carrying him farther from life and closer to death. Closer to the edge of this disc world.

Fear haunts me now, and yet I try to hide it from Wilder. I know that I'm in the process of destroying our future together, but I cannot do anything about it. Or rather: I do not want to do anything about it.

In the real world, I live with a man who doesn't know that I have visited Henri every day for almost five weeks now. I barely know how each new day is going to turn out. I'm filled with an intense and malignant sensation of having lost something vital, so vital that no laughter or beautiful place or new day means anything anymore. Infinite grief has taken hold of my chest, my stomach, and my neck.

A blackness has engulfed me, and I am drowning in a great, dark, deep lake.

Is Henri dead?

I listen out for Wilder's breathing, but he's lying quietly beside me in bed, one of his legs on top of mine. I bite my fist to stifle the sobs. I push Wilder's leg off mine as carefully as I can and get up.

The pain is more piercing than last time, when for months I didn't know how I would survive if I couldn't see Henri again, touch him, talk to him, see his smile, and feel his eyes and his hands on my skin. If I no longer felt loved. To be lovesick is to die, leaving only a husk of oneself in suspended animation.

I walk across the waxed wooden floorboards in my bare feet. I take a large mug, hold it under the tap to fill it, and then greedily drink the cold water. It tastes of the salt that was on Henri's lips when he kissed me just now.

My husband is dead.

I don't have the faintest idea why that word came into my mind. Henri isn't my husband.

It stems from that extraordinarily intense dream. We were married, and everything was different. The chapel with the red door stood on a grassy cliff above the sea. Samson was the sea chapel's patron saint. We promised to meet there if we ever lost contact. That was the deal.

The day after tomorrow Wilder is traveling to

the United States for a reading tour to promote his new book, **See You Later**. It's about people who simply walked out of the door and never came back. He searched for people who had been abandoned in this way and listened to their heartrending tales about breaking up and starting all over again.

A professor who slipped out without a word during a family dinner to go and live in the Canadian wilderness. A woman who was going on holiday announced that she needed to go to the toilet as the train entered a station and then simply got off the train instead. A golfer who left the fairway to search for his ball in the trees and just kept on walking away from his former life. A sick little girl who set out one night from the hospital to look for the sea.

I'm relieved that Wilder will be away for a few weeks. I'll be able to sleep at the Wellington and spend the nights with Henri. At long, long last. I don't want to miss the moment he comes back, and yet I feel guilty about planning my time with Henri as if he were my secret lover.

DAY FORTY

Sam
—//—

Something is different. I notice it as soon as I step out of the lift on the fifth floor. It feels as if disquiet, concern, and frenetic activity have united to create a storm at the end of the corridor. As I get closer I see that three people are attending to Madelyn—Benny, Dmitry, and one of the doctors Dmitry calls the "gas men."

Nurse Marion is wearing a face mask and casts me a backward glance that suggests, **Oh no, not him too.** But all she actually says is, "Would you please wait outside, Sam?"

"What's going on?"

"Please wait outside."

"What's wrong with Maddie? What's wrong with her, Nurse Marion?"

She doesn't answer, and Dr. Benedicta and Dmitry the Russian nurse attach further machines to Maddie's body with swift, precise movements. Intravenous catheters are inserted into the backs of her hands and below her collarbone, and catheters and drips are made ready. All of a sudden, like my father, she's entwined by the machines' antennae, at the center of a cobweb of total surveillance. One of the machines measuring the oxygen content of her blood is blinking in a way I have never seen my father's machines do. There's far too little oxygen in Maddie's body. Dangerously little.

Her eyes are closed, and she's pale and sweaty.

"Time since oxygen deterioration?" the doctor asks. I now recognize him as the anesthetist who is often on duty in the intensive care unit to monitor the level of the induced coma.

"Twenty-five minutes," the nurse replies. "Throat swabs and skin biopsies are under way. Central venous pressure still falling."

"We have one hour at most to administer the correct antibiotic and six to stabilize her blood pressure. If not—" Benedicta breaks off her sentence when she catches sight of me in the doorway. The tension in her body is palpable.

Marion pushes me gently toward the wall of the corridor.

"Let me see her!" I beg. "Please!"

"Not now, Sam. You realize this is a crisis?"

Yes, unfortunately I do. **Crisis** is an alternative word for **catastrophe**.

The automatic lift doors slide open and Dr. Foss

appears, followed by God. God's presence is a very, very bad sign.

He glances at me, only for the five seconds it takes for him to approach and pass me and enter Madelyn's room, but in that time everything happens. In those five seconds that seem to stretch on for thousands of wordless years, life passes like a slow-motion video and my blood turns to ice. God's message is that they don't know what to do because they've never had to treat anyone like Maddie before.

God tells his team, "We have very little margin for error in our choice of therapy. A broad-spectrum antibiotic, please; an antifungal drug. Ask the pharmacists to prepare fresh antimicrobiotics. Raise the head of her bed—I don't want her lying flat. Crystalloid fluid therapy. Start with thirty mil. We have to get her arterial pressure up. How far have we got with the blood cultures?" he asks last, quietly and calmly.

"Proceeding but not yet analyzed."

"Have you removed the blood from the catheters? I hate those things, they're only good for cultivating bacteria."

"Yes, but the results are negative."

"Marion, signs of sugar?"

She shakes her head. She's in shock, her face as white as a sheet.

"I suspect it's a bladder infection," Dr. Foss interjects.

"The urine analysis doesn't confirm that, Foss. How are her teeth?"

"Fine. Ultrasound reveals no lesions in the jaw or any other clue as to the source of the sepsis," Benedicta says.

"And why the hell is it taking so long to do the blood cultures? Liquor, please!" God is raising his voice now.

Nurse Marion rolls Maddie carefully onto her side and disinfects a spot on her coccyx, and Dr. Foss, who has pulled on some gloves, inserts a hypodermic needle into her lower back. He extracts something and fills three little tubes.

God watches this very carefully and holds up the vial containing the spinal fluid to the light. "Crystal clear," he says pensively. "Practically rules out meningitis."

"Should we do a CT—" Foss begins.

"She'd fall apart on the way there," God interrupts him. "And how could a foreign object have gotten into her system to cause this inflammation? She's been here for over six months."

"A wandering fragment from the accident, perhaps."

God considers this and then nods. "But first we must get her blood pressure down and stabilize her condition. The pharmacists need to get a move on, but I'm going to administer the bolus myself. Please hurry up."

As God is leaving the room I call out, "Excuse me, sir!"

He turns round. His face is deeply wrinkled, and his different-colored eyes are red and hard. "What do you want, Samuel?" he says quietly.

"I . . . I told Maddie that if she saw my father she should tell him . . ." I falter.

Wearily God says, "What, Samuel? What should she tell him?"

"That I knew he was on his way."

God nods. He runs one hand over his face and it remains hovering by his mouth. When people do that I know they're trying to control what they actually feel like saying. "I like you, Samuel, but now you're behaving like the boy you still are. You have nothing to do with this. Madelyn has blood poisoning. Sepsis. We don't yet know what caused it." He pats me on the shoulder. "And, Sam," he adds in a low voice, "Madelyn and your father are each in their own universe, wherever they may be. Do you get that? However comforting you may find the idea, they are not somewhere they might be able to meet."

"Aren't they?"

"Of course not." He turns away.

I stare after him, my eyes tingling. I heard my father call me, and I can feel that Madelyn's looking for something. She's searching for something, and that's why she has escaped from her solitude.

I know this, but I'll never be able to prove it. Perhaps I am crazy because I've been crazy from the very beginning. I know that synes-creeps like me can often go mad without any warning because of a sudden shock provoked by too much suffering, too many emotions, too many sensations.

SHORTLY AFTERWARD, Maddie is pushed past me on a wheeled bed. Dmitry and Benedicta hurry almost at a run to the lift. I see the doors open and swallow them, and then the numbers light up one after the other down to 2. Intensive care.

Nurse Marion appears by my side. "Go home, Samuel," she says softly. "Your girl's in good hands."

That's right; she's **my** girl.

"What happens now?" I whisper.

"They're going to try to identify the cause of the blood poisoning. Bacteria, fungi, a foreign object, a virus, meningitis . . . There are many possible causes." Her eyes dart anxiously to the large clock in the hallway. Too anxiously.

"What's wrong? Why do they have to hurry?" I ask, seized with red panic.

Nurse Marion's jaw clenches. "Sepsis contracted in a children's hospital is worse than any you can get outside, Sam. There are too many germs here, too many resistant fungi and bacteria. You see, Dr. Saul has to decide within the next half an hour which treatment to give and which antibiotics to use to combat the pathogens without completely paralyzing Maddie's immune system."

Half an hour? What if he makes the wrong decision? Oh please, please don't!

We learned in biology that antibiotics always kill off a whole load of healthy cells.

"But he's good at it, Sam. He really is."

"Is she going to die?"

"Only the next six hours will tell. And tonight."

Only six hours and a night. I should have been home long ago by then. In six hours' time my mother will have had her shower and be drinking her glass of sparkling wine. I can't leave now!

More to herself than to me, Nurse Marion says, "I always feared that one day it would come to this, and Maddie would make a decision."

"What decision?" I ask.

"Which path to take, Sam. Whether to leave or to come back."

No, that's not right! I want to say. She's escaped from the place where she has been for weeks now, alone, surrounded by an impenetrable layer. She is now on the way to herself, only she isn't taking the direct route but searching for something else first instead.

But that might not be correct either. Maybe I simply wish to believe that Maddie's disappearance is the beginning of a trajectory that will bring her to me, because I want to see the change in her eyes when she gets her first proper look at me. I'm scared that she won't like me as much as I like her, but I'm even more terrified that she'll never open her eyes again. I can't go home now.

OUTSIDE IT'S GETTING dark. My mobile buzzes, but I ignore it. Scott sends me some WhatsApp messages. I send one back, asking him to lie that I'm staying at his house.

My mobile buzzes again, and again I ignore it. My mother leaves me a voicemail message to say that she hopes Scott and I have a good time at the cinema.

If Maddie goes, I'm going too. No one knows where I am. No one knows where Maddie is. She seems to be getting ready to swap sides.

Henri

————//————

The sinking has stopped. So have the flowing and roaring, the voices and colors.

Never turn your back on the sea: the first and most important rule.

I sit up. The sky arches overhead but has condensed into a black ball that completely encloses me. My chest hurts, covered with bruises that bear down on my ribs, my skin, and my clavicles. Breathing is painful. I feel as if I've slid down an endless pipe lined with a thousand sharp-edged welding seams.

There's no horizon: the sky and the sea have melted into one. In the darkness above, the motionless stars. In the darkness below, like heartbeats rising from the dank, deep darkness, stars move on the sea's swell, giving the impression that they're floating and twinkling on the water. I can tell that the tide is approaching by the way the water rushes and rocks around me in the dark.

Then I figure it out. Everything. The realization drips into me with the searing burn of acid: I'm floating in the sea of the dead. Again.

This sea again, this boat, this endlessness: I've been here before! I thrash the surface of the sea with the oars, and an icy chill seizes my painful, battered chest and tightens its grip on my heart.

Maybe they haven't noticed I'm not dead and they're burying me?

A flurry of thoughts, colliding with one another as they grope for the moment before the incident. **Where was I before I was here? Where was I, and who was I? Or rather, was I still me?**

And then I realize everything. I've lived so many lives. I'm caught in an endless loop of being trapped in between. I didn't want to acknowledge that my father was right from the very start: it's dangerous to wander in between, along the boundary between life and death. As a man, a ghost, a demon, or as nothing. I should have stepped straight through that door.

Maybe this is hell. Yes, this must be hell. To live over and over again, through countless variations, repeatedly starting from scratch and committing the same mistakes and new mistakes, and then back to the start. And not to recognize any of the fresh repetitions as things that you're experiencing for the second or fourth or thousandth time.

Which life have I just lived? In which goddamn fucking real world?

The no-Sam world, in which Sam was never conceived?

The Eddie-dies world, in which my wife's life is snuffed out on her forty-fourth birthday because we argued and she drove along the coast road drunk? She often drank because I made her unhappy. She drank Talisker. She was sitting in a car that accelerated over a cliff, arcing outward through the air before tumbling down and down and smashing on the rocks.

Was it the best of all possible worlds, in which my father was still alive, holding his granddaughter Madeleine Winifred Skinner in his arms? Winifred after Eddie's grandmother.

Was it the world in which I told Eddie I didn't love her and in which I never saw my son?

How could I fritter away my life in such fear and on so many refusals, saying "no" at the wrong forks in the road and "I don't know" at the important ones? If only I'd recognized the vital, significant moments! I scream in desperation because I don't even know what I've done wrong this time. I fall to my knees and curl up in a ball.

Thirst. I need to drink, an Orangina, water, an ice-cold Coke. Such terrible thirst.

If I were asleep I could wake myself up by staring at my hands. I lift my trembling hands, although I know they don't actually exist, that they're merely motionless claws and maybe even those are no longer there. They fade into the darkness and become invisible.

Waves close in on the small blue boat, growling like large, disgruntled dogs. May it capsize! May it tip us out! Let's play with it! The sea can drown me, for all I care!

But it doesn't. Instead, it seems as though the sea brightens, so to speak, where my eyes pierce it, and there I see them again, their arms and legs sticking out in strange positions as if they were sleeping upright. Floating figures that have risen from distant depths, pulled up by fine yet firm threads. Some are naked, while others have fluttering shirts and smocks. Their eyes are closed.

Who are they? The dead, those who remained behind over the centuries when their ships went down.

"No, they're the dreamers," the girl says.

She's sitting on a black rock that rears up behind me like a stone whale. Low tide has uncovered the outcrop, whose sides, submerged twice a day, are overgrown with shells. In a few hours the waters will have risen again.

The girl has crystal-blue eyes and fine blond hair. She looks about eleven, and my heart tightens at the sadness in her eyes.

"How did you get here, my child?"

"I'm dying," the little girl replies. "Like you."

"No," I say quickly, "you're not dying. Neither

of us is. We can go back, you know. As long as we stay on the surface, we can go back."

"You know the way?" The way she asks this suggests that she knows I have no idea where I've come from or how to get back there.

I shake my head. I feel a spasm in my heart, fear creeping into its every nook and cranny along with despair at the thought that, as with the previous child, I am unable to protect her.

"Come on, I'll help you off that rock," I say to the child. I stand up and stretch out my arms toward the girl. The boat sways.

She doesn't move but merely stares down at me. "Have you ever been touched by a ghost?" she asks.

"I don't think so," I reply. "Come on, jump! I'll catch you."

She turns to face the sea again. "My mother touched me," she says, "when she died. Shortly after her death, she reached for me. Her ghost did. Here." The girl points to her cheek. "I felt her dissolve, turn to air, wind, and sea. She was transformed into the pages of the books I read and the music to which I danced. That's what happens when you die: you become the things you love."

"You're not dying," I helplessly reply. "Come on! We'll find the way."

Now she smiles, and even her smile is lonely and sad. "What do you love?" she asks.

I was never very good at loving, but now I love life so dearly. How I miss it!

"The dead don't know whether they're living among the living or among the dead, and ultimately there's no difference. Being dead is like dreaming without realizing you're dreaming," she whispers.

"Come," I beseech her once more, stretching out my arms. "Come with me, please. You don't have to die."

She gazes at me with her beautiful, bright eyes and in a quivering voice calls, "I do want to, but it's so hard. Did you know that it's hard? I'm not capable of it. I don't know how."

And now she claps her hands to her lovely, small face and weeps. Sobs shake her delicate frame. I can't even touch her feet to comfort her, and the whale rock is high and slippery. I can do nothing but stand there in my tiny, swaying boat below the weeping child who wants to die.

She sobs through her fingers, "I was a dancer all my life. I danced Marie in the **Nutcracker Suite**." Another fit of sobbing convulses her body. "And once when my father didn't take the motorway but drove along country roads, I broke my ankle by stumbling into a ditch after a picnic and I couldn't dance Marie. That was such a wonderful summer because my father carried me all the time, everywhere. In a different life, I lived to be old, very old, and I had children and a husband called Sam. Samuel."

Samuel!

My heart shatters into a thousand pieces.

The girl slowly withdraws her hands from her face. It is clear now, washed clean by her tears. "Sam asked me to tell you that he knows you were on your way and that he's waiting for you. He can see you. He can see me too."

The girl gets to her feet, takes a deep breath, and jumps with a ballerina's grace into the dark, star-studded water lapping against the base of the rock. She propels herself with powerful strokes down, ever deeper, toward the dreaming shadowy spirits.

Then I see something else, another shadow, emerge from the darkness and, with movements reminiscent of a mermaid or a siren, swim silently in the direction of the girl. I kneel down in the swaying boat and try to shout, "Go away! Leave her alone!" at the shadow. I see the floating figure reach for the child's foot and drag it down toward itself, snaring the girl's calves in long, dark fingers. Long strands of hair wind themselves like creepers around the child. I see the girl contorting and twitching, but the figure simply entangles her even more firmly, and then the two of them sink down into the dark depths.

The child doesn't attempt to break free. She gazes up at me, just as my father did while he was sinking into the sea all those years ago, with his eyes open, looking at me as the deep enveloped him. And I did nothing. Nothing.

My heart screams with fear, but I have to do it. I breathe in and dive headfirst into the sea. The water is cold, salty, and familiar. Down in the silent depths something is waiting for me. It raises its head and watches me as I attempt to plunge after the child.

The first cramp I feel in my calf is the cold clasp of a hand. I feel the tug of the undertow, pulling me out into the Atlantic and its thousands of miles of unbroken water.

The girl gazes at me and I can see her face and her sea-blue eyes merging into the waters beneath her. She has a look of desperation on her face, as if she cannot believe that it is not as she thought it would be. She seems to want to head back to the tiny dot of light above us and above the waves. My lungs and my head are burning. My pulse is hammering against my skull.

A second bout of cramp. I won't have enough strength. I dive and dive, and when I can no longer feel my feet, my legs, my lower body, and my face, the creature that is holding the child in an iron grip and dragging it downward turns to face me—and I recognize her.

Her gaze is a blinking light in the darkness. A moment later I feel the pull. I'm incapable of following them any farther. I must breathe, I must return to the light! Only for a second and then I'll try again. Again and again!

I swim up and now I can discern the brightness

playing on the surface. My lungs are ready to burst. I need air. I'll reach the surface any second now. I stretch out my arms, give one last powerful kick with my legs, expending the last of my strength. In a second I'll be able to take a breath, my fingers are already breaking through the waves . . . and then they hit a glass barrier.

Panic! Desperately I try not to open my mouth, but I still do, I can't help it, I need air. But I swallow only sea, the sea pours into me.

Help me, Eddie, I beg you!

Eddie

Wilder wants me to be part of his world. He discusses his writing and shows his manuscripts to me. He's introduced me to his mother, a woman who adores professing her love with gestures as well as words—the latter on their own would be too little. She loves to iron her son's shirts and cook for him. She tells him how beautiful and polite she thinks I am and showers praise on his most recent book. Certain people can add a touch of love to everything they do, as if they've tucked it into a small envelope and quietly slipped it to you with a cheeky grin.

I let him take me along wherever he goes. Sometimes I even forget that I have a life of my own. I bask in his reflected glory and find it intoxicating to accompany him to the kind of get-togethers I've always shunned: parties thrown by publishers with

332

five-story headquarters on the Victoria Embankment and offices in New York, Berlin, and New Delhi, and dinners with media-savvy judges and journalists whose opinions fuel nationwide debate—people who live grander, glitzier lives than mine. In their company I can hide away, drink deeply from the cup of life, and find enough distraction that I don't have time to think of Henri's inflammation from the catheter or the newest cramp in his instep, and all the manuscripts I don't read with the necessary care. And Sam, whom I worry about, because he's growing up far too fast.

I live in two separate worlds—one internal, one external. Outwardly I pretend to listen, put on my "Aha?" face, and nod when I feel it is appropriate to do so. But inside I am with Henri.

In the street I have learned to recognize those people who are caught between two different realities. They look without seeing. They no longer perceive the beauty of the world around them, and, focusing entirely on their sorrow, they are walled up inside themselves. I seek out and hold their gaze and for an instant I forget my shame about my own mask.

I may be physically present, but my thoughts and my feelings are at the hospital. As I take a sip of expensive chilled Sancerre white wine, with a feigned smile on my lips and my head tilted to suggest that I'm listening to the immensely sophisticated conversation, it happens: all of a sudden Henri's there, very loud and incredibly near.

Help me, Eddie, I beg you!

For one magical split second, I even have the impression that I can see him. At the end of the table, over in the shadows on the other side of the room. His face is twisted into a grimace, a picture of absolute panic. He's drumming on the glass coffin lid.

No, Edwina. You're so tired you're hearing voices. Don't pay any attention to them!

Help me, Eddie, I beg you! A second time I hear Henri loud and clear. It has nothing to do with the wine: I've only just taken my first sip.

I must get out of here right now.

"Excuse me," I mumble, shoving my chair backward. The legs screech on the floorboards and the chair topples over with an embarrassing crash of lacquered wood on parquet floor. On all sides of the long white-clothed table in the publisher's spacious dining room the monologues abruptly cease. The publisher interrupts his merry anecdotes, the artist breaks off his well-considered opinions, and the critic stops making studied quips. Everyone stares at me, half expecting terrible offense to be caused, half shocked by the unfolding scene.

Wilder, who has been engaged in a secretive conversation with his publisher about his new book, turns to me. "Everything okay, Eddie?"

Breathe in, breathe out!

He picks up the starched napkin that fell from my lap as I leaped to my feet. "Edwina?" he asks again, his gaze more intent now.

I **must** get out of here. I place one foot in front of the other and walk out of the warm, jovial, candlelit dinner party, my bearing restrained and upright so that nobody thinks that I might be drunk or angry or crazy.

Breathe. Breathe in, breathe out.

The heels of my pumps echo on the floorboards because everyone's attention is on me as I leave the room. Their eyes are burning holes in my back, and I suddenly feel overdressed.

Out in the hallway I quicken my pace, snatch my leather jacket from the coat stand, and hurry down the stairs, feeling nothing but the smooth handrail against my palm. I'm running now.

I can't stand this any longer. I cannot sit next to Wilder, repeatedly glancing at my damn mobile under the table, waiting for Nurse Marion to send me her nightly status report on Henri's pneumonia, kidneys, and fever. Every evening she announces his temperature; every evening she tells me if his position on the margins of life has changed. It hasn't so far. But she's three-quarters of an hour late today. **What if Henri's dead?**

As I dash down the stairs from the third floor and race through the entrance hall of the Kensington town house, I hear Wilder calling down to me over the clatter of my heels on the black-and-white tiles.

"Eddie?"

I heave open the heavy eight-foot-high wooden door and, with a deep breath, suck London's cool, roaring, fume-filled, rain-soaked air into my lungs.

Wilder doesn't deserve any of this. Not my lies or the fact that I get drunk when I'm with him to forget another man for a few hours. He should never be any woman's second choice, and yet I wish that he'd take me in his arms so I might confess everything at last. Still, it has only been forty days: some women have affairs that last for years. I've no idea how they manage, but obviously they do.

Help me, Wilder. No, I can't expect that of him. Briefly I rest my finger on the host's doorbell. I can't see the camera, but I know it's peering out from behind the black glass ball next to the buzzer, and that upstairs Wilder can see me.

I hear the crackle of Wilder's voice over the interphone. "What's going on, Eddie?"

"I . . ."

I should let you go, but I can't because I need your arms around me at night. I need you as my lover so I can cope with Henri. It's crazy, isn't it? I love you and yet I don't love you.

My feelings for Wilder used to be clear and pure. A fresh start, a different man, new emotions unlike those I had had for Henri. Not as fiery, not as confusing. Just good feelings. Honest feelings.

But then Henri came back—more or less. Rather less, but still more than ever before. All of a sudden, those two sets of emotions were in conflict.

Two kinds, two colors, two weight categories. Or
were they?

"Edwina?"

"Wilder."

**Good old Wilder. How much I love being with
you. How deeply I am caught up with Henri. You
do know I was never a woman for two men?**

"Would you like me to come with you?" he asks.

His warmth. His closeness. His intelligent, warm
eyes in that famous face with the laughter wrinkles
that has been staring out from so many posters on
bus stops since he recently won his second literary
award. His hands that work such wonders with me,
whatever they're doing. A feeling of being on the
same side of life. And yet . . .

I stare into the fish-eye camera. In its reflection
my eyes look brighter than in reality. I can see a
thousand white lies in them. And that is the only
reason I shake my head.

Silence. Then Wilder says, "I've been through
times like this. You can't be with or behave with
other people any longer. You have to get out or
else you'll choke to death or rage at everyone
because you feel pressure from all sides to behave,
adapt, and belong. To act **properly.**"

Breathe in, Eddie, and breathe out.

"I'll justify it to the others as a quintessential
moment of literary quirkiness. After all, they almost
expect us to be peculiar!"

My body is longing to run and move. I'm cold, but I want this cold—it'll keep me awake and remind me to breathe.

Wilder's words flow out of the interphone into the darkness. "I can live without you, Edwina Tomlin, but I don't want to. I want to go through life by your side—now, tomorrow, for as long as possible. I love you."

I'll never forget this moment when, for the first time, he tells me that he loves me. He can see me as he declares his love to my image, whereas I have no idea what **he** looks like as he pronounces those words.

I should now gaze at the lens and say that I love him too. It is now that he most deserves to hear it—and I the least. I kiss the index and middle fingers of my hand and silently tap the camera.

I run and run and at some stage I take a taxi. I weep the whole way home. I hate Henri. I love Henri.

I love Wilder. I must let him go.

I can't do it. I cannot bear to be alone again, without loving and being loved, without touching and being touched.

BACK HOME, I take my phone and sit down in Henri's chair. I've taken to having a drink as covertly as I make my daily visits to the Wellington.

Just a little tipple, I think, but I know I'm fooling myself, all the time. I'm struggling to keep everything together, while every thought and fiber of a different me is at the hospital, waiting to hear Henri's voice again.

But there's nothing to hear. Nothing at all. I don't know what he's doing on the other side of that barrier of skin and silence. I hate this half-dead man. I'd kill him if he were alive.

I call the speed dial number 1. Someone picks up after seven rings, and I hear a hoarse voice on the other end of the line.

"Hello, Mrs. Tomlin. Can't you sleep? Neither can Henri," Nurse Marion says.

He's alive! I'm so incredibly relieved that instead of greeting Marion I start to sob.

"What's wrong, Mrs. Tomlin? Is everything all right? Are you crying?"

"I thought he was dead," I whisper when I'm finally able to speak.

"No, no. Nowhere near. People don't die so quickly, least of all your Henri. He's a fighter, and he has unfinished business to take care of. It's good that you're thinking of him. Thoughts give patients strength too, you know. Are you still planning to come tomorrow and stay for a fortnight?"

"Yes, of course," I say.

"Excellent. That'll be good for him."

I don't ask what Nurse Marion means by

"unfinished business," nor do I consider how I'm supposed to manage everything.

Secretly redirecting phone calls from home to my mobile so Wilder doesn't notice while he's on his reading tour.

Ralph, Andrea, and Poppy.

Our books and the book fair.

Life and death.

Sam.

And Madelyn.

It feels as if I'm leaping from one stepping-stone to the next with no shore in sight. As if I have more balls in the air than I can juggle. When will I finally get there? When will I drop the first ball that brings all the others crashing down after it?

Sam's being very brave, and I have to make sure that I am too—for his sake. So there's no way I'm going to tell Henri's son that sometimes I can't go on. But I cannot go on, I really can't. Not one inch farther.

I breathe in and out and then I get to my feet and carry on.

I take another long swig of Talisker. Nurse Marion once said that she could feel that Henri was close at night, as if he were encased in a cocoon of rubber, and his vital functions seemed robust. She could determine his "sleep architecture." Another of those expressions you learn on the brink of death: sleep architecture.

I wish I could go back to being myself. However,

for some inexplicable reason I know who I am when I'm with Henri.

I hear footsteps coming up the spiral staircase toward me.

"I have to go," I say.

Nurse Marion's voice is urgent now. "Henri's very restless tonight. He's recovered from the pneumonia and all his broken bones have healed, but I've given him something against the pain as well as opiates to calm his anxiety. Nevertheless . . . he seemed very unhappy today."

I wish I could crawl into his world and join him.

"It was something about his posture," Nurse Marion continues. "I don't know if you can understand, but over the years I've learned to tell how my dreamers are feeling from their position in bed. Henri was seriously unhappy, as if . . . I don't know. Has something happened?"

The footsteps are close now.

"Eddie? Is everything all right?" Wilder stands blinking at the top of the stairs.

"Yes, I'm having a whiskey." I hang up and put the phone down on the table.

He walks slowly toward me and looks me straight in the eyes. "Eddie," he whispers once, then again, "Eddie." He brushes a few strands of hair from my face. Lowering his voice even further, he says, "We need to talk about Henri."

Sam

———//———

The stage is dark. Voices and a tinkling of glasses are audible through the theater's closed doors. As I walk down the aisle toward the stage, past rows of red folding seats, the crystal lights on the walls begin to glow and so do the curved balconies of the boxes. I thread my way past the orchestra pit and up a small flight of stairs onto the stage, slip through a gap in the drawn curtains, and then grope my way through the dimly illuminated spaces and corridors in the wings.

I know she's here. I can sense her presence. Opening a door, I find myself in a dressing room. There's a line of mirrors along the side wall, each with spotlights on both sides and a leather revolving chair in front of it. The dressing room is full of women and girls at various stages of dressing up and having their hair and makeup done. I walk past the revolving chairs. No one pays me any attention, and I'm not visible in any of the mirrors.

Maddie's sitting in the last chair, and a woman is combing her hair and pinning it up into a tight bun. Maddie's wearing makeup that makes her eyes look huge.

"Hi, Sam," she says quietly, her gaze ricocheting off the mirror and straight into my heart.

"Hi, Maddie," I answer, and it's then that I realize I'm dreaming.

When she's ready, the silent woman helps her put on her costume and as she steps out of the dressing room into the dark corridor, a nutcracker sprints past.

"I'm going to dance the part of Marie," she explains, speaking without moving her lips. "Do you know the story of **The Nutcracker**? Marie turns twelve, meaning she's no longer a child but not yet a woman. She's in between, you see, Sam—like me."

She scurries ahead of me along the corridor that leads to the stage. I can see she's gasping for breath and sense the nervous flicker of her fear. The narrow corridors are never-ending, and we lose our way. She starts to run and has to flatten the airy white flounces of her tutu against her body to prevent them from scraping along the dark walls.

Breaking into a run to keep up with her, I notice the glittering, silvery fingerprints her fright leaves on the walls. I get the feeling she isn't running toward the stage but away from it.

"In the ballet, Marie has a dream and in that dream she dances for the very first time en pointe. She falls in love for the first time, she becomes an adult, and never again will she believe that toys have souls. But they do, don't they, Sam? Everything has a soul, and everything recurs."

I don't know, but her desperation is overwhelming me and so I say, "Of course it does, Maddie."

She sets off again and I pursue her. The labyrinth seems to have doubled or tripled in size. We race back and forth, and then the theater bell rings once and then a second time.

"I must find the stage!" she cries desperately. She stops, and turning to face me, she beats the wall with her fists.

Closing my eyes, I listen and hear the murmur of the audience. I take her by the wrist.

"Come with me," I say.

She lets me pull her after me, tripping along on the points of her ballet shoes like Marie in **The Nutcracker,** and I can feel her pain, as if she were walking on broken glass. The murmur grows in volume as we near the stage. A beam of light splits the darkness, illuminating tiny, floating specks of dust. I can already see the red velvet curtain, already hear the sounds of the instruments in the orchestra pit and the stage manager preparing to pull the cord that will haul up the curtain for Maddie's entrance . . . But then Maddie freezes.

"Sam," she croaks, grabbing both my hands with hers. "I'm so scared."

"What of, Maddie?"

"Going out there," she whispers, glancing around her in panic.

We're standing very close to the edge of the stage. I hear a rustling sound and muffled conversations. There are hundreds of thousands of people on the other side of that curtain: I can feel the heat of their bodies. The stage lights emit a low hum. The air is heavy with expectation.

"I've seen you dance. You're beautiful and you can do this!" I tell her.

"I can't do it. I can't go out there." She makes to turn and flee into the dark labyrinth, but I stop her.

"I can't do it. Let me go!" she begs again.

"Why? What are you scared of?"

"They'll point and laugh at me. They'll say, 'She's no good.' They'll see how ugly I am!" Two tears detach themselves from her lovely eyes and trace long, blue-silver lines across her delicate white skin.

It dawns on me that she's not talking about dancing but about a completely different performance, a completely different form of "stepping back into the light."

"What are you most scared of?" I ask.

"There's no one there, Sam, nobody left to love me." She crumples in despair on the boundary between light and dark, when all she needs to do is take one step—one tiny step—back into the brightness and warmth of life. I can tell how she longs to whirl across that stage, watch the curtain rise, and then dance and live and laugh, lost in the music, the light, and the waves. She wants to live, but she fears life more than death.

"I'm here, Maddie," I say gently. "I'm going to sit in the front row and clap. I won't take my eyes off you, and no one will say you're ugly. I love you. I'm here."

I pull on one of her arms, then the other, but she stays slumped on the floor at the back of the stage. When a roving spotlight grazes her arm, she shrinks back as if burned. Tears stream down her cheeks as she tilts her face toward me, and the misery in her eyes is heartbreaking. Such despair, such desire, such loneliness.

"But what happens if you leave me too?" Madelyn asks.

"I won't."

"Everyone leaves someday. Everyone." Frantically she jumps to her feet and staggers off into the darkness. Her silhouette seems to fray, her white outfit fades, her arms and legs become feathery shadows, and a heartbeat later she has melted into the surrounding blackness.

"I'm not leaving," I call after her quietly. "Did you hear me, Maddie? I'm not leaving!" I scream, but she doesn't hear me. She simply doesn't hear me and if she does, she doesn't believe me. The day is sucking me away, but I don't want to leave her. I want to stay with her and sleep forever, yes . . .

DAY FORTY-ONE

Sam

It feels as if I'm being thrust upward out of the strange, foaming depths. I wake up in bed. My heart's beating so hard I can feel its pounding in my neck and temples. It wasn't a dream. No dream could ever be as close and as real as Maddie's fear, voice, and hands.

I throw back the covers and all the accumulated warmth instantly escapes. I get up and feel an immediate longing to visit her. What lessons do I have this morning? Assembly, then English. They never check attendance at assembly so I could arrive late.

The Nutcracker, I think. I have to find and listen to it.

I glance at the clock. It's still early. My mother will be helping Malcolm to get ready, so there's no way she'll notice that I'm leaving home earlier

351

than usual. Then, just as I'm hurriedly packing my rucksack and heading out of the house, it happens. The telephone rings.

My mother appears from the kitchen, spots me, signals for me to wait, picks up the phone, and after a couple of seconds, exclaims, "Oh, Madame Lupion!" It flashes through my mind that I've missed something or forgotten to take something into account.

My mother listens and replies, "What?" then "No, not that I know of," and finally "Oh, really? No, he's fine. He was at Scott's and . . . What? Yes, of course." She hangs up and catches me just before I make it out of the door.

"Samuel!" she hisses.

Steve, freshly out of the shower, comes down the stairs and says, "What's going on? Hey, Fanman."

My mother's eyes are glittering with fury, disappointment, and surprise. "I didn't realize you were a diabetic and have your blood purified three times a week."

"What?" asks Steve. "How come?"

"Nor did I know that my son is undergoing pain therapy," she says, ratcheting up the volume. "And I had no idea that I'd written all these things to your teacher and that you'd missed the entrance exams for St. Paul's!" She points to the kitchen. "Please go in there and sit down."

Steve slowly follows us into the room, glancing first at me and then at his wife in bewilderment. I take a seat. My mother gives me a glare I've never seen on her face before, and my shame is dark red. Malcolm comes into the kitchen, stammering, "M-Mum? Sam?" but she gestures to him to leave.

"Well, you owe your mother an explanation!" Steve orders.

"You keep out of this," I can't help saying.

"Wow," says Steve, "where did that come from?"

It's very quiet in the kitchen. The only sounds are the ticking of the small clock on the oven and a buzz as the fridge springs into action. My mother looks so tense that I'm scared she's going to start shouting or spank me.

So what she actually does comes as a huge surprise. She pulls up a chair, takes my hands, and says, "Samuel, I've loved you ever since you were born. Sometimes you're a stranger to me. You seem peculiar and that feeling has only intensified now that you're a teenager, but I love you." Tears are running down her face. "Whatever you've done, I guess you must have had good reasons for doing it."

I swallow hard. How long has it been since we last held hands? Not since I was really small, I reckon.

"Samuel. I'd like you to tell me, right now, what drove you to . . ."—she gropes for words to describe my faking excuse notes and counterfeiting her signature—"go to such great lengths to play truant and even skip the tests." She waits, still holding my hands, and her kindness and her concern overwhelm and envelop me. "Are you scared of someone at school? Are you being bullied? Or—"

"What?" I'm genuinely stunned. "No!"

She lets out a cry of relief, whereas I am overcome with shame and appalling guilt. Not because I lied, but because I dared to imagine that my mother didn't really love me. Not as I loved her. Not to the point where she could never have lived without me. And because I didn't trust her to care for me.

"Pre-exam stress?" Steve asks, only making things worse.

I shake my head. "I was with my dad," I confess.

"Oh," is all my mother says. She slumps back against the arm of her chair. One of her hands releases mine, but she immediately puts it back again.

More ticking from the clock on the oven.

The whoosh of the boiler. The buzz of the fridge. The drip and puff of the coffee machine.

Malcolm standing wide-eyed in the doorway, staring at us.

The scent of Steve's aftershave.

My mother's eyes gazing at me, blinking with the colors of distress, anger, pain, and helplessness.

We hold each other's gaze and for the first time it is as if we're really speaking openly with each other—all without uttering a sound. Our muteness says everything there is to say. I realize I've hurt her, not by loving my father but because I've gone behind her back. She offers me a glimpse of her anger, but she bottles it up. Her fingers clasp mine even more tightly, as if she can barely stop herself from yelling or weeping, but she keeps her emotions in check. For my sake and hers.

Abruptly my mother draws herself upright, and her breathing settles. She looks at me and gives a faint smile that contains sadness and pain, resignation and tenderness.

"When I first got to know him at Charles de Gaulle Airport, I thought he was the most arrogant person I'd ever met." She's still staring at me, but her gaze passes through me into the thicket of bygone days. "Two days later we were in Sudan. A child soldier shot at us. The boy was the same age as you are now, Sam. That day I took the photo that later won a prize: the cowrie necklace lying in a pool of our dead driver's blood."

Her eyes are once again focused on me. She stretches out one hand and strokes my cheek extremely gently with it. Her voice has subsided to a whisper as she says, "I never took another portrait photo after that—not a single one."

A tear trickles down her cheek, and I remember how she used to lay that cheek on mine when I was ill or running a temperature. **How could I have forgotten?**

"Your father saved my life by shielding me with his body. Can you imagine what it's like to think that you've reached the end of your life?"

Yes, I can. That's where my father is right now.

"The only emotions that really change your life, Sam, are fear and love. I was so afraid, and I'd never loved anyone. I had nothing to cling on to as the end approached." She's smiling and weeping at the same time. "Thinking of your father reminds me of the moment I realized that there'd been more fear than love in my life. I always held that against him. I was ashamed. I'm still ashamed. I've sought to lead a life that exposes me to as little danger as possible."

I pause before asking, "And now?"

"Now it's the other way around," she says. "I have more love and less fear."

Steve exhales. "Well, that's a relief, Marie-France."

"How is he?" she asks me, calmly and gravely.

"Not good," I whisper. "Not good at all." This time it's my turn to have trouble controlling my emotions. I'd dearly love to throw myself into her arms, but I know that would be too much today. "He's wearing my scoobie. He's in a coma, and no one knows if he'll ever come back."

"Oh sh—" Steve exclaims, aghast.

"And that's why you've been to see him so often," my mother concludes, gulping hard.

I could tell her about Maddie or Eddie. I could tell her that I now know three things: I'm in love, I'm not going to stop going to the hospital, and I've just realized that I really do want to be a writer. No, not "want"—must. I don't have a choice, but only

356

now has that become clear to me. It feels as if it's the only way to make sense of everything—people, colors, emotions, landscapes, and rooms I can read as if they were books. And Maddie too.

A story found me in Oxford. That's what always happens: stories find you.

There's one thing I'm not going to do for the time being, though, and that's go to school. I couldn't sit in class at Colet Court while Maddie would like to live but longs to die. I can't study math and electrical circuits and French while my father's fighting for survival. I must go to Maddie and tell her that I've understood and that I'll be there for her.

Malcolm is perching on the bottom step out in the hallway. When I wave to him, he gratefully jumps to his feet and comes into the kitchen. My mother puts her arm around him and hugs him tight. Steve has placed his hand beside my mother's on the plastic tablecloth, and they link their little fingers.

"Why didn't you tell me?" my mother asks in a faint voice.

"Because you've got one another," I answer honestly. "You, Malcolm, and Steve have got one another."

And that's exactly how they look as they face me. Without realizing it, they are intertwined.

Tears well up in my mother's eyes, and she lifts her hand to her mouth. "I had no idea that's how you saw things," she says. She opens her arms wide.

Come to me! her empty embrace cries, and very cautiously we both stand up and I hug her and she hugs me. I hadn't noticed I'd grown, but almost overnight my mother and I are the same height. As we stand there, it's clear that everything has changed.

I realize at that moment that you can always decide: nothing simply happens. It's always possible to decide whether to lie or tell the truth, whether to be an asshole or not to be an asshole.

Steve claps his hands and says, "All right then, I'll drive you to the hospital and then to school, okay? We'll tell the head teacher that you're going to take a break this year. But no more lies, do you hear? Marie-France? Sam?"

I nod and say, "I'll wait for you outside, Steve."

My voice has broken. I can feel the sound of my words echoing inside me. It is deep and calm and green. Dark green.

Henri

The barrier is a smoky gray and like glass. It's never-ending, reaching down as far as I can see, and no edges to it are visible to my left or right or above me.

I don't know what happened just now. I cannot remember having opened my eyes or waking up. Dark, turbulent depths gape beneath my feet. It's as if something far below was propelling me upward and is now pressing me against an obstacle whose origins and nature I cannot discern.

It has no tangible surface, and yet it stretches as taut as skin above me. I float within touching distance of its underside, which hovers like a coffin lid over my head. I'm so thirsty, and I struggle for air.

I can feel myself breathing. Air flows into my lungs but is then sucked out of them again, leaving me constantly short of breath.

Then I spot them, on the other side of the glass. Shadows coalesce into men and women in blue or purple trousers and shirts going about their mysterious business.

"Hello! Please, I'm thirsty!"

Nobody hears me.

"Hello!" I cry. "Please, over here!"

They pay no attention to me whatsoever.

It is a continually shifting landscape of people and shadows. Intermittently, for a few short, jerky moments, the scene comes into focus, and I glimpse neon tubes, walls, and machines, but nowhere the blue brightness of day or the pitch-blackness of night.

Someone moves my arms and legs—at least I think they're my arms and legs. I recognize my own hand by the familiar colorful band on my wrist. I try to waggle my forefinger, but I don't succeed. I can't feel a single part of my body. It's as if I consist exclusively of water and darkness, with my thoughts swimming in circles on the surface.

I can feel the air, though. I can make out the electrical odor of machines and the reek of smoke clinging to the hair of the men and women. I can sense the crackle of thoughts. I feel as if I'm a silent island surrounded by a sea of other people's thoughts. These alien thoughts come from the figures leaning over me, and they glance off me like marbles.

I don't know why I'm doing this. It makes no sense.

I could simply stay here tonight.

I can't put up with another night when she doesn't even look at me.

How about I make a salad rather than steaming some vegetables? Salad's a negative-calorie food. Or maybe I'll have a tiny piece of chocolate after all . . .

I'm working too hard. It must end sometime.

I feel sudden, acute pains, as if I'm being run through with a spear. They crush my heart, burn and singe and scorch me. The agony of it makes me want to scream. It is my lack of all bodily sensation that's splitting and tearing me apart—and this impenetrable barrier.

I must be asleep, but very soon I'll wake up. All I need to do is wake up.

A fragrance assails my nostrils—the aroma of a mild summer's evening on the coast of Brittany, redolent with jasmine, pancakes, salt, and caramel.

Oh my darling! For an instant the pains soften. Any moment now I'm going to wake up, and Eddie will be by my side. My darling Eddie. I'm filled with such love and then such yearning, followed by a deep and plaintive sense of loss and a horrible feeling of shame. I used to be with her. I was once at the dawn of life. I was once immortal. Now I'm dead, or as good as. And I'm not asleep. Oh no, I'm not asleep—I'm almost dead! That's the truth. Or is it?

A crackle of fear. A hum of tiredness, like a

drowsy bumblebee. A flicker of worry, like a defective neon tube.

What is this? Where am I? In a bed? This bed is somewhere in a world from which I'm gradually fading, having already lost my arms, my legs, my body, and my voice. The people on the other side of the glass ignore me, even when I call out to them. I might as well be invisible to them.

How did I get here? Suddenly a memory looms before me, opening like an enormous door through which I could hurry back the way I've come.

"I love you," said Eddie. "I want you, forever and beyond, in this life and every other."

"I don't want you," I replied, shattering our relationship. I broke our relationship, as Eddie's expression turned to ice.

The black silence beneath is pulling at me, dragging me back down.

"No," I yell. "No!" **I haven't yet drunk my fill of this woman—nowhere near! I have to let her know that I was lying!**

My heart aches more and more with every beat. It's the only part of me that continues to respond as I weep bitter tears of fear and horror and pain at this disembodied nightmare in which I'm trapped.

"Here," I call, straining every nerve. **Someone must hear me, surely!** "Please! I'm here!"

But nobody comes. I weep tears that will not flow from eyes that no one sees. I hurl beseeching cries at the barrier, but they go unheard. Then I remember the girl who was bent on dying. I can feel her presence close by. She's there on the other side, and yet she's also in the depths below me. She's putting up a fight, but her strength is waning. I haven't combed the sea thoroughly enough; she's still out there, lost among tides and dreams.

Where is the girl? And where am I?

Eddie

My room is on the same floor but a different corridor. The guest room—or "family room," as they call it here—is as plain and functional as one would imagine a monk's cell to be: a narrow bed and a bedside table, a desk and chair, and two armchairs with a coffee table between them. The view makes up for the lack of comfort somewhat. I stare out across the roofs of the city at the setting sun painting fire on the graphite-gray clouds over London.

I spot the winking lights of a plane taking off. Maybe it's Wilder's. Three hours ago, as he set off along the traffic-clogged roads leading west to Heathrow, he said to me, "I can understand why you're doing this. I'd do the same. Exactly the same. The trouble is, I'm not you. I'm the man who wants you, who wants to live with you. And who cannot share you, Edwina, not with anyone, whether that person's a man in a coma or someone else." He set me an ultimatum.

To be completely honest, I'd have done exactly the same in his position. Understanding, yes, but self-sacrifice? Only if I was number one. No question of being second choice.

Wilder said, "When I get back, I want you to tell me if your heart is free for me."

I take the bottle of Talisker from the wheeled suitcase I've packed for the Wellington. There's a sealed disposable plastic cup in the tiny shower cubicle–cum-bathroom. I tear off the wrapping and pour myself a large shot of whiskey.

Wilder stretched out his arms to give me a hug and said, "I'm sorry, Eddie. That ultimatum was stupid. Forget I ever mentioned it, please?"

I told him that I didn't need an ultimatum. "My heart isn't free," I answered, but even as I spoke those words I wanted to beseech him to stay. I'd already gone too far, though, incapable of pausing, reaching for Wilder's hands, holding on to him, and taking everything back. What else could I do but release him? He deserves to be loved exclusively.

I drink. In the mirror I see a woman who's weary of fighting. For the first time I notice I've aged. Wrinkles, a faded complexion, a lack of luster in my eyes. I'm losing touch with myself in this tug-of-war between Henri and Wilder, between my old life and my present one.

After my answer Wilder kissed me, and his kiss had a bitter, shocked, bewildered taste.

The hair on his head is blond. On his chest it is dark, almost black, and between his legs it's light brown. Naked, he looks completely different from Henri. He is completely different—always in the here and now, never in the past or the future. He bears no grudges. He has no trouble saying "I love you" or "As you wish. So is this the end?"

I nodded, noticing the moist gleam in his eyes as he brusquely turned to leave.

Another sip, or more like a swig this time. I'm no beauty. I resemble a goblin in the wrong light and a relatively pretty Irish boy in the right conditions. But Wilder loved this nonbeauty.

If I have even the slightest feelings for Henri, then I was obliged to let Wilder go. It's only fair. I can't keep him on the back burner.

"Take care, my girl, and make sure you bring him back!"

I'm touched by that expression "my girl" and also by the fact that he had a good word for Henri, his rival in a coma who beat him to the prize without even entering the contest. I regret never having dared to share the whole truth of my life with Wilder.

I take the candles out of my suitcase, light them, and turn off the dazzling ceiling lamp. I go over to the window. The fire in the London sky has been extinguished, and the world is turning its face to night.

In a film or a novel, I think, Wilder would be the willing victim who loves his girlfriend so much that he's even prepared to accept that she cares for the comatose love of her life. The hearts of female viewers and readers would go out to him.

But that's not how it works in the real world. I know why I publish new future and dystopian novels rather than romances. Because in principle loving means repeatedly coping with despair and uncertainty and change. Love changes as we do. I don't know if I could have loved the way I do now when I was in my midtwenties. Someone who wants to write truthfully about love would need to write a new novel about the same couple every year in order to tell the story of how their love evolves, how life comes between them, and the color their affection takes on as the days darken.

I drink my Talisker, breathing in its notes of toffee, earth, and ether. How must they all feel, all the people whose beloved lies in a coma? Do they remain "faithful" in the most innocent sense of the word? Do they long for sex, the touch of skin, laughter, and shared moments when life is full and sweet? Or do they die, a little at a time, because they no longer dare to live? Do they abandon their lives completely and devote themselves entirely to caring and comforting? Or do they conserve some of their strength for themselves?

I drain my glass. The whiskey burns my throat. Then I brush my hair, go to the small chapel to gather my courage and tenderness, and set off to see my oblivious husband.

"HOW'S MADDIE?" I ask Dr. Foss, who's standing on the low dais in the center of the intensive care unit and peering at a monitor over another doctor's shoulder.

He turns to face me and purses his lips. "I'm afraid there are no grounds for optimism," he says quietly, his eyes scanning the space behind me, as if he's worried that Sam might be there. "She's still running a high temperature, and we haven't been able to locate its cause. One of her kidneys has stopped working and her left lung is infected. Things don't look good."

I utter a silent prayer for her. **Not the girl, please.**

Henri and Maddie are now lying side by side in intensive care. C6 and C7.

"What about Henri?"

"No change, Mrs. Tomlin. His body appears to be stable, but he's showing no signs of consciousness beyond that."

He studies my face carefully, and I worry that he can smell the whiskey on my breath. I go over to the two beds, which the nurses have arranged so that Sam can sit with both of them at once. They've also granted him permission to stay overnight at the hospital. He's been given the smallest room in the "family section." Nobody's informed the health insurance because there's no budget for accommodation if there are no surviving relatives. Dr. Saul has ignored the rules in Sam and Maddie's case. I felt a momentary flash of love for the doctor for this show of kindness.

"Don't go thinking I'm a good person, Mrs. Tomlin," he said. "I cannot stand good people."

"It didn't even cross my mind, I assure you."

He flashed me a quick grin, and to my surprise I returned it. I'm afraid that we might actually grow to like each other.

Unlike Henri, Maddie is a ward of the state, and the state doesn't sit on her bed for half the day, whispering words of encouragement to her as Sam does. The state doesn't bring her light and beauty and cake as Sam does.

She seems so tiny and vulnerable. Around her bed they've placed a transparent protective box, equipped with a filter to purify the air. I've read up on sepsis. Blood poisoning is one of the most common and fatal diseases. I stare down at the girl with her drawn features, the tube in her mouth, and her frail, sunken frame. Her sudden illness is a mystery, but her struggle for life has galvanized everyone. Her small body is increasingly tense, her head and her calves bent back almost into a C-shape. Nothing moves and torments the entire intensive care staff more than the sight of Sam, swaddled in overalls, face mask, and plastic gloves, sitting at the foot of Maddie's bed, quietly reading aloud to her or recounting an anecdote or simply being there and holding her hand for hours on end.

I turn to Henri and give a stunned gasp. He's opened his eyes!

"Henri!" I whisper. "Oh, Henri!" But those are the only words I can utter as laughter comes bubbling up inside me. It soon dies in my throat, though, because his gaze passes straight through me. He's completely lifeless.

"Dr. Foss!" I call, or try to, but the only sound that comes out is a high-pitched squeak. I automatically feel for Henri's pulse. He's there: his skin is warm.

Dr. Saul joins me at the bedside. He pulls out his light pen and shines it into Henri's eyes, causing me to wince in spite of myself. Standing up straight again, the doctor announces, "His pupils don't react. He can't see us."

I lean down close to Henri's face. It's been such a long time since I saw him—and now he's ignoring me. I feel distraught.

"Look at me!" I beseech him. "I'm here. I'm not leaving, so don't you go either, Henri, my heart, my darling."

"He can't hear you either."

"How do you know?"

Dr. Saul gives Dr. Foss a signal. They're so bloody used to this life shorn of miracles.

"The spontaneous fluctuation of activity in his

auditory cortex alternates between internal and external stimuli approximately every twenty seconds," he says.

"What does that mean?"

"That we try not to miss the moments when Mr. Skinner regains consciousness. We monitor him continuously. It's almost out of the question that we'd fail to notice if he were to hear, see, or try to establish contact with us."

" 'Almost' isn't good enough."

Dr. Saul sighs. The two doctors bend over Henri, speak to him, touch him, and examine him. I loathe the almost imperceptible shakes of their heads and acquiescent glances with which they increasingly exclude me from their deliberations. It's obvious, though: Dr. Foss and Dr. Saul are beginning to give up on Henri.

My thoughts fly back to that moment in the past when he and I were sitting facing each other across my kitchen table. He never wore shoes in my flat and would always sit on the same chair with his bare feet on the wooden floor. Even all these years later, I still don't like anyone else sitting there. Occasionally I'll sit opposite his empty chair and stare at it for minutes on end.

"Henri," I say, clasping his lovely, kind, warm hands. Feeling how tense they have become, I start to massage and move them the way Liz the physiotherapist taught me so that the tendons and the ligaments remain lithe.

Dr. Saul and Dr. Foss, the cynic and his gentleman companion, continue their visits.

I can't get into my routine today. As always, I breathe in and prepare to tell Henri who he is, why he's here, and why I'm here. Except today it seems like mumbo-jumbo, and so I tell him what's on my mind.

"Madelyn's in a bad way, Henri. I'm worried about her and Sam and you and me too. The rules in this place instruct us to speak calmly and optimistically, but you opened your eyes and yet you can't see anything. Or can you? How about briefly squeezing my hand, just a little? Neither of those moronic doctors ever needs to know. You can continue to string them along if you like."

His hand doesn't move.

"You could blink. Once for yes, twice for no."

He doesn't blink.

I RECALL our first kiss. We'd already spent two nights together without exchanging a single word, although on the second night our hands and our eyes spoke. I'll never forget the ballet our hands performed as they stroked and cradled one another. Never before had I had such intimate sex with a man as during that second night, as Henri and I lay on my bed and our hands made love. Those movements contained the future, and our fingers sketched out and agreed upon every encounter to come—desire, tenderness, seduction, arousal, and release.

On our third night together we kissed. Earlier, we had walked through the dark streets of London from which everyday life had withdrawn and been replaced by street cleaners, and all the bars, so recently thrumming with fate and desire and drunken merriment, had tidied away their chairs and with them any promise of bliss. We walked across the Golden Jubilee Bridge from the Victoria Embankment. I leaned against the railings with my back to the river.

"Never turn your back to the sea," Henri said all of a sudden, his voice calm and imposing. He placed his hands on the railings on either side of my waist, creating a protective bubble with his arms. I could feel the warmth of his body as at last it came closer to mine.

"I'm not turning my back to it. I can see it reflected in your eyes," I said.

Then he kissed me. He kissed me so firmly and sensuously that it seemed as if that kiss opened up entirely new vistas. Our bodies put into practice the deal our hands had sealed and answered the questions our fingers had posed.

NOW I PRESS his unresponsive hands to my cheek and forehead. His uninhabited eyes look like empty windows.

I won't cry. I don't cry.

Darkness is closing in, and every bed in this warehouse of wandering souls stands in its own pool of light. Around us I can feel the souls trying slowly to free themselves from their bodies, like tiny sparks detaching themselves and floating into the air.

I gaze at Henri and quietly tell him what it was like when we met. I recount everything, every day we spent together, and I continue by telling him about the times when my father would sing to me and other times when we would run out onto the lawn where the grass reached his chest and was taller than I was. When it was raining he would sing and I would dance, and he said, "You're unbreakable, my girl. No soul is ever erased." I could feel what he meant, even if I didn't understand his words. "Every day is a step, Edwina. Every day is another step toward a distant goal."

I imagine that I'm a lighthouse, emitting a beam of words, memories, and songs that will guide Henri out of the darkness between the worlds.

DAY FORTY-THREE

Henri

I cling with waning strength to the glass barrier, and below me loom the watery depths from which I propelled myself upward. Death lurks in the surging, roaring, gurgling blackness, but it's farther away than I feared.

I can feel my heart thumping, as if something just caused my heart to race. Something is amiss. It feels as if all my nerve ends are spreading out like jellyfish tentacles, and I use them to explore the other side of the glass. Something is different from normal. From normal? From yesterday? From a year ago?

There are no more blinking emerald lights, none of the annoying beeping or the electrical odors of the monitoring devices. There are no longer any shadowy figures whose thoughts about dinner and dieting lap against the shores of my lonely island, no voices counting drops or murmuring medical terms. There's something else, though, shimmering like the air above a fire.

Thoughts! But they make no sense, they belong to . . . **the wandering souls**. Who pronounced those words?

The fine threads that constitute my invisible feelers are searching, revealing for the first time the dimensions of the room around me. It is large. No ordinary room. This room is filled with sighs— continual sighing as if people are letting go of things and people and times. And life. My mind goes back to a door—a door on an island—and to the kindly face of a woman embracing a girl under- water. Then I hear the child weeping. The child on the rock. Madelyn.

That's her name? How do I know that?

Other things occur to me, as if chestnuts were raining down from an invisible tree onto the ground before me.

Scott wants to study psychology, specializing in psychosis. Who's Scott?

Madame Lupion has a squint and a kitchen crammed with handwritten recipe books, includ- ing one for tarte tatin, which you bake facedown with caramel in a special flat pan. I've no idea who Madame Lupion is, but my grandfather Malo had one of those pans for making tarte tatin.

Greg was here and so were Monica and Ibrahim,

who has a tattoo and says he's going to go to work for Amnesty International as a human rights lawyer.

I have the impression that I'm leafing through a book I didn't know I wrote. I also notice that something else is different on the other side of the barrier. The light has a different quality, quieter and more sheltered. My chest hardens into a rock with a heart of stone beating inside it. **I'm alone. Completely alone!** I panic, I want to scream, I want . . .

"Calm down, Mr. Skinner," a woman's voice says. "Everything's fine. Nurse Marion's with you. Shush, everything's all right. The stars are breathing and so are you. Nothing bad can happen to you. You're safe here."

Nurse Marion? I cannot see the woman with the vaguely familiar, croaky voice, which smells of cigarettes. It's a welcoming aroma, like coming home. Soon my heart is beating more calmly, no longer flapping frenziedly like a bird in stormy waters, no longer begging so urgently to be heard.

"Hello, Henri Skinner," the voice says softly.

"Hello," I answer. **Can she hear me?**

"Mr. Skinner, every night I analyze your sleep architecture. I'm certain you're awake, but you can't express yourself."

Yes, yes! A gentle coolness floods my veins, and my fierce, black pain subsides, burning me less, no more than a flickering candle flame now.

"It's almost half past three," Nurse Marion tells me, and the scent of smoke reminds me of childhood nights by the fireside. Central heating came late to our village by the sea, and every house was heated with firewood in winter, its fragrance only fading when warmth arrived with the summer breeze at the end of spring.

The voice says something else: "Madelyn, my dear."

I think, **Madelyn, are you there?**

There is no sound. The end of my world in this hall of the "zombies." That's the ceiling; this is my phantom body. I drift away. I fly through a purple sky—below me the sea, above me the barrier. The glass zone. I fly for days and days. I can feel sparks breaking off me as I begin to dissolve and disperse across an endless space. . . .

"Good morning, Mr. Skinner."

I'm startled. The sky recedes with a whoosh. **Good morning, Mr. Skinner?** The words are buzzing in my head. Is there someone who can hear me on the other side of the glass?

"My name is Dr. John Saul and I'm your doctor, Mr. Skinner. I'm a neurosurgeon and I've operated on you several times. You had a cerebral contusion. You sustained a tear to your spleen and fractures in your right arm, knee, and five ribs."

What?

"Your name is Henri Malo Skinner. You've spent the past forty-two days at the Wellington Hospital in London, Great Britain. Britain is still a part of

Europe, although a majority of Britons have recently voted to change that. It's late June 2016, shortly before seven o'clock in the morning. The city is full of tourists from places where we go on holiday. It's ghastly."

"What happened to me?" I ask, but he continues without answering my question.

"You've been living in a coma for twenty-eight days, Mr. Skinner, ever since you suffered a cardiac arrest that left you clinically dead for several minutes. You've already survived two bouts of pneumonia and the onset of thrombosis."

I was dead? I suddenly understand. My father, the sea, the island, that door. I died and on the way to death I ended up—what did my father call it?—"in between."

"If you can hear me now but cannot speak, I would ask you to give me a different signal. First, I will squeeze your hand and would be very obliged if you could give mine a short squeeze back."

"I **am** here!"

He doesn't answer.

Oh no, no, no! He can't hear me either, and I can't feel his hand. I cast around despairingly inside my numb body, but I feel nothing—no hand and no pressure. I try with all my might to imagine fingers clenching.

"Oh well, shaking hands obviously isn't your thing but then it never really has been."

What does that mean: never has been? How

many times has he squeezed my hand before? He told you, Henri: twenty-nine mornings in a row. But what am I doing in London? It's not possible. First I lived in Paris with my boy. I got married to Eddie, and we lived in . . . we lived . . . where did we live?

No, I didn't marry. Or did I?

Coma, I'm in a coma. That's what Dr. Saul said.

Fear overwhelms me. It's like brackish water, gradually submerging a deep, stagnant underwater prison cell. I feel the pull of the silence beneath me and try to press myself against the glass, try not to fall asleep, not to let go. I don't want to sink back down there; I can't bear the thought. The glass darkens, as if someone's lowering a blind over the glass barrier. But then I recognize a face and moving lips.

"Mr. Henri Skinner, I've said your name so often I'm starting to sound like one of those irritating call-center assistants, but in my case I was testing whether you can hear while unconscious."

Yes, for hell's sake, I'm here. Here! Please get me out. Wake me up, damn it, wake me up. Do something, please! I'm here!

"Your name is Henri Malo Skinner, Malo being the name of your Breton grandfather. You were born at the northwestern tip of Brittany, and you grew up on the coast of the Iroise Sea."

I know where I was born, for God's sake. But he doesn't care. He can't hear me. He keeps saying that I'm living in a coma, and I want to tell him that everything is very different. **I'm here. I'm really here!**

He talks about a form that appoints Edwina Tomlin to decide on my fate. But where's Eddie?

I'm supposed to squeeze hands, lift my arm, move my nostrils, blink, and swallow, but I can't do any of those things. He says that he's given me a gentle pinch, but I don't feel anything. Next he claims that he doesn't like doing this, but it's necessary. I have no idea what he's talking about. He apologizes again, saying, "I'm sorry, you're bleeding a little. Some tests are brutal."

Maybe I'm paralyzed!

Then it's over. Dr. Saul mumbles, "I visit you ten times a day and every four hours at night. You've been through a scanner three times, revealing no significant streams of consciousness."

Well, buy a machine that works then, idiot!

"Mr. Skinner, you're nearer to us than to our strange friend Death. Come toward us. We're here, and you're safe with us."

Death isn't my friend, I feel like saying. **Also, didn't you know that Death is a woman? Death is a woman!**

I can sense that Dr. Saul is contemplating me, as if a message just got through to him. My anger, perhaps. I have to make myself angrier. I perceive his presence like a huge, cragged rock amid the foaming waves, weary from many millennia of erosion by salt and wind, but solid nonetheless. And very, very lonely.

Lonely old Dr. Saul reassures me again: "You're safe here, Mr. Skinner."

I don't feel safe. I feel as if I were buried up to my mouth in asphalt at the end of an empty street.

Dr. Saul walks away.

I try to listen out for any sounds in the world beyond the glass barrier and penetrate it with my sensory antennae. There's someone else there. I can feel a presence, calm and majestic and attentive, but it's out of reach. Is it Dr. Saul? Or Nurse Marion with her cool, soothing fingers?

What is watching me?

I continue to search for the girl and find her very close, directly by my side. She's in a frightful state, but she no longer wants to die. She's fighting. She seems to be desperately dragging herself toward life, yet something is holding her back with an iron grip.

The darkness approaches tantalizingly from all sides with a peaceful, soft blanket, trying to carry me away, and I anticipate the sweet slumbers that it brings. I put up a fight. **No!** I want to open my eyes wide, squeeze and crush Dr. Saul's hand. I want to tell him not to leave me and that I've been here, close to the glass, many times before, always too briefly, and now I want to wake up. I want to tell him to help the child, because the little girl is never going to make it alone. But it's as if someone has turned off the light and . . .

DAY FORTY-THREE

Night

Henri

The next time I drift up to the glass barrier, the air is different, cooler, as cold as groundwater, and a lush, black veil is lying on it. I can feel the depths of night have settled over the room; it has a different weight from the day.

At my side is the rock called Dr. Saul. He whispers, "It's two o'clock." He's searching for me, but he can't find me. He explains that they tested me in my "absence" for Guillain-Barré syndrome, a form of rapid-onset paralysis, and for polyneuropathy, a different disorder of the nervous system that makes it impossible for the sufferer to move. However, it isn't my body that's resisting—it's my brain.

"Your son once said that the brain was a church built of thoughts. I like Samuel. He has an inner dignity most people will never attain, even if they live to be a hundred."

My son! He's here? What does he look like? What's he doing? How is he?

Dr. Saul doesn't tell me. I suspect that this doctor never leaves the hospital and has set up his camp bed in a room on a forgotten corridor somewhere.

Light stabs at my pupils. I can smell Dr. Saul's breath. It smells fresh and warm, and his body radiates the same warmth. I envy him for being able simply to get up and walk away. I can see him, as if through a reverse telescope, a hundred yards above me, his face the size of a pin.

I call out, "Where's Eddie? What's wrong with Madelyn?"

"We must work in a guilt-free space, Mr. Skinner. We doctors, I mean. We shouldn't beat ourselves up about our mistakes. Fuck that. The older I get, the more of my mistakes I'm able to visit, either here in the unit or out in the graveyard. No brain surgeon is free of guilt. Are you there, Mr. Skinner? Can you hear me?"

Yes I can, but why can't this idiot hear me? Dr. Saul's faraway face vanishes. The world beyond the barrier starts to shift and begins to swirl and eddy, like drifting smoke. Through the smoke I can make out my father's outline, sitting on a bed in the background. I recognize his striped sweater, his jeans, and his bare feet.

Am I dying? He shakes his head and says, "I'm just waiting." Those who love us wait for us. "Henri, did you know that I let go of you, not the other way around?"

I don't believe him.

Being in a coma is like being buried alive, and nobody knows that I'm here. **Here!** What happens if they never hear me? If they think I've died? If they bury me alive? I can't go on, I don't want to go on.

DAY FORTY-FOUR

Henri

—— // ——

A hand brushes against mine, then something seems to try to escape from the room. It is quick and as light as spray, and for a while it flits about between the beds and past the machines. It keeps banging against the windows, growing more and more impatient, like a moth desperate to escape.

Soon afterward there's a rumpus. Doctors and nurses gather around a bed, which is now empty of the essential. **You're too late**, I could tell them. **The husk lies there, but the core has gone.**

I smell smoke, and Nurse Marion says to the others, "He just passed me in the corridor," but although this is true, no one listens to her. She goes quietly and alone out into the corridor because she's not needed at the deceased's bedside, and a few seconds later I get a whiff of fresh air. Marion has opened a window, and whatever it was that was desperately seeking to exit the ward and touched me on its way past is relieved to be able to escape. I savor the unexpected aromas. It's as if the air has wandered the streets of London throughout the night and is now bringing the whole city to me: the smell of beer and the echo of loud music, the odors of people on the Underground, cinnamon, and the dirty brown water of the Thames.

The dead body still gives off the occasional spark as it is wheeled out of the ward. I can see this and more, but I'll never be able to tell anyone.

I've had time to think, to think properly about the situation. I've never had as much as now because I am made up entirely of thoughts. And thirst.

I'll probably never make it back to the other side of the glass barrier. Not today, not tomorrow, not easily. I'm buried alive inside myself, condemned to remain "in between" forever. Before the disc zone, as I call it—the narrow band on the edge of reality and the plain where something is always driving me toward the shores and decisive forks in my life where I was in the wrong or my spirit was weak. That something allows me to experience what might have been if I'd acted or decided differently between leaving and staying, kissing and running away; if I had said yes instead of no.

I have searched and searched for the right life—and never found it. None of the lives was perfect, no matter what I did or didn't do. And out there, where I can see and hear real people more clearly with every passing hour—although **they** cannot see or hear me—I realize there's a second world, which seems to shimmer like a mirage or sparkle through water vapor. Nobody's aware of it, maybe not even Nurse Marion, although the night nurse does appear to be more sensitive than the others. I've always found her thoughts to be the clearest.

She calls the dead "the others," and it's an accurate description. I sometimes call them "the watchers." Like my father, who's waiting out there somewhere for me, and whom I am only able to see because I myself am half dead. He's watching me, as he has probably been doing for decades, although I've been almost unaware of it.

"Almost," because I could sense him at certain precious moments, although I denied it and wouldn't allow him to offer me any encouragement, wouldn't believe that he would occasionally borrow my body to walk or smell, briefly and breathlessly, or to feel the touch of a soft hand on his cheek.

The "watchers" are everywhere, especially those who have unfinished business with the living. Sometimes they show themselves in a reflective surface—for example as sparkling light on the surface of the sea, in the gleaming chrome of a speeding car, or in a passing glint in an Underground tunnel. Most clearly, though, they reveal themselves to us just before we fall asleep, and we also notice them in opaque, confusing, and fleeting dreams. We think they're apparitions, but in fact they're the "others."

I wonder if you need to be dead to infiltrate the dreams of the living, or almost dead.

I sense four others standing more and more frequently at Madelyn's bedside, observing her. They pace around the ward, listening here and there for sparks, for breaths, and for news of the outside world. From time to time they vanish, as if they merely wanted to take a lungful of London air, and I imagine their taking the last empty seats on a bus or the tube, the ones passengers usually shun, although they don't know why.

I must learn to understand this in-between state. **Bar-khord.** Between everything and nothing.

I once wrote a portrait of a hundred-year-old Persian tutor who, until the early 1970s, taught the children of the Iranian royal family the art of being a king and acting like one. I can still hear the old man's wry voice and his cultivated Oxford English through the mists of my constantly shifting memories. With the same caution with which you might extend your hand toward a cobra, I had asked him for his opinion on the culture clash between the British and Iranian monarchies.

He pondered my question for a long time, his fine features half obscured in the dim courtyard of his house in Tehran's old quarter, then replied, "The English language, like all Christian-dominated,

Western languages, describes the meeting of two opposites in violent terms, as a 'clash,' a 'crash,' a 'rupture,' or even an 'attack'—always as hostile and aggressive. It is undoubtedly an effective means of promoting prejudice and fear, for there is nothing better than seeing things as black and white, don't you agree?"

He slowly raised his glass of mint tea into the sunlight of the hot, sandy afternoon and took a sip. The bright blue light filtered through the slatted roof that created a pleasant shade in the courtyard.

"In Persia we call the meeting of two opposites **bar-khord**. **Bar-khord** happens when two strong elements touch and something new forms at their point of intersection. It is not a clash of opposites—not like flesh on the metal of a car— more like an intermingling. Do you understand? This in-between state is in constant flux. It doesn't set opposites against each other; it is the source of a third element, something completely new that draws on the opposites and bears no major similarities to either one or the other. It's like a child that grows into something very different from its mother or its father, you see?"

I nodded.

"**Bar-khord** is this tea—hot water and mint combining to create poetry and comfort. **Bar-khord** is when blood mingles with blood, when migrants find a home and love in a new country. It's a new life. Not war, not peace, but a fresh start." He sipped his tea. "And the highest form of **bar-khord** is dying. When death and life meet in dying, they create . . ." Here he paused. "What do you think, effendi? What is created between being and nonbeing?"

I answered, "Fear."

Bar-khord. Between being and nonbeing. I'm at the spot where life and death create something. It sounds like a riddle to me, but if I solve it, will I be saved? What is born when dying begins?

THEN THE MIRACLE happens. I sense her presence before she has crossed the ward, even as she's still passing the "watchers." Some of the others say, "Hey, here she is again."

I'm filled with gratitude and anticipation. I can smell her—oh, her fragrance!—and it brings everything flooding back. She approaches and then . . . the long, gray day is finally over. "Eddie, my love," I whisper.

She looks at me, and nothing in her beautiful, proud face suggests that she has heard me. Or did she hear me and is now tormenting me with silence? Is she even real? My sense of salvation is soon chased away by doubt and panic.

She sits down and it is as if the shape of the air has changed, becoming more supple and warm. A sense of enormous well-being flows through me. Yes, she is real. Eddie is reality.

"Hello, Henri," she says, her voice dark and gentle.

"Hello, my darling," I reply.

I want to lift both my hands to draw her face to my burning, frozen heart. I want to feel her and watch her bold lips as she speaks and laughs and demands to be kissed. I want her eyes to rest in mine, as they often did—so fiery and good, knowing and inviting, tender and grand. Nothing about her was ever hard, neither toward me nor toward anyone else, even when she flew into a rage.

Her anger was only ever directed at herself. Apart from that one, fatal time when nothing could pierce her armor.

"Please forgive me. I love you. I love you." Her eyes seek mine, but the harder I try, the less success I have in drawing her gaze to mine. I say, "I love you, in this life and every other."

Nothing. I can feel the crinkle of her fear working its way along invisible threads to me. She doesn't notice me. She looks at me, and I look at her, but there's no meeting of eyes, no recognition. I'd love to wipe away the tear that's creeping down her face. **Oh God, I don't even know if I have a hand.**

"Henri, just in case Dr. Saul hasn't come by to read you the weather forecast and your biography, you should know that today is a fine day for open-air swimming. I'd love to go to the pool with you, but Liz is on holiday . . ."

Who's Liz?

". . . and so I'm going to take over her job. I hope you don't mind my exercising your arms and legs?"

Oh thank you, my darling. I wasn't aware that I still had arms and legs.

She's here and she does things with me that I can't feel, and yet it seems as if I'm lying in a warm bath of silk and scents, soft, sweet oil, and safety. She sings "Lullaby of Birdland," interspersed with descriptions of what she's doing. She washes my feet, she moves my ankles, works on my knees and legs, my hands and shoulders, and then she tells me that the hardest part is next. She rocks my head gently back and forth, using my nape as a fulcrum, singing as she does so. It is as if she were painting a wonderful garden with her voice. Dappled sunlight falls through the treetops; the weather is mild, and fragrances rise from the jasmine bushes and beds of wildflowers. She sings of all these things.

I am completely in her hands: it's the safest place in the whole world.

"My darling," I whisper again. **Why are you here? I want to ask. Why haven't you given up on me?**

Her face is very close to mine, and quietly she says, "I must kiss you every time and hope that you consent."

With a gargantuan effort I try to summon some sensation in my body and conjure up a twitch of my finger, toe, or eyelid. Something to tell her, **I'm here and not only do I give my consent, but I need your kiss and you if I am to survive.**

"Are you there, Henri?" she asks.

Yes! Her eyes seek mine, and I concentrate on boring through the glass to Eddie. **Please, Eddie, can't you see me?**

She breathes out with resignation. I can feel her heart sink, but then she pulls herself together. She won't give up. She might not know it yet, but she never gives up. All the stories she has read have shown her the fantastic, unbelievable, and yet feasible twists and turns life can take. She can imagine anything, both beautiful and terrible, and she never averts her gaze.

"Do you remember the drunk wine waiter at that Swiss hotel?" she inquires, and for an instant it seems as if she can see me.

I'm electrified.

"A few nights ago I dreamed of the sea. You and I were by the coast, in a place where there was a small chapel?"

Saint Samson? Was it Saint Samson?

"We . . ."—her breath is close now, her words shrouded in warmth—"made love on the rocks. But then . . ."

I know, I want to say. **But then the wave came. I know that life! Did you dream of it, Eddie?**

I don't have time to consider this further, because just then I feel another presence. It is as if all my sensory antennae form a hot ball. I know it's him. Samuel Noam. So this is my son! He has a fine soul, and he has a great deal of Malo in him. A very great deal.

Far under his skin, I see a tall, intelligent man growing inside him, ready to emerge one day and replace the boy.

"Hi, Ed," Samuel says in a deep voice, and they bump fists. Then he's in front of me, saying, "Hi, Dad!" and we see each other. No, his gaze is like Eddie's: just past me.

"Hello, Samuel," I say anyway. I'm overjoyed to see him. My happiness and affection and pride and also despair overflow because this child is so dear to me. Every single moment of my life, my imperfect life, now makes sense because of Sam. Because I have unwittingly gotten something right. I look at him and love him with a desire to protect and touch him that leaves me in despair.

My child. My longing to see my son grow up pulls me back toward life. I want to see what he's like, what he wants from life, what he'll do with his.

Just as I think these thoughts, there's a spark of interest in my son's eyes and he focuses his attention afresh. Apparently he can really see me. Yes, he can!

"Hi, Dad," he repeats, but this time in a far softer voice. "So you're here." His face glows with unbridled joy as he raises his eyes to Eddie on the other side of the bed, and then the words spill from his lips. "He's here, Eddie. My father's here."

Sam

—⫽—

I cannot bear to watch their attempts to wake him or, rather, to get him to a state they think resembles "waking." He's come a long way, from the outer edge of life to here, a hair's breadth from waking. He gives the impression of being trapped in amber, voiceless and motionless, but I know he's there. He radiates warmth, but that warmth is only perceptible on the underside of one's skin.

I wish I'd kept quiet. They're pestering him now. They want him to breathe independently and so they are frequently turning off his air supply for a few seconds. They wave objects before his eyes. They knead his calves so hard that their red fingerprints mark the skin where they've rolled and pinched a bunch of muscles.

Standing at the head of the bed, Dr. Foss is trying

403

to startle him. Out of the blue he claps his hands, making everyone jump apart from my father and Maddie. They push things into his hands—soft massage balls and toothbrushes—but he doesn't grasp them. They ask him to blink, look to the left, say his name, or calculate the sum of one and zero.

"I wouldn't answer that kind of question even if Claudia Cardinale were putting it to me," I hear Scott whisper inside my head.

My father doesn't move. No fluttering of the eyelids, no quickening of the pulse, no twitches anywhere.

"I'm sorry, Dad," I murmur.

Dr. Foss changes position and takes a mechanical pencil from his top pocket. I know what he's going to do because I've watched him carry out similar tests on other patients in the intensive care unit. He's going to insert the lead under the nail of my father's big toe and then under his thumbnail.

I sense my father's presence and the black pain that's threatening to engulf him because he cannot do what they're demanding of him, and because there's another greater pain. And thirst. And anger. Bright-red, foaming anger at what they're putting him through.

Now they're pulling his tongue. It hurts me, and I hear a sharp intake of breath from Eddie.

Dad's despair is a strange blue inky color that seems to smudge, as if he were weeping tears that mingle with the ink. But I realize that the cause is not the tests but rather that Eddie cannot feel him.

She's standing by the wall with one hand cupped over her mouth and the other resting on her stomach. Her eyes are glued to my father.

I've moved over to kneel down beside Maddie's bed and stroke her hand. Both of us are wearing antiseptic gloves. She's receiving artificial respiration, and her left kidney failed this morning.

"He was here, Maddie," I whisper, "and he looked at me as . . ." As nobody has ever looked at me before, as if I were the most important person in the world, as if he were expending all his capacity and strength and experience to tell me that he was proud of me.

But of course I cannot say any of those things aloud. I can't even really put them into words. Wimpy tears crowd into my throat, salty and bitter. Bitter because this is so good and so new, and yet it's almost over before it's even begun, and because I had no idea how amazing it feels to mean the world to someone. I mean the whole world to my father!

There's not enough room inside me to cope with this sensation, and so I weep furious tears and clasp Maddie's hand. I imagine that **she's** holding **my** hand instead and drying my tears. This would have embarrassed me in the past—seven weeks ago, when I was still a child.

"Stop it!" I hear Eddie implore loudly but calmly.

The nurses have just stretched out my father's arms and legs to allow Dr. Foss to carry out his pain test.

"But, Mrs. Tomlin, I need to stimulate the reflexes and muscle tone to check his motor functions."

"Don't, Dr. Foss. Stop bombarding us with medical jargon to justify hurting him. Stop it." Eddie's intimidating manner as she strides toward Dr. Foss forces him to retreat. "Leave him alone. Now! That's enough!"

Fozzie sighs and says, "All right, if that's what you want." He clicks the lead back in and stows the pencil in the breast pocket of his coat. "However, to ensure that we don't overlook—"

Eddie gives him such a withering glare that he's unable to finish his sentence. "The patient may well be conscious but have no control of his motor system. Perhaps you're simply causing him pain while he is incapable of defending himself. As his representative, I forbid you to torture him. Is there no other way?"

Dr. Foss glances at Dr. Saul, who turns to me and says, "Our managers are well known for their penny-pinching, but as we have the monster, we may as well use it."

By the "monster" he means a special functional MRI scanner that measures activity in specific areas of the brain. It cost two million pounds and is referred to as England's "mind reader."

Dr. Saul once explained to me that he's one of only four neurosurgeons capable of carrying out reliable tests with it. "The monster peers into the brain for us. We can ask questions such as 'Did you eat a clown for breakfast?' and see if there's a response in the middle prefrontal cortex. We can inject a fluorescent substance into the patient and measure his or her glucose consumption. If the brain continues to consume nutrients, then there's a high probability that the patient is using them. We can even stimulate his or her motor imagination. 'Play tennis! Hop on one leg! Imagine that you're clenching your fist!' We can do any of those things and the lights would start to blink, but unfortunately hardly anyone can interpret the signals. Nobody knows if it's a reaction or simply a loose contact. The machine is smart, and we are stupid."

Nevertheless, God says to Dmitry, "Please prepare Mr. Skinner," then motions to Eddie and me to follow him into his office. I take my time getting to my feet. Eddie brushes the remaining strands of hair next to the scar from my father's operation out of his face. Her gesture is full of love, fear, and infinite sadness. Then she looks at me and says, "Come to us," reaching across my father's chest. I remove my disposable glove, take her hand, and then clasp his right fingers. She grasps his left hand and we stand there, united.

Eddie checks that we're alone and asks, "Tell me how you do it, Sam. Will this work?"

I immediately understand what she means, but I don't know how to explain it to her.

I hear Scott's grave future-psychologist voice echoing in my mind. "**Mon ami,** your only hope is occasionally to make contact with the outside world. Use pictures to explain. People like pictures."

So I try to put it into pictures. I can intensify my perception of everything I see by combining the senses, as if I were dialing up the volume or pushing a button up to maximum. Bright numbers, scented music, fragrances that paint pictures, colored pain, lies, anger, emotions, echoes from buildings.

"Is he here now?" she asks.

I stare into my father's open, unresponsive eyes. I can feel he's there below the surface, just as you can perceive someone's presence behind a door. The atmosphere is different—denser, warmer.

"Yes," I reply.

She gasps, her expression a mixture of disbelief and devotion. "Can he hear me?" she asks with longing and doubt in her voice.

"What do **you** think?" I say. Maybe she too has an amplifier inside her. Maybe everyone does but simply doesn't know it.

Eddie gazes at my father, and the words wrench themselves from her lips. "Oh—H-Henri," she stammers. "Oh, Henri, I love you."

She raises his hand to kiss it, and I peer at the EEG monitor. Three spikes in quick succession.

She casts a desperate but hopeful glance in my direction. "I'm sorry, Sam. You must think I'm incredibly stupid, but I'm going to have to ask you to give me a simultaneous translation."

Her smile is gentle and lopsided, and I'd love to be able to comfort her by saying, **Of course I will!**

"How can you sense he's there?" she asks.

"I don't think about it."

"And what do you feel?"

I study my father's face and once again I can feel the echo of the sea's swell. "Love, burning, and thirst," I say softly.

She lets go of my hand and reaches into the box behind her before carefully dabbing my father's lips and palate with a damp swab. As she does it, I try to open myself up even further, turning up my inner amplifier far into the red. It's almost unbearable because I pick up not only my father's presence but every other sound, and that's far more than a normal person can hear.

There are so many intense emotions in every bed in the ward. One person has gotten lost in a very dangerous place, another is hounded by mortal dread, and yet another patient is running a fever. I sense fatigue and tension, as if there were taut strings and elastic bands crisscrossing the room. Concern, aches, and fear.

"Sam?" Eddie asks, on her guard, with crackling, quivering anxiety. "It's fine. Forget it. Stop now, you don't have to do it." She lays her hands on my shoulders.

Dizzy from holding my breath for so long, I breathe in sharply. I need to tell her, though. "It's as if there's a different quality of light falling on him, darker, brighter, or colored, and it tells me how he's feeling. If he could speak, I'd be able to tell by the tone of his voice if he were hiding something. I can see from his body if he's there. It's . . ."—I try to think of a simile—". . . like a needle coming down on a record; you know something's there even before the music has begun. Or when there's someone in a pitch-black room: there's a tension in the air."

I can tell from Eddie's face that she isn't sure whether to believe me. I can sense that she's wondering if I haven't just made all of this up to console myself and not lose hope.

"He wants to live," I say.

"But is this enough to live?" she says bluntly, pointing wearily to his helpless, near-defunct body.

My father is in turmoil, as if he were hurling himself, over and over, against the bars of his inner jail. But Eddie's right: none of this is obvious from his face or his pulse.

Maybe I'm kidding myself? No. No way. I can feel my father as clearly as if he were talking to me.

"Come on," she says. "Let's go to see Dr. Saul. He'll tell us what he can do."

Eddie

"Fish don't plait their hair," says Dr. Saul. "Dragonflies write poetry."

Ten times he utters a completely nonsensical phrase in order to activate particular areas of Henri's brain that only respond when the brain registers something absurd or must solve a puzzle. Henri's brain appears to have no interest whatsoever in riddles, for Dr. Saul shakes his blond-haired head again and again.

"Hello, Mr. Skinner? I'm your doctor. Your name is Henri Malo Skinner, and you've been at the Wellington Hospital in London for the past forty-four days. You're living in a coma, Mr. Skinner. You've been transferred to a brain scanner that is measuring activity in your middle prefrontal cortex."

Sam is standing beside me. His attention is focused on the huge, humming apparatus into

411

which his father has just been pushed—the MRI tube, otherwise known as the "monster." A ring fitted with special cameras is revolving inside it, dividing the brain into slices, alert for any light signals that might emerge from the darkness.

"Imagine that you're standing on a golf course, hitting a ball," Dr. Saul says now.

"That's stupid," Sam mutters, and I must agree. The fMRI is designed to highlight the same task-specific areas of the brain that are activated when the patient imagines particular movements—for example, while Henri is imagining swinging a golf club—as when a healthy individual dreams of standing on the fairway.

"In your mind, please clench your fist," the doctor orders. "Imagine that you're wiggling your toes." He also asks Henri to imagine that he's playing tennis and soccer and then dancing.

Electric sensors attached to Henri's head and chest register every signal so that Dr. Saul can identify—if not on-screen, then on the MRI printer—any response.

I want Saul and Foss and their bloody monster finally to confirm that Henri is truly there. Not because I don't believe Sam, but because I don't believe myself. I don't trust myself, nor do I trust the doctors to listen to us.

Nothing in Henri's brain suggests that he's imagining any of the desired movements. Nothing indicates that he isn't lying still simply because he doesn't know he's in a coma.

"Mr. Skinner? Mr. Henri Skinner?"

The theta-wave test. I watch Dr. Saul, but he's concentrating on the monitors.

Nurse Marion joins us. "If nothing happens, it doesn't mean that nothing's happening," she whispers. "We'll connect Mr. Skinner to electrodes for another twenty-four hours after we've completed these tests. I actually trust them more than this 'mind reader,' which only observes Mr. Skinner for an hour. That's nothing: he could be anywhere but here during that hour."

"How's Maddie?" Sam asks.

"She's fighting, Samuel. She's fighting."

"She wants to live, but she's scared," he explains.

"You must know her well to make presumptions like that, eh?" Marion teases him.

"No, she told me," he answers.

"Oh really?"

"Yes, in my dreams," Sam says earnestly. He states it in the same tone of voice that authors adopt when they tell me about their new ideas—calmly and with conviction. I've never found any of them pompous. Not even when a writer revealed to me that dreaming was when your spirit visited its soul mate, even if that person was already dead. Dream machines, lucid dreams, dream time travel: none of them ever struck me as absurd or crazy. Poppy,

Ralph, Andrea, and I have often debated the possibility of impossible things happening. I'm accustomed to the unbelievable. Literature exists to survey unfamiliar worlds. Who else but writers will gladly take on that task? Who else is duty-bound to consider, without inhibitions, "What would happen if . . ."?

And yet now I take a step back. This here is reality, not a book or some nerdy competition. That humming monster over there, Dr. Saul's questions, and Henri's ventilator, pumping air in and out of him eight times per minute: they're reality. Henri hasn't breathed independently for six weeks now. The time for miracles has come—a time when nothing's more urgent and nothing's rarer.

"When did you dream about her?" Nurse Marion asks slowly.

"The night after I found out she got blood poisoning."

"Do you mind telling me your dream? You know, dreams are definitely a means of communication and—"

"I'm going to get a cup of tea," I angrily interject.

I can't stand the way Nurse Marion is raising Sam's hopes, even at this juncture.

"Don't you want to hear this, Mrs. Tomlin?"

No. It breaks the last tiny, intact corner of my heart to look at the boy in this light and see his resemblance to his father. **I promise to protect you, Sam, even if I have no idea what you need** protecting from. Maybe from too many illusions? Yes, that's it—from the illusion that miracles occur when you most need them.

"Have you never dreamed of him, Mrs. Tomlin?" the night nurse asks in her smoker's voice.

The buzz of the neon lights on the ceiling changes in tone. What was it Sam said? How can he sense that Henri is very close, watching us and wishing to tell us something? It's . . . **like a needle coming down on a record**. I know that feeling all too well. It's as if the world were secretly catching its breath. It's the moment when the eyes of the entire orchestra are trained on the tip of the conductor's baton. But I cannot disclose it—not the dream in which I was making love with Henri. That was simply lust, no more than that.

But what if it wasn't only that?

"I dreamed about my father long ago," I reluctantly confess. "But only after he died. Often at first, then less and less frequently."

Nurse Marion nods.

Whenever I see my father, I immediately know I'm dreaming. That's what happens when we lose someone who meant the world to us. It tears a hole in our lives, and that hole sucks out our laughter and insouciance. The person's absence crushes us, and all at once the distinctions between truth and dream appear to us with great clarity. It's as if only death allows us to enter the world between the worlds.

Only occasionally do I hear my father outside of those dreams. One example was when Sam was lying in my arms in the hospital chapel and I picked up my father's voice, loud and clear, saying, "Seek out a place and sing it."

Twice I had an impression that he was me: once when I was riding my motorbike and the second time in Cornwall. The air smelled fresh and was still warm in spite of a first hint of autumn. The sea was singing, and everything was well with the world. It felt as if he were walking in my body and enjoying this unexpected opportunity to smell and feel the warmth of his own life, the tensing of muscles and the pounding of a heart. It must have lasted for four or five minutes. Yet despite their intensity I still regard those experiences as a successful piece of self-delusion. That's how people are: they imagine the most outlandish things as solace and deem them true.

"Mrs. Tomlin, have you ever heard of after-death experiences?"

"I've heard of **near**-death experiences."

"No, **after** death. You dreamed of your father. Did you also have the impression that he was there? Could you smell or hear him? After-death experiences are instances of interaction, experienced by people when someone they were very close to has died."

That's nonsense! I want to shout. That's what

I imagine Henri calling to me: **Help me, Eddie! Sancerre-sozzled nonsense!**

So I say, "No. The brain is an excellent self-deluder. We console ourselves by fancying that we can hear and feel and smell our loved ones. Self-healing is the best medicine. In truth, though, Henri hasn't given even the slightest response when I've been here. Nothing, do you hear? After death? Dreams? Spare me!" My voice thunders in my ears. Even Dr. Saul looks over from his Plexiglas cubicle.

After-death experiences. Dreams. Too esoteric, too few guarantees, too much wondrous wound-healing.

I stand up, walk out of the MRI room, and wander along the corridor toward the drinks machine. I feel like beating the walls with my fists or ramming my forehead into them. I want Henri back. I want my dad back. I want my life back.

"Dear little Eddie," I hear my father say softly, but only inside my head.

By the time I reach the drinks machine, I don't feel like a coffee. Instead I tiptoe back and lean against the wall beside the open glass door where neither Marion nor Sam can see me.

". . . and Maddie didn't want to go out onstage. She was longing to, but she was scared. Of life. I told her I was there, but I don't know if that's enough. Maybe I offer too little for a whole life."

Nurse Marion says in a kindly voice, "Sam, you're the best reason she has for recovering."

Sam's voice cracks as he asks, "Can my father dream?"

Marion sighs. "I've worked for many years here at the brain center, you know. I've often heard neurologists say that there's no chance of coma patients having dreams because they take place at a level of consciousness that isn't accessible from a coma. You see? The dream machine is almost at a standstill, but . . ."

I prick up my ears.

". . . but when coma patients return—and more of them do than you'd think—then they relate their experiences. Some of those experiences are hallucinations, as we know. The noise of the machines, the lights, the injections, and the doctors' conversations are all recast in the limbic system—the emotional part of the brain—and translated into new images. A ventilator becomes a submarine engine. The beeping of the EEG turns into a truck or a slot machine."

Silence, apart from the humming of the monster.

Dr. Saul announces through the loudspeaker, "We'll conduct one last series of tests with glucose."

Nurse Marion resumes her explanation at a slightly lower volume. "And then there are some patients who display no REM phases in their sleep cycle, meaning that at no stage do their eyes move under their lids."

"The dream phase," notes Sam.

"No, that's old hat," Marion contradicts him. "We now know that dreams occur during any phase of sleep. But . . ."

"But?" I ask, reentering the room.

"But the question is: if someone is in as deep a coma as your Henri, for example, far beyond sleeping and dreaming, then as far as modern medicine is concerned, he's unable to dream because the brain won't allow him to do so in his condition. But what does that say about returnees' accounts? Do you see? If people in comas are unable to dream or receive any stimuli from their surroundings, then where were they? What are returnees talking about if it is neither reality nor dream?"

Before I can really process what it might mean if comatose patients' experiences weren't dreams but . . . well, what? . . . the loudspeakers crackle again. Dr. Saul has obviously forgotten to switch off the microphone because, without warning, he says, "Well, Fozzie, I'd be amazed if we receive any sign of life from Skinner before we retire."

Nurse Marion waves a warning and strides rapidly toward the doctor, but he doesn't notice her and continues, unaware that we are unintentionally listening in. "Whatever the boy's beliefs, this man is not going to recover. If the twenty-four-hour electroencephalogram doesn't register anything, we should consider persuading Mrs. Tomlin to interrupt the treatment and remove the ventilator and the feeding catheter."

Dr. Foss replies, "Yes. Simply extending life isn't valuable on its own. You have to be able to live properly."

The boyish confidence drains from Sam's face. He heaves himself out of his chair like an old man.

"They're wrong," he whispers. With clenched fists and wild eyes, he turns to face me. "They're wrong, Eddie! You mustn't do it. My father's alive. He's here."

Nurse Marion flings open the door of the cubicle with the monitors. Dr. Saul glances up in surprise and realizes that we must have overheard him. I see a flash of shame in his blue eyes. He glances at Sam and hangs his head. "I'm sorry, Samuel."

Sam rushes into the MRI room as his father is removed from the tube.

"Don't worry, Dad," he blurts out. "I know you're here. Did you hear them say they were going to switch you off? Well, I won't let them. Don't be scared—I'm here and I know you are too."

But Henri just lies there the same as ever, a face with no twinkle in its eye, a beating heart, and an uninhabited body. Nobody knows where he is—including himself, probably. Nurse Marion seems neither a fanatic nor religious, and I see Sam, whose synesthetic sensory powers can penetrate skin and the boundaries of the visible world. What if the two of them are right, and I'm deliberately blocking out their knowledge?

I think of my father, and to be on the safe side,

I say his full name out loud. "Edward Tomlin." They say that the dead can touch you when you speak their names.

And immediately I feel him—for one, two, three, four, five seconds. I sense his presence diagonally to my left, on the same side as my heart. I couldn't care less if I'm imagining it or if the impossible has happened.

"Sam," I say calmly, "do you have your smartphone here?"

The boy gets up from his position leaning over his father. His face has twisted into a grimace. He nods.

"Please give me your phone. I want to check if there's a Saint Samson chapel on the coast of Brittany."

DAY FORTY-FIVE

Evening

Eddie
//

I feel like a bride. I'm trembling with panic and anticipation. I scan my mind and my body for the least doubt that might stop me from saying yes. I have many, the same ones as before, but none of them are loud enough to urge me to say no.

I'm lying between the crisp white hospital sheets of my bed in the sparsely decorated family suite, ready to dream. But I can't dream, now of all times. I've been running around for the past seven weeks in a state of constant exhaustion, but now, when my only goal is to sleep, I can't.

That dream of being with Henri at the church. It was more than a dream; it was . . . I don't know what you'd call that kind of experience. It was inexplicable.

The chapel dedicated to Saint Samson really does exist. It's a small stone church by the sea, with a red door and two small stained-glass windows, on the D127 to Trémazan, near the Saint Laurent peninsula, a promontory dotted with giant rocks and wild horses at the entrance to the Chenal du Four, the most dangerous stretch of sea in the entire world. The chapel lies in the parish of Landunvez on the shores of the Iroise Sea, between Porspoder and Portsall in an area known as Pays de Léon, the Land of the Lion. Henri's homeland.

I used first Sam's smartphone and then my laptop to travel through the area where Henri grew up. The images, maps, and blogs reveal a wild land, and I would love to visit it one day and explore it with him.

The cliffs are fringed with yellow gorse bushes, and to the south the Saint Mathieu lighthouse guards the entrance to the roadstead of Brest. Bright waves thunder against the cliffs, as translucent as fine bottle glass and a magnificent shade of emerald green. They are magical, hypnotic, and so alluring that people vanish into them.

That is how I would like to vanish into the night. I long to throw myself into a deep sea of dreams, where I will meet Henri again. It's of no importance what it's called, or how unlikely or inexplicable it is. But my heart is racing, and I feel no trace of tiredness. I don't wish to drink to hasten the onset of sleep. I don't want any whiskey-steeped fantasies.

I toss and turn on the mattress, get up, draw the curtains closer together, and place a rolled-up towel along the bottom of the door to banish the ray of light seeping through the crack there. I try counting backward from a hundred.

An hour passes, then another. I feel as if I've never been so awake in my entire life. As thoughts flash through my mind, I remember the many things I've forgotten to do over the past forty-five days. I've neglected to pay bills, haven't answered emails, and have overlooked invitations. I haven't cleaned my flat, gone to the hairdresser's, or enjoyed sleeping in once, and yet still I'm wide awake.

I get up and wander along the permanently lit corridor in my pajamas. I pad down the stairs in my socks to the intensive care unit. I put on the rustling smock and pick up a mask.

The lights in the ward have been dimmed for the night, and on the central podium, half illuminated by the blue glare from the monitors in front of them, sit the watchmen over life and death.

The doctors nod and ask, "Have you disinfected your hands and arms?" I say yes. I probably do it a dozen times a day, but still they check.

I'm drawn to Maddie's bed. They've closed the curtains around her cubicle. For the past four days her body has been powered entirely by machines. Should her liver also give out, she will die. Sitting beside her is Sam, kitted out in a nurse's green uniform, complete with mask and gloves, hairnet, and disposable plastic overshoes. He's reading to Maddie. He's blocked everything else out, and his whole world consists of her face and this ten-foot-square cubicle bordered by green curtains.

"Look," I whisper to Henri. "Your son's a great lad and a good person. I love him dearly, Henri." Henri's eyes are shut.

I study the notes detailing his "sleep architecture," but they still baffle me. The lines on the graph stream from right to left like the straight lines along the sides of a road. I dab his mouth with water, again and again, so that his thirst doesn't burn him up.

Every fifteen minutes one of the duty doctors does his rounds, examines Maddie, and gives me a nod.

I imagine telling Henri in my dreams to come back so that we can start afresh, saying that everything will turn out fine and we'll have each other forever. I imagine his overcoming every obstacle—cerebral contusions, clamping, bruising, fear, coma, rehabilitation—and learning to speak and walk and love.

At long last, for one wonderful moment, I'm able to draw a deep breath that isn't obstructed by the worry constricting my throat.

I sit on the bed and, taking great care, lie down beside Henri on top of the sheet with my face against his shoulder. I take his hand and stare up at the ceiling above, wondering if he can also see it. Can he see the dimmed lights, the oblique lamps, the reflected red, blue, and green dots from the computer-gray monitoring devices stacked on top of one another on the wheeled trolleys alongside each bed?

Planting a gentle kiss on his shoulder, I whisper into his ear, "I've seen photos of Saint Samson, Henri. I'd love to go there and to Saint Laurent and to Melon, where the winter storms batter the bay like nowhere else on earth."

I think of the lighthouses. A quarter of France's lighthouses stand on the cragged rocks and enormous stone islands of the raging Iroise Sea. There's no sea as hungry, no sea in the world that demands such a heavy tribute in people and ships. "So that's your home."

Despite having been there, my father never told me anything about Brittany. Even many years later, lighthouse keepers refuse to speak about what they've seen at night, out at sea. They say nothing, and their silence is as deep as the sea around them.

"Shall we meet there, Henri? In Saint Samson or the place where you were born, Ty Kerk? You showed it to me once on the globe in Café Campania. I'll be able to find it, the house between heaven and earth. I'll take Sam."

I notice I'm growing calmer in Henri's presence, lulled to sleep by the rhythm of his ventilator, with which, as always, my breathing keeps time. I feel very drowsy. Still squeezing his hand, I lay mine on his heart and fall asleep by his side.

Henri

I can feel Sam's incredible yearning and concern tugging at me like an invisible hand, reaching out with multiple feelers to check whether I'm here. However, most of his attention is focused on Madelyn.

I sense Eddie by my side. She's taking care of my son. She's stronger than she realizes. My child's fear, my wife's affection: one tears me apart, the other holds me together.

Eddie has just told me about Melon and Saint Laurent and the color of the waves that break against the shores of the land I call home. She's asleep, but I'm not.

How I'd love to do something taboo and appropriate the body of a real person! There's a doctor in the center of the room who's about my height. He has strawberry-blond sideburns, and I spot the mark

431

of an old injury—a scar at the top of his throat. Yet his body is so full of vivacity, blood, and nonchalance. Free of pain! If I could only borrow his body for a while, if I could only bend over Eddie's sleeping face and cover her lips with mine, taste the soft expanse of her mouth. At first she would still be dazed by night, but then she'd respond.

I'd feel her breath, then her hands running over the fabric of my trousers to grasp my hips. Her quiet, purposeful hands would undress, admire, and touch me. Skin, life, skin, warmth.

I long to feel warmth and moisture, the patter of water on skin. Eddie's skin and her whole body pressing against mine. An urgency in my abdomen, liquefying and hardening. Caresses, the heat between her legs, the softness of her breasts against my chest, my mouth closing first on one nipple and then the other.

Molding my palms to the contours of her upper arms and elbows, the swell of her backside, the curve of her thighs.

The changing texture of her skin as I approach her center.

Kissing every inch of her.

Hearing her moan.

Seeing her eyes gazing up at me, the laughter in them as her lips remain delicately parted and she says, "Taste me."

I become absorbed with the idea of borrowing and inhabiting the young body of the doctor on the far side of that screen. Just briefly, for a short time, so I can touch my darling.

Would she see me inside that other body? Would she know I was paying thanks and homage to every inch of her being? The moles on her left breast, her rangy limbs, the swirl of hair at the back of her neck, those delightful laughter lines at the corners of her mouth, those eyes that contain the sea, life, dreams, eternity, everything.

"My summer's day, my wintry sea, my home," I whisper.

A wave of calm and peace ripples out from her and mingles with my vibrating senses. Tentatively, my thoughts venture into this peace. I have to think hard to know which direction to take.

I start with the girl. Madelyn told me that in one of her alternative lives she was married to Samuel, with whom she had grown happily old. If what I'm gently turning over in my mind is true, namely that all our alternative lives—in dreams, in dying, as a memory that can't actually exist, as déjà vu, or when one feels a chance slip by—come into contact, then there must be one of Madelyn's alternative lives in which she steps out of the shadow of her fear, survives sepsis, wakes up, recovers, escapes the last shadow that is imprisoning the girl beneath the waves, then takes the path on which my son, Sam, becomes her husband and they grow old together. That path will only be possible if Madelyn lives. And if I . . .

I can feel the tugging darkness below me, pumping and pulsing an insight up to me that I don't yet fully grasp. When I do, it is as if I am jumping over the side of an enormous tanker that's plowing through the sea at full speed, leaping out into empty space and—eventually, somewhere—crashing into the water, then sinking, my eyes riveted to the retreating world, life, and the last receding light.

I think it through a second time and fix every individual step in my mind. It's like solving a formula whose X and Y are known only to the dead.

I've made up my mind. Eddie's deep peaceful sleep was the key, but from now on I go it alone. Backward. To the edge. All I need to do now is allow myself to topple into the dark, billowing night waiting below, and then watch the ship continue on its course. All I have to do is let go.

Adieu, my darling. Adieu. It was the best of all lives.

DAY FORTY-SIX

Early Morning

Sam

It's half past two. I sit down next to Maddie. My voice is cracking. I'm reading her **A Song of Ice and Fire**. George R. R. Martin's epic tale will last us for a while, and I imagine her wanting to hear how it continues, refusing to die before we've finished, and then recovering so that she can read it herself.

Maybe it's a stupid idea, but I don't see what else I can do to detain her and bring her back. Occasionally when I'm drifting off to sleep, I can hear her in the maze of corridors behind the stage of **The Nutcracker**. She runs desperately through the wings, up and down stairs, calling my name. She calls for her mother and her father. I sit on the stage and wait. I cannot follow her into the labyrinth. I can only . . .

Hang on a second. What's this? How long has this been going on?

"A bloody long time, **mon ami**. Now go!"

I've become so accustomed to my father's dark pain and the tangible tension in the air by which I can tell he's there, that I didn't notice that there's been a shift. His shimmering pain has turned to a gentle light, which is far more scary. It's like the quiet that follows the final note of a symphony, the silence of a final exhalation, an empty room.

I hurriedly put down the book, get up, and open the curtain that has been drawn between C7 and Maddie. Eddie is still sleeping, with her hand on my father's chest. I take a step closer, searching for him but not finding him.

"Dad?" I whisper. "Dad!" **He's gone. He's no longer here!**

One stride and I'm at his side, touching his hand. **Please, please, let him merely be sleeping!** Panic steals my breath. I check the machines. Pulse, heartbeat, sleep phase. Peaks and troughs and spikes. He's alive, but he's gone, I know it. His body is completely deserted.

It's as if he has entered a zone that Dr. Saul didn't sketch out. An unfamiliar zone between coma and death. An area between life and death, which no one has identified because it's always moving.

I glance at Maddie, then back at my father, then at the heart monitors, and for one absurd moment I have the feeling that their two hearts are perfectly attuned, beating in time as if they were walking side by side. This moment lasts for a few seconds, but the lines suddenly diverge. Maddie's heartbeat accelerates and my father's slows down more and more.

I know what's about to happen and yet I'm powerless to move or call out. It's like a countdown to something, as my father's heartbeat falters. Four, three, two, one, zero: everything happens exactly as planned, in every respect.

Henri

—//—

Each time the oar dips into the water, breaking the reflection of the sky and the stars, I see Eddie's face on the surface and watch her wake up. I see Sam as he realizes, and then I'm ready.

The sea is calm beneath a sunny winter's day. This color was always my favorite—this bright metallic blue, as translucent as glass, the same shade as the sky.

I stand up and the boat wobbles. I pull in the oars. I won't need them again. Then I leap into the water. I have to dive deep to find the girl. The sea has taken her far, far down. It wants to keep her there among the rocks and the shells and the dread. Her hair floats around her head like seaweed.

She's lying in the embrace of the final shadow, the beautiful woman who'd like to make the end of our lives easy. She would gladly carry us to the island, free of pain and fear. But she too has her task and her element, and she cannot do everything; she can only be there when the time comes. She looks at me without surprise.

I pull Madelyn toward me by her blond seaweed hair and grab one thin, slippery upper arm. As I tug her toward me, I swallow a mouthful of icy, salty water. Gulp by gulp, it cools me down and takes hold of my entrails and lungs. Eventually it will encircle my heart.

The sea takes me fully into its embrace, as if it were happy to see me after all these decades, so happy indeed that it refuses to release me. There'll be no need.

The delicate, strangely familiar face floats toward me. Maddie stares at me with a mixture of endless questions, trust, and hope. I cling to the child more tightly so that both the shadow and I are now embracing her.

When I reach into the shadow, it feels as if I'm grasping seaweed, as if I were running my fingers over a wet flowery lawn, wild and tall and . . .

Eddie
—————//—————

"Look, little Eddie, I haven't mown the lawn. I've left it to grow. Is this how you want it?"

"Yes, Dad," I say.

"Will the unicorn like it?"

"It'll love it."

My father smiles and walks to the center of the lawn. The poppies sway for a moment, and then my father is gone. My heart sinks to see him leave. There's never enough time. But the dream continues, and I know I'm dreaming. A blue moon is riding in the sky. I'm walking through the tall grass behind our house. The stems almost reach my chin, and I can only just see over the tips of the ticking grasses. Dawn is breaking, and out of the glittering thicket, through the dewy stems and the blue half-light, the unicorn steps out of the dark. I hardly dare to greet it.

It's magnificent, a great, strong, beautiful beast, but I can tell from its gait that it's injured. It's injured in the only spot where unicorns can be wounded—in the heart.

It sends me a thought: **I know I'll be safe with you**. Then it wends its way deeper into the grass and very slowly, with a pain-filled expression in its otherwise shining, lively eyes, it lies down.

I tread carefully across the damp lawn past the poppies, the cornflowers, and the sunflowers. I kneel beside the unicorn I have been awaiting for so, so long. It is a timeless creature. It is afraid of nothing, not even death. But I can see and I know that it's going to die. It gradually lowers its head until its glittering horn sinks into the thick vegetation.

It's safe now. I stroke its head, my fingers oddly accustomed to its shape. Its shiny, fearless eyes are so vulnerable and inviting. I want to explore the spaces behind them—those dark, deep, never-ending spaces where no fear or sadness exists.

What does it know? What secrets will it tell me? I have a thousand questions, but only one is truly essential: "What must I know?"

The unicorn stares at me, and there is a change in its shining gaze. Suddenly the world tilts. Henri and I are lying in the grass among the bamboo groves on the roof of the old tulip warehouse. The trapdoor leading to the staircase down into my loft is open.

"Make love to me," I say.

"Of course," he replies. "Always."

He turns onto his side and draws circles with his warm, knowing finger on my naked stomach, small ones radiating out from my belly button at first, then larger ones that run across my stomach, my chest, my mound of Venus, and my thighs. He kneels beside me and caresses me with both hands, and I feel like weeping with relief at how beautiful it is and how long it has been.

He says, "You know that small chapel at Saint Samson? When you make it there, I'll be there too. I'll be everywhere, always. I'll accompany you and I'll wait for you and for Sam."

His hands pause.

"Carry on," I demand.

"Sometimes impossible things happen," he adds, and his hands also perform impossible things that make me feel so good. "The inexplicable is part and parcel of life."

"Will you make love to me again?"

He smiles. "Yes."

Henri covers me with his body, obscuring the sky and the stars with his kisses, and at first we simply lie inside each other, and all boundaries dissolve. The boundaries of my body have dissolved: Henri is in me, and I am in him. He slowly rises to a sitting position, pulling me up with him until I'm in his lap, kneeling at first, but then I push out my legs and interlock my ankles behind his back. He holds me in his embrace.

We gaze at each other, and the wind circles us, the blue moon holds us in a pool of light, and a distant sea rolls across my husband's eyes. He lays his hand on my heart.

"I'm so sorry, my darling. I've always loved you, and I'd have gladly been your husband."

"You are my husband."

He smiles. "You must live, Edwina."

He withdraws his body from mine, leaving an absence, an emptiness that grows bigger and bigger and I know will last forever. He releases me.

"No," I try to shout, "don't go!" But he's already leaving, retreating with increasing speed. He keeps his eyes on mine the whole time, and those eyes radiate love.

"Forgive me," he says.

Just before he plunges over the edge into space, his gaze darkens into an expression of despair, fear, and formidable determination.

"Henri!" I scream as I awake.

Henri

— // —

So this is your choice? the final shadow asks. Like this? Then come.

The shadow loosens its grip on Madelyn. The little dancer freezes. She stares at me for a long time as she treads water, and then the child makes a push for the surface, toward life and light, and I hope that she won't encounter a glass barrier that prevents her from taking the final step.

I stretch out my hand to the shadow. However scared I am of death, it's the only solution, the only time I've ever made the correct decision and not flinched at the crucial moment. Eddie must live her life to the full, not linger with a man who'll never be anything but a breathing creature without a will of his own. Sam and Maddie are made for each other. It's good like this—the perfect outcome.

The shadow drags me through the water. The

446

pain is so all-consuming that I open my mouth and allow the sea to invade and take possession of me. I'm incapable of moving my arms or my legs, and they hurt like hell. Everything hurts, as if all at once I can feel every single cell of my forgotten, abandoned, defunct body. The pain is overwhelming; it roars and stabs, filling me with nausea. A loud, deep rumbling sound reverberates in my ears.

I'm sinking faster and faster, mingling and dissolving into the sea. I touch the sand and stone on the bottom, which opens and sucks me in. But as I disappear something completely unforeseen occurs.

DAY FORTY-SIX

Sam

Everything is in free fall: his temperature, his blood pressure, his pulse. It's like a stately old oak crumbling to the ground. At the same time his fingers are in spasms, clutching repeatedly at Eddie's as she stands by his side. His arms twitch, his cheek muscles tense and relax, and his eyelids quiver.

I can sense his arriving. No, it's more like he's being pushed; something is driving my father with great force back into his body. Now he's hammering his heels on the bed, and finally the machines also register the change. Spikes show up on the EEG connected to his head, alerting the doctors on their control podium. Within two minutes Dr. Saul is on the scene, the strains of a restless night evident from his face. He peers at the young duty doctor with the red sideburns and the scar on his throat.

451

"Stress-induced activity," the young doctor says. "He's coming back, but his circulation is on the brink of collapse, and the oxygen content in the blood is falling sharply."

"Can you hear me, Mr. Skinner?" says Dr. Saul.

"Please," whispers Eddie, pale but composed. She puts her hand on Dr. Saul's shoulder. He turns to face her, and she gently shakes her head. The doctor steps back from the bed.

"Samuel," Eddie orders. "Come here."

My father's sweating, and the ventilator's wheezing. It's as if he's trying to breathe and swallow on his own. Swiftly they remove the aspirator from his mouth. Eddie clings to Henri's hand, and I stand in the same position as I always do so that he can see me if he opens his eyes.

And then my father does open his eyes and he is here. **He is truly here!** He gazes lovingly at me, and the pain on his face almost overwhelms me. There's no means of alleviating the torment caused by his fever, inflammation, and fractured skull. No drugs, no sleep, nothing. He's being burned alive—but nevertheless, he is alive!

Then his eyes swivel with enormous effort to Eddie, and he stares unwaveringly at her.

I turn my attention to Maddie. She too has opened her eyes. She looks at me! Now I understand everything, but I refuse to accept it.

Eddie

"Painkillers, we have to . . ." "Blood pressure . . ."
"Hypertension . . ."

I want them to stop for a moment, all of them, and listen to Henri.

"Be quiet," I say, then I roar, "Will you please be quiet for a second! Shut up!"

At last they stop.

Henri's eyes are cradling me, and his hand is alive and squeezing mine.

"I love you," I say.

His gaze softens, and I can see the effort it requires from him just to keep his eyes open. He tries to say something, but all that comes out is a feeble sigh.

"Maddie?" he asks, attempting to turn his gaze to Sam. I don't know how he knows her name, but

Sam's answer is swift and reassuring. "She's going to recover, Dad."

Henri's features relax. Our eyes meet again. **You too**, I pray, **you too.**

"Don't go," I whisper.

With unbearable effort his lips articulate an "I," then "love," and finally "you." Last of all, in an exhalation, Henri pronounces the words "Forgive me" so loudly that everyone beside the bed hears them. This both breaks my heart and heals it.

"Of course," I say.

He squeezes my hand harder and harder, and again I whisper, "I love you, forever and ever." He continues to gaze at me with infinite love and unbearable terror in his eyes.

Henri doesn't breathe again. With an expression of stunned surprise, he falls back into a boundless void, leaving me behind. His hand lets go of mine, but I hold on to it. I hold it tight as Sam rushes to Maddie's bedside and grabs her outstretched hand, as Dr. Saul gives instructions for resuscitation, as Dmitry tries to push me aside, as the machine that has measured Henri's heartbeat for the past forty-six long days and nights draws a straight line under everything, as the final beep rings out—and I know that Henri will never return.

Nurse Marion flings a window wide open. I sense Henri Skinner linger in the ward for one minute more, and then he turns away and silently abandons life.

EPILOGUE

Henri

—— // ——

At certain times, herring gulls and great black-backed gulls wheel together in tight circles over the bay. One of those times is now, as the water takes on that metallic blue color and the setting sun spreads its lava on the surface of the sea.

I'm waiting for them and so when they arrive, I'm not surprised to see Madelyn holding my son's hand. They walk along the very edge of this small beach not far from Ty Kerk, a place where both the tides and the worlds blur into one another.

Eddie, Sam, and Madelyn. I approach them silently, without their noticing me. I lay my arms on Eddie's and Sam's shoulders, and together we watch the sun go down. These sunsets at the world's end—or, some would say, its beginning—are the most beautiful to be found anywhere on earth. Every day they paint the sky in different colors.

Today the clouds trail away into small blobs, and planes trace zigzag vapor trails across a white-gold canvas that brightens to the color of ripe apricots at the edges.

"Hello, Henri," says Eddie, smiling at the sea, and the sparkling light pours into her eyes.

"Hello, my darling."

It is always said that we may take no earthly treasures with us when we die. No money or possessions, none of our beauty or power. That is correct. Some who have switched worlds have been intensely bewildered at first that they were unable to carry anything tangible with them.

But there's a second truth. We can take anything with us that we could not hoard during our lifetimes because it could only be felt, sometimes for a few brief heartbeats, sometimes only in secret. We can take joy with us, and love. Every beautiful moment from our lives. All the light we have peacefully admired, all the lovely scents and laughter and friendship we have collected. Every kiss, every caress, and every song. The wind on our faces; tango; music; the rustle of autumn grass, stiff with frozen dew; the twinkle of the stars; contentment; courage; and generosity. All those things we may take with us. All that is in between.

"Don't leave empty-hearted," I whisper to them.

They take one another's hands and watch the sun disappear below the sea, guardian of us all, with our dreams and our lives.

Hand in hand, they walk back to Ty Kerk, and I go with them, invisible, casting no shadow. Wilder Glass has lit a fire in my grandfather's hearth, and when he looks at Eddie he is happy and still a little self-conscious. She loves him, and I seldom visit her in her dreams. I follow them singing, and as I sing, I recall everything I used to be.

I can see all the paths that lie open to Madelyn, Sam, and Eddie. I see the moments that will be decisive for them: they show up in a different hue. Still, their future path together is positive.

I sing of the dancing waves out in the Iroise Sea, and I know exactly how it feels when the summer sea leaps against the rocks and dances to the song of the wind. I evoke the complexion of the spring tide and the winter seas, of the light when it rains and the sky turns black and yet the sun still dapples the surface of the lead-gray sea with islands of brightness. I sing of dark blue, turquoise, midnight blue and morning gray, milk-white and bottle-green waves; of the sky's powerful love for that hot-tempered, multicolored woman, the Iroise Sea, so powerful that it both takes on her colors and lends new ones to her so that they might meld together as closely as love—boundless, inseparable, without distinction between above and below, without end, and without question.

Eddie turns around one last time before closing the door and says under her breath, "Henri Malo Skinner."

For an instant I feel the wind on my face and taste the salt in the air. I brush a curl from Eddie's brow. She smiles as if she can feel my touch. Maybe she can.

There's more between life and death than we can tell from here.

POSTSCRIPT

Afterword and Thanks

The better I got on with my father, the more scared I became that he might die and leave me alone in this life without the conversations, shelter, and inner peace that his presence gave me. For years I couldn't sleep because of a nagging, bitter anxiety that kept me awake at night: what if my best friend, my confidant in tax and "man" matters and my teammate in the George household, were really to die one day, this person whose love and insight and understanding I cherished, whose light and bigheartedness I needed?

"I'd never survive," I whispered desperately into the darkness of my room when I was in my midtwenties. Later, I numbed my panic with whiskey, a drink that gave me no pleasure. Later still, I reassured myself with the thought that he would die only a long way into the future. He was a strong,

463

energetic, and loving man, and so much life would be hard to extinguish.

It all happened in the space of eleven days, and on April 4, 2011, Wolfgang George died far too early, at the age of seventy-two. I was thirty-eight, and the person I was before did not survive.

My fear of Dad's dying, and then his actual, horribly sudden death, which blew a hole in the normal course of my life, have shaped my life and my writing. Dying and death. Mourning and surviving. Our own fear of one-day-not-being-here-anymore. The question: was that it? And the haunting doubt: when death comes, will I have lived the life I might have lived?

These existential questions about death have colored my last three novels, **The Little Paris Bookshop, The Little French Bistro,** and **The Book of Dreams**. To produce these books, which address issues of being and no-longer-being, have no happy endings, and are therefore not very "market friendly," I needed book people who were willing to tread this kind of literary path with me. First, an author as manic as I am—my husband, Jens. He's always the first to fan the sparks of my ideas, saying, "Yes, do it. Break through boundaries. Why write otherwise?" Discussions with him open thousands of doors in my mind.

My second traveling companion is my editor Andrea Müller, a woman who never lies. This can occasionally cause me pain and shame, but her critical enthusiasm is the foundation on which I build my stories, in the certain knowledge that Mrs. Müller will always make the good things better and give me an earful about whatever didn't make the grade.

The reactions of initial readers such as my congenial final editor Gisela Klemt, my congenial agent Anja Keil, and my meticulous webmistress Angela Schwarze tell me if I've "bared" my soul enough in my manuscript. I would also like to thank Barbara Henze and Marion Barciaga for their ideas and feedback.

And, last but not least, I would like to thank you the bookseller, you the sales representative, and you the reader. Books are the only works of art that only really come into being in the mind and soul of their audience.

If you notice any mistakes in the novel, rest assured that I am entirely to blame. Please write to the publisher, and we'll try to rectify them in a future edition.

The Book of Dreams completes my cycle of novels about mortality. I needed to write about fear and transience and to portray the points where life and death meet as a sort of fairy-tale place brimming with parallel realities, a transitional zone among all worlds, heaven, and earth. None of us knows if this zone really exists or if it is born of our thoughts and hopes and fears.

Only now do I feel that I am emotionally free enough and, being in my forties, have enough "living" under my belt to devote my next major novel cycle to life.

More reading soon!

Regards,
Nina George
Berlin/Trévignon, December 27, 2015

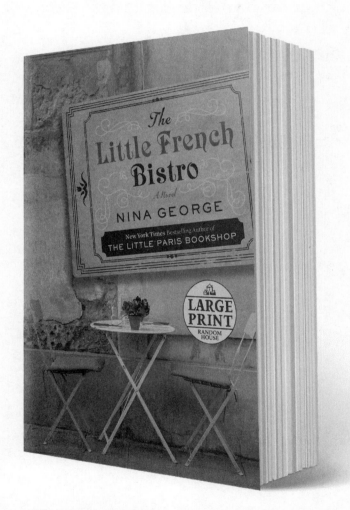